BROKEN WARRIORS

INTERGALACTIC ENOSIS: THE PYXIS SYSTEM

AURORA WELKIN

ALSO BY AURORA WELKIN

INTERGALACTIC ENOSIS: THE PYXIS SYSTEM

Fallen Warriors (Arana - Origin Story)

Saved Warriors (Arana, Rorc, Mes, & Kali)

Divided Warriors (Urien, Thora, & River)

Broken Warriors (Callibohr, Brarn, Hunter, & Lyra)

Healed Warriors (Callibohr, Brarn, Hunter, & Lyra)

INTERGALACTIC ENOSIS: THE SOLAR SYSTEM

My Destined Aliens (Kanurn, Kadohl, Kaer, & Sammie)

My Stubborn Aliens (Aux, Dagoner, Pirhanh, & Audrey)

BROKEN WARRIORS

INTERGALACTIC ENOSIS: THE PYXIS SYSTEM

BOOK 4

AURORA WELKIN

Hardback ISBN: 978-0-6454825-4-6

Cover design: Kasmit Designs

Editor: Ce-ce Cox, Outside-Eyes Editing and Proofreading

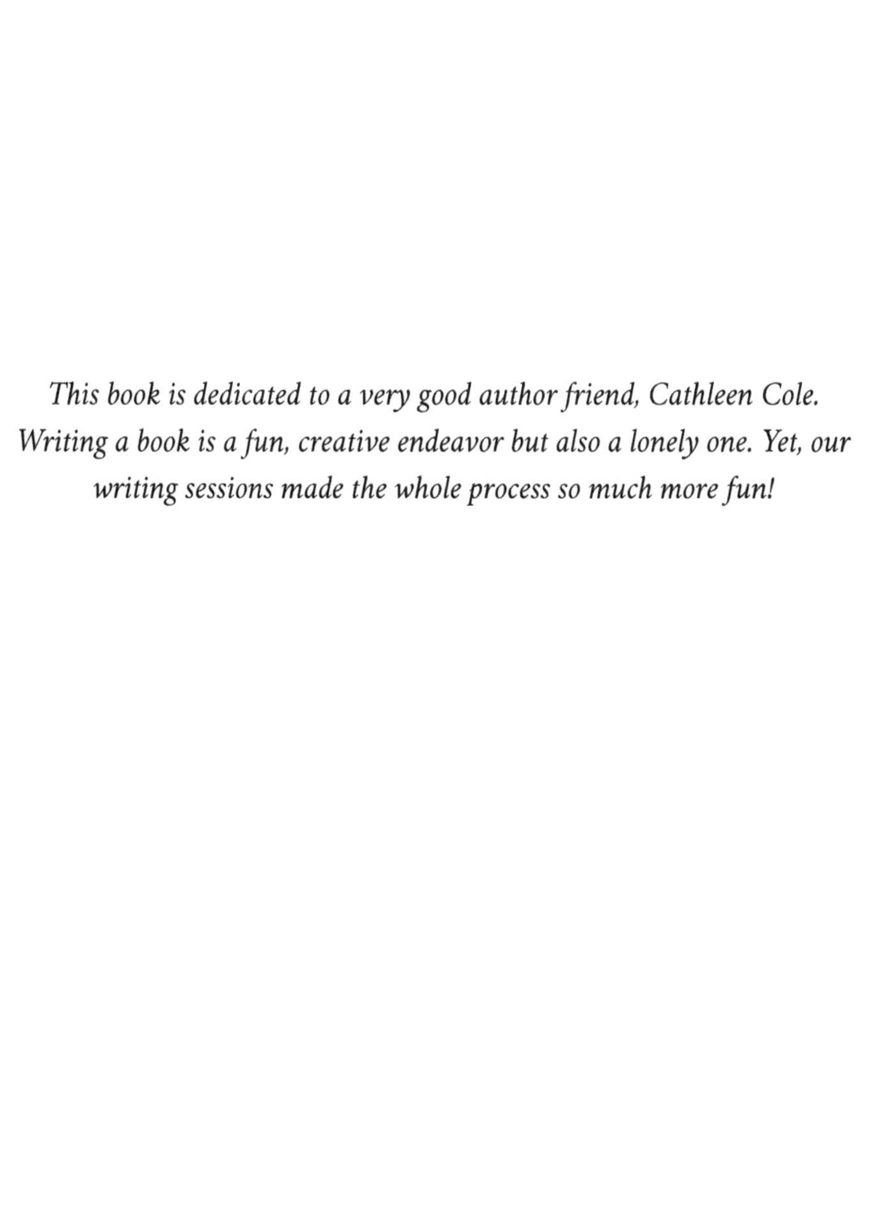

This book is dedicated to a very good author friend, Cathleen Cole. Writing a book is a fun, creative endeavor but also a lonely one. Yet, our writing sessions made the whole process so much more fun!

TRIGGER WARNINGS

This book is intended for mature audiences due to explicit language and sexual content. Contains steamy group scenes, but there are no M/M scenes. No cheating. Includes warfare and violence, as well as death by overdose (secondary characters). Includes domestic abuse (secondary characters). **If you find this type of content triggering or offending, please do not read.** Books should offer an escape from our daily routines, not cause us extra nightmares.

Broken Warriors, book 4 in the Intergalactic Enosis: The Pyxis System series, is a science fiction alien warrior why choose romance featuring a human female and three males—two aliens, one human—that are determined to claim their fated mate. Broken Warriors is the first part of a duet and ends in a cliffhanger. Healed Warriors, the second part of the duet, ends in a happily ever after!

NO PLACE OR PERSON WAS SAFE

LYRA—10 YEARS OLD

"Lyra," my mom called from downstairs. "We're going to the PCP. You'll wait for us here." She sounded way too excited for someone heading to the doctor, and the click of the door sounded before I had a chance to respond.

My parents didn't seem to be ill, yet it was the fourth time this month they'd left me alone at home to go to one of their checkup appointments.

"Michael, here...here...pass me the ball!" Jordan's voice reached my ears even though I was up in my room in the attic.

I put on the first things I grabbed from my closet and lifted the window. The other kids were playing my favorite game—football. Hopefully, Kyle, who was older and for some reason hated me, wouldn't be with them.

Grabbing the lanyard with my key, I put it around my neck and under my tee so I wouldn't lose it, and went out.

"Hey! That's not fair. I scored," Jordan, the youngest of the bunch, yelled.

Mary, Jack, Erik, and Dwight had formed one team whilst Anne, Michael, and Jordan another. Great, they had room for one more person but as soon as they saw me running toward them, they stopped talking and started whispering.

The gentle but constant buzzing in my head became louder, but I ignored it this time. I wasn't in danger because there were a lot of people around. While growing up, I'd thought everyone had an internal warning system like mine in their heads, but when I told my friends at school, they started calling me names and making fun of me. I never spoke about it again. "Hi, guys!"

One of the girls whispered something that sounded like 'slug-slimed freak alert,' and the boys snickered.

Slowing down, I furrowed my brows. Anne must have been talking about something else. She was my friend. "Can I play, too? That way we'll form two teams of four."

Someone knocked into me from behind, and I almost face-planted. "We don't need another player, sack-of-rat-guts-in-cat-vomit," Kyle said, and my heart sank. "Are you going to cry, fart-knocker?" he asked and threw the ball at me, hitting me on the head.

I lost my balance and landed on my butt, scraping my hands while trying to break the fall. "Ow." Momentarily, the buzzing in my head drowned out all other noises, and I lifted my palm to rub the sore spot. Instead of making it better, the sting made my eyes water, but I wouldn't let them see me cry.

Defeated and hurt, I got up and turned around to leave when a loud thud made me look over my shoulder.

Surprisingly, someone had tackled Kyle to the ground. He wasn't one of my friends—they stood frozen on the sidewalk as the new boy started hitting my bully. He and his family must have been the neighbors who had just moved in next door.

So many emotions filled me and I didn't know what to do with them.

"Stop," I said, and the boy turned my way while managing to keep a now weeping Kyle still.

His stormy eyes widened as they fell on me, and my cheeks burned with embarrassment, but I had to warn him nonetheless. "You'll get in trouble, and I'm not worth it."

Without waiting to see what he'd do, I fled to my house, smiling the entire way because Kyle was wailing and calling out for his momma.

The rest of the day, I stayed in my room, looking out the window, hoping to see the boy again. It was three o'clock when he went outside to their backyard, holding a small box in his hands. He reverently put it down, then dug a hole.

"What are you doing?" I whispered while I curiously kept watching.

He grabbed two stick-like things and raised them to his eye level. They wiggled suspended from between his fingers before he lowered them into the box.

He's feeding a birdie! I clapped inwardly with joy. Birds were my favorite animals, and I wished to be like them; they could take to the air and escape. Someday, once I grew up, I would join them in the sky, and...maybe the boy would come with me.

Our front door opened, and shut, before a woman's voice—more lucid than I was used to hearing it after their return from the doctors—slipped through the cracks of my bedroom's door.

"Last week, new people moved in next door, Michael. Maybe we should pay them a visit…to welcome them of course." My mother's laughter covered my father's response if there even was one.

My parents' social call would not be a good thing for the new neighbors because they liked to collect things…other people's things.

"I'll bake them a pie," my mom said, and my dad added, "We'll go drop it off this evening."

I raced down the stairs, and into our kitchen. I needed to stop them. "You can't go to their house."

"And why not?" my mother sneered.

Suddenly, my throat felt too tight, but I pushed the words out. "Their son was good to me, not like the other kids who bully me. I don't want them to go." My voice got lower and lower with each extra word uttered.

They both laughed at me. "Of course the other children bully you. Look at you, whining about everything." Her words hurt more than the worst injury I'd gotten that had needed stitches.

I wouldn't give up, though. "I'll tell on you, so they know not to open the door!" I yelled, angry at both of them.

The sound reached my ears a second before my cheek felt like it was on fire, and I stumbled backward, afraid my father wouldn't stop there. Tears wet my fingers as I cradled the side of my face. The pain throbbed along with my heartbeat.

"You will do no such thing, ungrateful little wench. This is how we put food on the table. Maybe it's time you started paying for the things we give you," he bellowed, stunning me with the vehemence in his voice.

"Dad—" My mom interrupted me by pinching my arm hard while pushing me out of the kitchen.

"Go to your room! Nobody wants to hear your ugly cries," she told me, then turned to my father and said, "How on Earth did we end up with a daughter like her? I swear they gave us the wrong child at the hospital."

"Family are those we choose, Judy, not those who carry our blood."

I couldn't take any more of their words. They were even worse than their actions, and they verified that once again I wasn't good enough. Once in my room, I threw myself on my bed and cried until I had no more tears.

Fear of what would happen if my parents found out kept my feet locked in place, but my conscience gnawed at me. I ought to tell them.

The neighbors had done nothing wrong. They seemed to be good people, and I wanted them to stay. Their son was nothing like the other boys. He was nice, my heart insisted, and I had to warn him. He would know what to do because he protected others... although, after I told him about my parents, he wouldn't want to be my friend.

Well, that was okay. Miss Kayleen at school said we should always speak up about acts that were wrong even if it was uncomfortable to do so.

By the time the sun went down, and the stars started twinkling in the sky, I'd made up my mind. Arranging the pillows on my bed to appear like I was sleeping—not that my parents would come to check on me, they never did—I climbed out the window.

The attic of our house was my room. When I was little, my daddy had told me I was his princess and that was why I had the best room in our castle. It was one of my favorite memories, but it'd been a while since he'd spoken to me with warmth in his voice.

I carefully walked across the porch's roof, knowing by now

where the creaky parts were and avoiding all of them. The jump off the lowest part of the roof was still a long way down, and I needed to focus on what I was about to do. Taking the leap was the easy part, landing unscathed on the other hand was tricky, but I'd been practicing.

Taking a deep breath, then slowly letting it go, I jumped—eyes open wide. For just a moment I was weightless, flying, and then I landed on my feet, without breaking anything. This time I didn't even feel the jarring in my bones. I was getting good at this. A giggle escaped my lips, and I slapped a hand on my mouth. Standing still—barely breathing—I listened for sounds from inside the house.

My heart beat fast. *Should I climb back up? If my parents find out I'm gone...* I couldn't even finish that thought, but when no one stirred, I ran stealthily across our yard, making sure to remain hidden in the shadows.

A fence divided our yards, and I leaped over it like a cat before stopping in my tracks.

Do I knock on the front door or climb up the wooden strips attached to the sidewall? Our houses were exactly the same on the outside, and his room's window was the one above their porch's roof.

I chose the latter. Finding the foot holds was easy, and in no time I was knocking on his window. It was shut but the curtain was drawn to the side, and I could see him, sitting at his desk doing something.

The knock didn't startle him; instead, he slowly turned around, then approached me and lifted the pane.

He had the most striking eyes I'd ever seen. They reminded me of the lively color of a clear blue sky.

"Hi," I awkwardly greeted him—the absence of noise in my

head, momentarily distracting me from saying anything else. It was never quiet in my world. The buzzing that always warned me when danger was near was quiet. That was how I knew for certain he was a good boy, worthy of my trust.

He smiled, and butterflies took flight right where my heart was, but then furrowed his brows, before wrapping his arms underneath mine, and pulling me inside his room.

Was he afraid I would fall?

"Don't worry, I'm good at climbing and jumping off the roof." I wanted to reassure him because he hadn't let go yet.

Looking around at his room, I noticed his desk was empty. I wanted to ask him what he'd been doing there, but that wasn't important. My reason for coming over, though, was. "Thank you," I blurted out.

Clouds obscured his eyes as he looked at me, puzzled.

"For earlier with those boys. They were mean to me, but they are my only friends," I stuttered. My chest felt tight, and my tummy felt funny, but my mind was quiet, and it was all because of him.

"They aren't your friends." Anger made him drawl the words out. "I'll be your friend and I'll never be mean to you," he vowed and hugged me tight.

My arms, which had been hanging awkwardly at my sides, wrapped around him. He felt warm and safe. Hopefully, he wouldn't hate me after I told him about my parents. "Do you promise?" I whispered because if he did, then he couldn't take it back.

"Yes." There was no hesitation, and I breathed a little easier.

We let go at the same time and sat across from each other on his bed.

I had to tell him quickly, like removing a band-aid so one would only feel pain for a little bit. "I came here to warn you—" But suddenly, I couldn't utter another word.

Even though the boy tensed, he didn't push me. Instead, he folded his hands on his lap and waited patiently.

My eyes followed the movement, and I was able to build my courage. It was easier to talk when not looking at his face, so that was how I confessed. "My parents are going to visit yours. They are bad. They will take things from them and then drive your family out of this house, but you're my new friend and I don't want you to go."

His breath whooshed out of him, and his body sagged. "My parents are bad too," he whispered.

My eyes rounded in surprise, then met his. This time the blue sky was stormy, and I understood—his life was like mine. I threw myself at him—knocking him backward on the bed—and hugged him tight. "I'm sorry."

He pressed his face between my shoulder and neck and shivered.

"My name is Lyra." My voice trembled, and he disentangled himself so we could look at each other while we talked.

"Mine is Hunter. Not everyone is bad, you're safe with me." This was his second promise to me, but I didn't want to make him sad by telling him I was big enough to know no place or person was safe, the same way I knew Santa wasn't real.

MY GIRL

HUNTER—11 YEARS OLD

"Please, Jack," my mom cried out and grunted in pain, but then silence followed and it was more terrifying than anything else.

No, no. We had moved to this place for a new start; he'd promised he'd change.

I took two steps at a time going down the stairs, nearly tripping over my feet when I stopped abruptly because she was sprawled on the floor, unmoving.

Dark shadowy wisps reached for her defenseless form causing cold chills to race across my skin. "Mom—" I didn't get the chance to say anything else because the monster, who I called dad, turned his bloodshot eyes toward me.

Dread, the kind only he could induce, exploded inside me, causing my body to shake.

His lips lifted in a lecherous, sardonic smile, and he pulled his foot back, getting ready to deliver another kick to his own wife.

Get up...get up, I prayed but she didn't even blink. Her chest barely rose and fell.

Terrified, but determined to protect her any way I could, I threw myself on my father, managing to knock him off her. The action, though, drew his attention to me, and that was never a good thing.

It might have been a couple of minutes or a few hours, but as I lay on the floor, the monster's fists still raining down on me, I stopped feeling—my body no longer my own but a rag doll in the hands of the person whose mirror image I was.

I could no longer see my mother's still form, just the dust particles rising in the air, then falling all around me, before darkness pulled me under, and I knew no more.

Intense, unbearable pain racked my body as someone shook me. Electricity zinged through my aching muscles at the same time pins and needles dug into my vulnerable flesh, making me cry out.

"Thank God, you're alive! I thought I lost you," my mother cried out while hugging the life out of me.

I wanted to be strong for her, but couldn't stop the tears and the groans that escaped. Then I noticed her black eye and busted lips. "Momma, Nana taught me that boys shouldn't hit girls, and I'll never hit you...please, let's run away together," I begged, hoping that this time the answer would be different.

She pressed her face into the nook of my neck, and I felt her body tremble. "Nana taught you well, but it was my fault this time, Hunter. Papa loves me very much, and it hurts him when he has to discipline me."

My heart sank inside my chest. Every time it was my mom's fault. She was too friendly with Mr. Harrison, our old neighbor.

She smiled too much at the grocery store and the other men would find her too provocative. She didn't cook our food to his liking. There was always a reason.

"You shouldn't have interfered, sweetheart...please, never get in the middle again." A sob burst out of her. "Sometimes, he can't control his strength, and now look at you—" Another sob stole her words, but she swallowed it. "Do you still have Nana's medicines?"

My grandma was a Healer, and before she died she taught me as much as I could understand because she insisted I had the gift too. The old suitcase with all the herbs, poultices, and roots that had been passed down to me was my most prized treasure.

"Yes," I replied and braced for the pain that would come when I tried to get up.

With her help, I limped up the stairs to my room and managed to reach my bed. At the last moment, my legs gave up and I fell onto the soft mattress.

"I don't want you taking medicine on an empty stomach. I'll bring you some food first," she said and draped a blanket over me.

The cocoon of warmth pulled me under fast, and I wasn't strong enough to resist sleep from claiming me.

For five days, I did little else but sleep. My body needed the rest to recover, and my mom made sure I ate broth and soup, so it had the necessary fuel to speed up the healing process. But on the sixth, the pain had disappeared, so I got up, dressed, and was out of my room in no time.

I hesitated on top of the stairs, but the house was overly quiet so I felt safe to descend. A loud growl echoed around me, and I clutched my aching belly. Finding something to devour was a priority, but my father didn't allow us to eat unless we were all sitting together at the table.

Maybe if I grabbed something from the back, he wouldn't notice before I told my mom and she replaced it. In the second cupboard behind the dry foods, I noticed a single can. I pulled it out but couldn't tell if it contained meat or fish inside.

I had no choice but to eat it because I wanted to get strong enough to defend my mother and stop my dad from hurting us. Sighing, I pulled the metal lid backward and practically inhaled the disgusting contents of the can, then gulped two glasses of water to wash down the aftertaste.

The combo did the job of quieting my stomach, and I pushed the evidence of my disobedience to the bottom of the trashcan, wondering what I should do next.

Noise from outside startled me, but it was children's voices, cheerful voices. Looking out the window, I saw them playing football on the street. We'd already been here for a week but I hadn't met any of them yet.

Well, now is a great time.

I put on my shoes as fast as I could and went outside.

Something moving high on my periphery drew my attention. The girl next door was walking on the roof slowly.

My heart beat faster in my chest. A fall could take her life. I wanted to call out to her, to be careful, but it was like watching an agile cat. Not wanting to frighten her, I remained silent.

She stopped near the edge.

There wasn't a ladder nor a tree nearby that she could climb down from. *How will she get down?* I wondered when she answered my question by jumping.

Oh my God! I ran toward her when a giggle full of delight stopped me short. I expected to see her sprawled on the ground, but she was glowing as she started toward the other children, oblivious to my presence. For reasons unknown to me, something about her held my attention, and did not let go while I followed at a distance.

I was so focused on her that I missed what the others were doing until a boy knocked her to the ground, then said, "Are you going to cry, fartknocker?", before he threw the ball he was holding at her.

My reaction was instinctual. Anger exploded inside me, and I released it on the boy. Like my father, he didn't know that we should treat others with respect.

The girl said something, but I couldn't hear the words over the boy's cries. Then the other kids ran to their houses, calling their parents.

Not wanting to get in trouble with my father again so soon, I raced back home, looking for her on the way but she was nowhere to be found.

Disappointment filled me because I didn't get to speak to her, to make sure she was all right, and to tell her that what those boys had said didn't matter because they didn't know better. But as I stepped into the safety of our house, a horrific realization hit me. I had become my father. I had used my fists to beat someone. Guilt nearly drowned me, discovering I was just like him.

The front door opened but I stood frozen in the middle of the hallway leading to the entryway.

"Hunter?" my mom asked. "What is it, sweetheart?" Her voice was always gentle. Her touch was always loving, and I recoiled when she lifted her palm to my cheek.

Chin trembling, I blurted my shame, "I'm just like him." The words wobbly and barely audible but somehow my momma knew who I was talking about and she enveloped me in her arms.

"You may be your father's son, but you'll never be like him." Her vehement tone made me pay attention. "You're a Healer, like your grandma. You're incapable of hurting others."

Wrong.

She was so wrong, and she'd never forgive me, but I had to tell her. "I hit a boy earlier...with my fists—" I couldn't keep talking.

I expected to see disgust on her face, instead, her eyes softened, and she tightened her embrace.

"Did you hit him for no reason?" she asked and ran her fingers through my hair.

"No. He threw a girl to the ground then hit her with a ball..." My voice trailed off trying to understand where my mother was going with this.

She smiled; her eyes lighting up. "Then you did good. You protected her with the means that you had." She kissed my forehead. "You look like him, my handsome boy, but you'll never be him. Let's go make dinner," she finished and I could breathe again.

Much later, once it was dark out, and the house quieted, I sat at my desk to count the bills I had hidden in my shoe box. Fifty-seven bucks—not enough to buy two tickets out of here for me and my mom. Maybe I could help the neighbors with their chores for money. Summer was less than a month away, and I could help with the grass cutting—

A knock interrupted my thoughts.

Blocking the view with my body, I slid the shoe box behind my bed and turned to look at who it was.

Hiding my surprise, I tried to act cool. Her almond-shaped eyes looked solemnly at me, watching my every move as if waiting to be ignored or something. Silly girl, I couldn't pretend she wasn't there...I didn't want to.

"Hi," she stuttered the moment I lifted the window pane but didn't try to get in.

I swore this girl loved heights and had no sense of danger. What if she slipped? She'd hurt herself. I wrapped my arms around her torso and pulled her in. She didn't resist.

Instead, as if reading my mind, she said, "Don't worry, I'm good at climbing and jumping off the roof." Despite her reassuring words, I couldn't shake the fear that gripped me, and when I didn't let go, she added, "Thank you."

I furrowed my brows in confusion and was about to ask her why, when she beat me to it.

"For earlier with those boys. They were mean to me, but they're my only friends." Her soft voice was what I imagined an angel would sound like.

The need to protect her rose to the surface along with the anger I'd felt earlier. "They aren't your friends," I snapped at her, then gentled my voice because that boy's behavior wasn't her fault. "I'll be your friend and I'll never be mean to you," I promised and hugged her tighter because she seemed so lost. When her arms wrapped around my back, my heart fluttered in my chest.

She twisted my t-shirt in her fists, and murmured, "Do you promise?"

"Yes," I replied, knowing already that we would become the best of friends.

I couldn't keep her in my arms forever, so I let go and we sat on my bed. She rubbed her palms down her pants legs, then scratched her cheek but flinched and pulled her hand away. Something was bothering her, and I waited patiently for her to tell me as I scanned her face. One side of it was light pink, the other light ivory; and on her right arm, the black outline of a bruise was visible underneath her sleeve.

"I came here to warn you—" she started then halted, and I held my breath, waiting to hear I was in deep trouble for what I'd done earlier. "My parents are going to visit yours. They are bad. They will take things from them and then drive your family out of this house, but you're my new friend and I don't want you to go," she confessed, surprising me with her words, and I exhaled the air I'd been holding in a rush.

Suddenly, I didn't feel alone anymore. And even though fear of being heard kept my tone low, I looked straight into her hazel eyes, so she knew I wasn't lying, when I admitted, "My parents are bad too."

Her reaction caught me by surprise, and I buckled under her weight when she jumped straight into my arms. We fell backward but she didn't seem to mind.

"I'm sorry," she said and once again hugged me tight.

Two simple words…that meant the world to me. I was sorry, too—for both of us.

"My name is Lyra," she said shyly as she got off me, but something in her voice changed; the tremble betrayed her true emotions of vulnerability, maybe even fear.

Exposed was the last thing I wanted her to feel, so I decided to give her something of myself. "Mine is Hunter. Not everyone is bad, you're safe with me."

Ly, it seemed was one of those people whose face never hid their emotions. I saw the denial of the truth I had shared with her coming, so I took a leap of faith and opened up some more to her.

"I have a secret, only two people know, my mom, and my nana

who was like me. I have the gift of healing, and when I get older I'll become a doctor and save as many people as I can."

Both of her cheeks turned bright pink, and she raised her hand to cover the injured side. She shouldn't be embarrassed, though.

"Does it hurt?" I asked and held my breath. Would she trust me as I trusted her?

She nodded her assent but remained silent.

"Can I make it better?"

Another nod.

I pulled out my most treasured possession from under my bed. Reverently, I opened the lid of the small suitcase. It was filled to the brim with notebooks and little tins and bottles with labels, so it wasn't hard to find the ointment that promoted the healing of skin injuries, and would make her bruises disappear in a couple of days.

If I was to protect my girl as well as my momma, I needed to train to become a better Healer sooner rather than later.

YOU NEED TO BE IN CONTROL

CALLIBOHR-13 ROTATIONS OLD

Sweat beaded on my forehead, but I didn't dare move my hand to wipe it away for fear of losing my concentration.

"Keep your shield steady, Callibohr," my mother advised. "Imagine it is a bubble that encircles Meskiagkasher...a fully formed sphere that has no points of entry," she continued guiding me as she withdrew her own shield completely, leaving both of us vulnerable to Ameelon's attack, which never wavered.

A thousand knives slashed at the mental armor I had erected around my brother. Immense pressure threatened to crush me, but I would not yield this time, not when I knew what the attack would do to my brother.

"Focus is important, but always be aware of what is happening around you, of what the natural rhythm is communicating to you," she warned me, and I heeded her advice, taking in my surroundings.

Using my basic senses wasn't enough. My chest tightened

slightly, and my stomach quivered at what I was about to do. Would I be strong enough or would I fail to control it again?

"You're doing great, son," my mother, as if having sensed my inner turmoil, encouraged me.

I took a deep, centering breath that quieted the pandemonium threatening my control.

My most dominant power unfurled, and a lively beat—one only I could feel—came from the palace behind us that was bustling with activity. In front of us, the surface of the pond was tranquil, its ancient song calming me further. The gardens around us pulsed in tandem with my heartbeat. Nothing was amiss.

See...my gift is not just a curse, I lied to myself, doing my best to ignore the pain the vibrations caused the moment they entered my body. Every living creature emitted them. Some were calm, some violent, but they were always seeking, and I was a magnet pulling them to me.

Our lives would have been very different if I or Mes had been born Shields, like our mother. Alas, that wasn't meant to be, and we both had to learn to protect ourselves because our abilities left us wide open...vulnerable. What made us powerful could also lead to our ruin unless we mastered them.

In my case, it had cost me one of my senses, too. No matter how tremendous my efforts, the moment I touched another person, their vibes would assault me, sometimes to the point of incapacitation. So far, practicing daily until I became an exhausted heap on the arena's ground had helped little with stopping them from invading my body and announcing the other's emotions or intentions. Every win—big or small—mattered, though, and I was determined to succeed, to do whatever it took.

From the periphery of my vision, the slight movement of my mother's nod brought me out of my reverie.

Suddenly, a ripple disrupted the vibrations emanating from the Royal Trainer, broadcasting his intention faster than any words would.

My blood turned cold. Horror for what such an attack would do to the offspring in my mother's womb incapacitated me, and I lost track of time and space. With my focus scattered, the shield disintegrated. Mes's grunts of pain became my own, and I collapsed under the continuous pressure as the vibrations around me bombarded my unprotected body, stealing my breath in the process.

Black spots darkened the edges of my vision. I'd failed and was going under when sweet relief filled me and oxygen entered my lungs as my mother's shield formed a protective cocoon around me and my brother, protecting us from the world.

Ameelon approached me and offered his hand. I grabbed it and pulled myself upright. Then, upon seeing my brother and mother standing unhurt, the tension coiling in my body unwound.

"You were about to attack my mother," I accused. Lifting my eyes to his, I let him see the darkness that swirled in me, always trying to escape my control. "That wasn't part of our training regime."

He bowed his head in acknowledgment. "Prince Callibohr, the enemy never asks for permission. This is an important lesson, and upon the Queen's request, I added it to today's practice."

"Thank you, Ameelon. It's enough for today," my mother said, dismissing him before she turned her unusual colored eyes my way, a silent rebuke in them. She was one of three Wravukians with deep red eyes that not many had the courage to face.

He bent at the waist, then walked away, leaving us alone.

I opened my mouth to speak, but she beat me to it. "You have a role to fulfill, but that doesn't mean, my little Prince, you have to be perfect all the time. It's all right to make mistakes, to let others see the real you. Both of you have so much to learn, and it's okay to fail before you succeed," she said; her voice carrying the love she felt for us.

"But every time I fail, Mes will pay the price," I interjected, not really accepting what she was telling me.

"The darkness the two of you carry is both a gift and a curse… it's a weapon that will turn the tides in your favor in battles that are yet to come, and when the time is right, I'll tell you more about it." She closed the distance between us and lifted her hand to caress my cheek. "You need to rise above it. Learn to control it, instead of letting your emotions hold its reins. Only destruction lays down that path." Her hand smoothed over her swollen belly before she bent and kissed my forehead. "I believe in both of you—" she turned to my brother and smiled at him "—you will tame your demons and rise above them." Abruptly she stopped, frowned, then flinched.

"Mother?" Mes's voice trembled as he rushed to her side, placing one of his palms on her belly, the other at her back, then closed his eyes in concentration before his breath hitched.

"No, no…it's too early…the Keon Healer is not here yet," she mumbled as her knees buckled and she started falling.

Reacting on instinct, I wrapped my arms around her too, and we lowered her to the soft grass. The moment my flesh came into contact with hers, only one steady rhythm connected to mine. The other was broken, flickering in and out of existence.

Mes hovered both of his hands above our mother's midsection.

"Something's wrong with the offspring." Light emanated from his palms, and he grunted in pain.

"I've summoned your father," she whispered, then grabbed his hands to stop him from trying to heal her. "Your gift is powerful, but you're not ready yet, little one, and that is all right. Be strong for mommy and let go."

The sound of my heartbeat thrashing in my ears drowned the noises my father and the Royal Healers made while they raced toward us. Pain in my chest—as if someone had speared the damn organ with a sword—caused black spots to fill my vision, and the tick their vibrations reached me I staggered.

"Callibohr, raise your shields," my mother croaked, and I felt her power envelop me, offering a temporary reprieve.

A sob burst out of my lips at the realization that while she was fighting for her life, she cared more about my pain. "Please, Mother, save your strength."

Right as I finished the sentence, we were pushed aside by the Healers. "Move away," one of them ordered, and we obeyed.

Our father spared us a glance before he knelt next to her. "Hold on, Love."

"The offspring, Nathraichean. Save him."

It was too late for our unborn brother, but I didn't have the heart to tell my mother the grim news. The Arch-healer used a wand to scan her body from top to bottom, then locked eyes with the King of Wravuk and shook his head.

"Save her, Elirs," he ordered through clenched teeth while the Queen's body was prepped for transport.

Among the crowd surrounding the Queen, I noticed a shadowy being moving a few paces away from them only to stop as if an invisible rope tethered it to my mother. What was curious, though, was that it had its own separate resonance—I'd never seen anything like it. Anger at its inability to escape reached me before it braced itself, then launched and slammed into her body, disappearing from sight. Upon impact, her vibrations diminished, terrifyingly so, before they rose again as it came out of her to then repeat what it had just done.

"Mes are you seeing this?" I whispered, and when he nodded—confirming what I was seeing—I yelled, "A shadow is attacking her." But they paid no mind to me. As if the fact wasn't important. As if they already knew.

"Where is the fucking Keon Healer?" The King growled, ignoring my warning. "She will pay for this."

Nobody replied to my father. Our Healers were some of the best in the Intergalactic Enosis. I didn't understand why we would need a Keon one. Mes moved next to me. Heat was coming off of him in waves. He didn't just enjoy healing others; it was a compulsion he couldn't deny. Watching them—forbidden to help—was torture.

My ears started ringing, and an icy stream of light-headedness crashed over me from the effort to keep everyone's energy at bay and away from me. Their vibrations were unrelenting, and I felt battered inside. The weakness in my legs was yet another sign my shields were crumbling. Soon I'd be exposed…completely vulnerable.

The ground under my feet shook, and something in me stirred as if trying to ascend to the surface. It was ready to lay to waste everyone around me, and its malicious intent rocked me to my core.

The shadow attacking my mother froze. It turned my way and braced itself.

"No," she screamed, somehow wrenching it back to her.

Terrified, with all my might I pushed against whatever was trying to escape from me. My brother laid his hand on my shoulder. Warmth spread from the point of contact, easing my burden as it dispersed, making breathing a little bit easier. He didn't let go until I had successfully trapped the darkness within me.

Raising my head, I caught my mother's tear-filled gaze. "I'm so proud of you. I love you both," she said before she was whisked away.

Mes and I rushed after them but were locked out of the Healers' Chamber. We had no option but to sit and wait. There was an unnerving silence during which intrusive thoughts ran rampant in my head, mocking me for my inability to keep the most important being in my life safe; taunting me, for I was too weak to prevent my loved one from being taken away from me.

"She's not gone. They're fighting to save her," Mes said as if I'd spoken out loud, and he was right. I shouldn't lose hope.

Much later, the crimson door blocking our way opened to reveal a figure I barely recognized. His golden skin was tinged with gray, wide shoulders bowed, and his arms dragged while he took faltering steps toward us.

Raw yellow eyes that were tinged with red met mine, and the condemning stare in them didn't need the help of words to convey the meaning. It said I should have protected her; that I should have called for help earlier. Being the first in line for the throne, I should have been stronger, yet I was weak and had allowed someone we loved to be taken away from us.

"Your mother is gone." His voice was devoid of emotion as it rang clear, shattering my world. Ice emanated from his pores where warmth once had been. Before either I or Mes could reply, he pivoted and walked away, leaving us alone.

Suddenly, my skin was too tight for my frame, and my stomach roiled, threatening to expel its contents. Guilt ate my insides. "What is the point of loving someone if it only ends in agony?" I muttered, the pain in the back of my throat making speaking hard.

Head hung low, Mes thrust his hands in his hair, fingers pulling the strands. "I don't know." His voice carried the suffocating anguish he tried to hold inside, but there wasn't any need for that.

If she—in her delicate condition—hadn't overexerted herself trying to help me learn how to shield, maybe both of them would still be alive. No, I deserved to feel everything for I had failed. I deserved pain.

Today marked one rotation since the life of the Royals of Wravuk had changed irrevocably. One rotation since the Queen of Wravuk had crossed the Vaults of No Return.

One rotation since our father had left to hunt, leaving Arwium —his Right Hand—along with the Elder Council to rule in his place until he returned.

One rotation since a female healer-maiden, Maiju, had been appointed to raise us in place of our mother. She had been the one who'd taught the Queen how to use her powers and, because of her experience, she'd been tasked with caring for the two motherless royal offspring as well as teaching Mes and me how to shield. She was doing her best, but it wasn't near enough. She'd never replace the one I lost, and I took every opportunity to remind her of the fact.

Lashing out at her was wrong, but it was as if I couldn't stop. I wasn't proud of the male I was becoming, but I hadn't found a way to let go of the shame from knowing that if I'd been stronger that fateful day, she and my other brother would be alive today; or to disperse the anger that was flowing beneath the surface, turning everything to ice until all emotions disappeared and all that remained was numbness.

"Prince Callibohr," Maiju admonished when I failed to maintain the sphere of protection around her. She tiptoed toward me the same way one would approach a scared animal, and even though her vibe was an almost indiscernible low hum, her rigid posture and wary eyes betrayed her unease since all I'd done during the last rotation was prove what a volatile monster I was becoming. "You've gotten stronger, and I know you're capable of holding the shield for more than half a spire."

It was my turn to stiffen when she cupped my face, invading my personal space.

"I miss her too, but she would want you to move on, to succeed in what she was teaching you. One day, you'll have great responsibility toward our people. You need to be in control."

Hating the reminder that one day I'd be King, because my father would leave big fucking shoes to fill and all I felt was inadequate, I growled, "You don't know what she would want." I intended to jerk away from her, but the growth spurt that would give me a warrior's stature and strength hadn't hit me yet, so when she pulled me closer and wrapped her arms around me, I couldn't escape. From every point of contact, warmth slowly seeped into my body, calming the angry waves and thawing the edges of the glaciers that were my insides.

"I help her sire raise her, Princeling. I trained her until the time came when she was sent to apprentice." She kissed the top of my head. The gesture was so reminiscent of my mother's affections that it caused moisture to gather in my eyes. Tears streaked down my cheeks, and a sob bubbled up in my chest. "Worry not, my little warrior, for you are powerful, and I will guide you until you harness your gift the same way Maysa did."

We'd both been so lost in the moment that when a loud snarl filled the chamber, sounding like a crazed beast had entered the palatial stronghold, we jerked apart. On instinct, I grabbed a sword from the weapons collection used for training and jumped in front of Maiju.

"How dare you raise a weapon to your King, boy?" The seething voice belonged to a figure I knew, yet failed to recognize.

He looked almost the same—a tall, imposing figure with muted gold skin and yellow eyes that could pierce one's soul to uncover what made them tick. The only difference…he no longer had a mane on his head, making his bloodline's brands on his scalp visible. It wasn't the slight change in appearance that made me hesitate and ask, "Father?" No, it was the complete lack of emotion in his eyes; the utter glacial demeanor of a being that used to be considerate and loving toward his offspring.

"Leave us," he barked. When the healer-maiden remained behind me, he focused his furious orbs on her.

I knew she wanted to protect me, but no one was a match for the King, and the promise of severe retribution made her scurry out of the stronghold. Then he turned those eyes that were the same color as mine my way. The hatred in them paralyzed me on the spot, for this might have looked and sounded like the King, but he wasn't my sire. My mother's death, or perhaps something in his rotation away, had irrevocably changed and turned him into someone I didn't recognize. Fear kept my fingers locked around the hilt of the sword I was holding. The realization that I'd lost both my parents and not just one cut deep, reopening the wounds that had barely started healing.

"If you're fool enough to challenge me, it's only fair I oblige you," he said, and I furrowed my brows, confused because I wasn't challenging him.

"I—" Any words I might have formed were cut off abruptly as he became a blur, and I went flying across the room and into the wall behind me. Upon collision, pain erupted in my head in a kaleidoscope pattern—fractured, intense, and spreading outward to engulf my entire body. I landed on the floor, my muscles refusing to cooperate when I tried to get up, but I managed to roll over onto my back.

The shields I had been working so hard to hone disintegrated, leaving me exposed. The darkness that had been growing inside me felt my weakness and unfurled, pushing to get out, but I didn't dare unleash it. That happened once by accident, and two Wravukian soldiers had paid with their lives before Maiju had managed to stop it and me. After that incident, she'd officially become my trainer.

As I lay vulnerable there, his vibrations reached me first, communicating his emotion, and the body I had no control over flinched. A choking sound in his throat was the only verbal indication of the disgust he felt.

"The healer-maiden should have been training you, not turning you softer," he spat, as I scrambled to my feet in an effort to level the field, yet he still loomed over me. "Good thing I'm back. Tomorrow, both you and your brother will join the Wravukian Fleet Boarding Academy."

My stomach turned to stone, and my hearts thudded loudly in my chest as horror filled me. He would take away the one person who'd been helping Mes and me learn control because it didn't meet his standards. I couldn't allow this to happen. "Maiju must keep training us. She taught mother."

"Quiet!" he bellowed, and I snapped my mouth shut. "I'll set the record straight for you, but afterward no one will ever speak about her again." He was seething. I'd never seen him this angry. "The Queen was one of the most skilled assassins in the Intergalactic Enosis. She'd be turning in her grave if she saw how soft you've become. But worry not, for the Fleet has never failed to turn a weakling into a worthy warrior."

Lies...he was spewing lies. Vibrations, though, couldn't mislead, and his gave away his intention to put some sense into me, not deceive me.

Our mother had been an assassin? How could that be? She'd been the sweetest female on the planet. Everyone sought her presence, craved the solace she spread wherever she went. Like all Wravukian females, she was soft and gentle, not a killer.

"At first light, be ready for transport to the academy," he said and left me there, reeling, still trying to reconcile the image of my mother as I knew her with what my father had revealed.

BAD. REALLY BAD

HUNTER—16 YEARS OLD

The moon beams spilled through the window, lighting up my room, and like every other night in the last five years, I lay awake thinking of her; of the most important person in my life, the only source of happiness in the hell that was my everyday reality once I got home from school.

I had been through a couple of growth spurts, and I was now taller than my father, but he was still bulkier than me, which gave him the advantage. He continued to rule our household with his fists, and so far I hadn't managed to stop him from hurting my mother or me. Training hard every day helped build muscle, and Lyra cheered me on every time I reached a milestone while she worked out alongside me.

It was an hour of bliss every day…it was an hour of torture because I was afraid to tell her how I actually felt. I'd known for a while that my feelings toward her were more than friendship; Mine was a love created at the bottom of hell's pits that we both called our life.

Revealing the truth had the potential to jeopardize everything, and I couldn't risk losing her. The guys in our neighborhood that had spent the past few years bullying her, had now started noticing how gorgeous she was, and had started hitting on the one person who was mine. Thank fuck for small favors, though, because she wasn't the least bit interested in them.

Loud voices interrupted the quiet of the night. I tiptoed toward the window and opened it slowly.

"Damn it," I cursed under my breath for the voices were coming from her house.

She had to be all right. We had a signal—turn on and off a flashlight three times—either one of us would use in case of an emergency. My eyes remained glued to her house as I waited with bated breath. My body, taut like the strings of a violin, trembled from tension. I didn't just want to know if she was safe, a deep-rooted visceral need that rocked me to my core demanded I ensured she was unharmed.

A quarter hour. That's how long I'd give her before I sneaked out and knocked on their door, consequences be damned.

Ten minutes of pure agony later, I spotted her climbing out of her bedroom window. Her dark clothes couldn't hide her lithe form as she followed the route she'd taken so many times before. I lifted the window, ready to bolt to her rescue if needed. I had gotten used to her unique way of traversing between our houses but my heart still clenched painfully in my chest and didn't let up until she arrived, unharmed, before me.

"Ly," I called out when she disappeared from view at the side of my house, taking longer than usual. I knew she didn't like abbreviations of her name. Others had painfully made fun of every variation of it they could find or make up. She had stuck her chin up and insisted her name was beautiful and hers, making me proud, but at times like this, when worry ate at me, I couldn't refrain myself.

Slowly the top of her head popped up, then her beautiful face followed. I gasped and cursed inwardly. Her bottom lip was split and her right eye was swollen and turning an angry pink.

The moment she was within reach, I pulled her in, then set her on my bed.

"I can walk just fine, you know," she snapped, but I knew it was shame and not anger that caused her irritation.

Without replying I pulled my Nana's suitcase out, then grabbed the salve for flesh wounds along with the one I'd concocted for swelling. Scooping up a generous amount, I gently applied both on her damaged face that bore all the pain in the world. The green of her hazel eyes was barely visible, and the inner honey-brown ring around the iris seemed duller than usual, further evidence of her inner turmoil.

Using my thumb, I lightly pressed the bones around her eye socket, checking for fractures when tears glistened in them. "I know it hurts, but I have to make sure, baby girl." Satisfied that nothing felt shattered, I pulled her in for a tight hug. "Are you hurt anywhere else?"

Times like these, when she was hurt—emotionally or physically —were the only ones she openly accepted my affection. When she shook her head negatively, relief washed over me.

"It'll be all right, Lyra." I tried to console her, knowing what came out of my mouth were empty words because I couldn't protect her yet, but I would be able…soon.

Sobs racked her body, and I could already feel a wet spot forming on my tee, but I didn't let go. She never revealed her vulnerable side to others—not even her parents—with me, though, she was open and never hid her true feelings. She trusted in me, knowing that I would never judge, or take advantage of her.

"They took my money, Hunter. The money I worked hard for and had been saving for college." Her breath hitched, and I felt her shudder in my arms.

I knew it was not so much the money gone that bothered her, as was their taking her options away. Our parents took everything away from us, and we could do nothing about it. They weren't model parents. They weren't even good at pretending, for the sake of others, but they gave us a roof over our heads, and for that we were thankful.

"They hurt me," she whispered in defeat.

"No one can hurt you, unless you allow them," I contradicted. "It's only money, babe, you can have mine." I'd do anything to make her feel better.

She pressed a kiss on top of my heart over my clothes, searing the damn organ with her innocent action. "You'd do that?" Her lips were a hair's breadth away from my chest, but the muffled words didn't conceal her surprise.

I was willing to give my life for hers, money didn't even present a dilemma. "Of course."

She hugged me tighter. "You are the best brother a girl could ever ask for."

Up to this point in my life, I hadn't known that such an innocent statement could wreak havoc, but it did…it tore me apart.

When she pulled back, I plunged my fingers into her chocolaty brown strands and pressed her head back to my chest. I needed a few seconds more, to compose my face.

Lyra was the one person I could be myself with. She knew my darkest moments, and I knew hers. Nothing was off limits during our long talks. From the moment we met, she'd been there to put me back together every time my father broke me apart, and I'd done the same for her.

Having to don a mask now was the hardest thing I'd ever done, but she'd told me how she felt, and I couldn't risk revealing my feelings and losing her. That meant she could never find out, and if the only role I had in her life was as her brother, I'd take it, no matter the repercussions.

"I can't take your money," she said, and I let her up to finish treating her wounds. "I'll just have to apply for more scholarships," she added when I was done.

While tidying my supplies for the next time we needed them, I debated whether to tell her about what could be our ticket out of this life.

Can I really be just her brother? My darkest thoughts took a voice of their own inside my head.

What happens when she falls in love with another guy? I shook my head, trying to dislodge the unwelcome speculations.

Mine. Only mine. The words reverberated, slashing deep with every rise in their tone. *Tell her,* they insisted, weakening my defenses, *then she won't have to stress...you're doing it for her.*

Didn't my father alienate my mother from her family so he could have her all to himself? My conscience scolded me, but it was too late.

Unable to resist the seductive whispers of a future I desperately wanted, I told her what I'd been keeping secret, "There might be a solution to our problem."

Lyra's blouse lifted, revealing creamy skin underneath as she stretched out her taut body on my bed. My cock stirred at the sight. "Move over, you bed hog," I admonished, making her giggle as she obediently scooted over.

Instead of hopping on the bed, I got up and pushed my dresser in front of the door, blocking it. I wouldn't put it past my father to barge into my room during the night, looking for booze or a fight. Switching off the light, I then shut the window and pulled the curtains. Thankfully, thoughts of my father helped my boner subside, and I could safely lie next to her.

Lyra tapped her fingers on the bed's wooden headboard; the rhythm hypnotizing. "Tell me," she demanded, making me chuckle —patience wasn't her strong suit.

"Enlisting in the military could solve our problem. Tuition would be covered, and at the same time we'd have a steady income while serving." I'd thought she'd be happy to hear there was a way to escape, to carve out a future for ourselves; instead, she turned her back to me, and curled in on herself.

I didn't like the distance she put between us, so I closed it by lying beside her, then turning and cocooning her. She wiggled in an effort to push me off the bed. Her bottom rubbing my pelvis, though, inflamed my desire. "Ly," I growled and placed my hand on her waist, restricting her movements.

"Talk to me…I know something upset you."

She cleared her throat a couple of times, then sighed. "If we enlist, they'll separate us, Hunter. And even though I want our independence, the cost isn't worth it."

The words were a balm to my tattered heart, encouraging me to divulge the next step in my plan to secure her by my side forever. "Not if we get married first."

She isn't a possession, my conscience spoke up, and I shut it, but then her body in my arms turned rigid, and I wanted to swallow back the words that'd just left my mouth.

"It's an option that would solve our problem, and when you're ready to have your own family, we'll get a divorce. Easy peasy," I backtracked, hoping to salvage the situation because I couldn't lose her.

"Okay," she whispered, surprising me.

Had my ears fooled me? "What?" I asked, needing the clarification.

"If marriage is what it takes, then I'll do it…as you said, we can always get a divorce later." Her voice was steady, neutral; her face hidden from me.

I couldn't get an inclination of her true feelings.

A yawn danced on Lyra's lips, and she flinched when the notion stretched her torn skin.

"Turn around. I need to see if your lip started bleeding again," I ordered, and she ignored me.

A heartbeat later, though, she added, "It hasn't. Don't worry."

"Then it's time to sleep, princess. Good night."

She mumbled something unintelligible, and before I knew it, her breathing had evened out. She'd fallen asleep.

I pulled the comforter over us, then wrapped myself around her, enveloping her in a cocoon of warmth, and myself in her soft scent. Unlike other girls, Lyra had an acute sense of smell and didn't like perfumes. She didn't need the artificial substances. The aroma wafting off her skin was feminine, soft, and sweet, reminding me of the flowers of the jasmine vines snaking around the pillars supporting our front porch. I closed my eyes, and let it lull me to sleep.

A whimper pulled me out of slumber. "Ly?" Instead of answering, she cried out and thrashed, her elbow catching my ribs—my breath exploding out of me. "Lyra, wake up," I ordered.

She was usually a light sleeper, but the nightmare that gripped her wasn't letting go. Heaving, she kicked wildly, fighting an invisible enemy.

I covered her body with my heavier one, trapping her legs underneath me, and shackling her wrists with my hands above her head. "Wake up, babe."

She sobbed.

Fuck.

"You're safe. It's just a bad dream. Come back to me, baby girl," I implored, hating that I couldn't shield her from whatever had sunk its claws into her.

A heartbeat. Two. Then she opened her eyes. "Hunter?" she croaked.

"Are you with me?" She nodded, and I released her limbs to get off her, but she stopped me by wrapping her arms around my torso. "I'm heavy, Ly."

"Thank you," she said and kissed the spot where my neck met my shoulder. Her lips lingered, causing goosebumps to rise on my flesh.

Unfortunately, something else rose as well, and was now pressing against her thigh. Mortified that she would tell me off… terrified that she wouldn't…I took the matter into my own hands. "We should get back to sleep. We have school tomorrow." My steady voice doing a fine job concealing my jumbled emotions.

Without a word, she let go and turned to her side once again. Not long after, her soft snores filled the room.

The alarm clock rang, the jarring tone rousing me from a fitful sleep. Sometime during the night, I had draped my arm across her waist and pulled her closer.

Damn it. I was sporting morning wood. Luckily enough, none of her body parts were near that area. *Thank fuck for small favors.*

Under my palm, the taut muscles of Lyra's tummy clenched and then expanded as she stretched while still within my embrace. Her tee had bunched up during the night, and her action now revealed the underside of her breasts, drawing my eyes and making my hard cock twitch in excitement.

Before I knew it, she'd pushed her bottom toward me—her firm ass coming into contact with my groin sent a jolt of electricity through me, and I froze.

Her body shook, and a chortle escaped. The sound brought me out of my stupor, and I all but threw myself on the other side of the room.

"Oh my God, Hunter. Overreact much?" she said between guffaws, "I know what happens to boys in the mornings." Then as if her words weren't enough, she placed her hand on top of her groin and raised her pointer finger upward, accompanying the motion with a whistling sound effect.

I walked to the window and pulled the curtain aside, hoping the bright light would chase away my dark thoughts.

Say something cool, act flippant, I ordered myself, but instead thoughts of her sleeping with other boys took over my brain. Jealousy overpowered good sense, and I growled, "How do you know? How many boys have you woken up next to?"

"You know this was the first time, Hunter." Her serious voice brooked no argument, and I looked over my shoulder at her. Something crossed her eyes but it was gone before I could decipher its meaning, so I turned my head back around, lest she picked up on my inner turmoil. "But I have watched porn, so I know what happens," she added.

The words would have shocked me, but dread filled my gut because black semi-transparent tendrils were slithering out of the crevices of the windows of Lyra's home.

I'd never seen so many dark wisps congregated together. Whatever awaited us in that house was bad. Really bad. What worried me the most was that I didn't feel pain emanating from the place, just cold emptiness. Early on, I'd discovered that my Nana had been right. I had a gift for healing. Most of the time, I could sense where someone's ache was located. I could feel the intensity and know instinctively what needed to be done. It was almost like the injury was talking to me.

What I was experiencing at this moment, though, scared me. I'd never felt or seen anything like it before. Watching the oily black fingers wriggling out of Lyra's house, as if trying to grab the unsuspecting victims within their proximity, made bile burn the back of my throat, leaving a sour taste in my mouth.

FOREVER ALTERED

LYRA—15 YEARS OLD

Hunter stood frozen, staring out of the window.

When our bodies came into contact, and I realized he was so big and hard, my body went into overdrive in less than a heartbeat; and if he hadn't jumped out of the bed as if I had electrocuted him, I might have done something stupid.

Feeling protective of him didn't stop me from being attracted to him on some level I didn't understand. We were brother and sister. We were family, even if it wasn't by blood. My emotions were…wrong.

His reaction hurt, but better get doused with a bucket of ice-cold water now lest I forget he thought of me as a sister too…which was safer. I wasn't willing to sacrifice our relationship for a fling. Besides, if I looked how I felt, the last thing one could call me was attractive with my split lip and black eye. Which reminded me, I needed makeup to cover the bruise before we left. The last thing I wanted was to touch my mother's cosmetics, but since I didn't own any, what other choice was there?

The tension was so thick in the air that when his alarm rang again, we both startled.

"It's the last day before summer vacation. We can't miss school," I said and went to bypass him without success—his figure blocked the way out. "I'll grab my stuff, then meet you outside in ten."

"No." His curt tone stung, but I chose to ignore it, certain that five minutes apart would help both of us calm down.

My second try to go around his bulk failed as well. "What?" I snapped, but then something drew my eye, and I gazed at my home.

Nothing seemed out of place, but the longer I stared, the more an ominous sensation slithered its way inside me.

Hunter enveloped my shivering form in his arms, and I pressed my face to the base of his neck. "We'll go together, all right?" The vibrations of his deep timbre soothing my nerves.

I nodded my assent, and waited for him to get ready.

Less than ten minutes later we were at my house. I raised my head toward the sky. Had the weather gotten chillier all of a sudden, or was it me who was freezing? I hesitated. My inner alarm system was shrieking at me. The buzzing in my head that always quieted whenever I was with Hunter came to life—the sudden noise made the world tilt on its axis, disorienting me.

Shaking my head stopped the cosmos from spinning, and I attempted to climb the side wall, when my protector wrapped his arm around my waist and pulled me backward. I stumbled, but his firm body stopped my fall.

"Do you feel it too?" he whispered, his soft lips brushing against the shell of my ear, quieting the loud murmur in my brain.

My weird extra sense had always set me apart from others. My own parents had never believed me; Hunter, on the other hand, was the only one who had. When I'd mentioned it to him, he'd confessed his secret to me, too. Upon hearing about his gift, all tension had left my body because I was no longer alone.

"Yes."

"I've never seen anything like it, Lyra. Let's go back to my place and tell my parents."

His words carried a heaviness that settled on top of me, weighing me down. But my parents were always civil in the presence of company. Maybe he was reacting this way because they hurt me yesterday. He was always overprotective after I got hurt. "No. We can deal with whatever is going on. We're safe; let's go," I insisted, not sure whether I was trying to convince Hunter or myself.

He released me, and with slow and measured steps, we climbed up the wooden strips attached to the side wall. The closer we got to my room, though, the heavier the pit of my stomach became.

The window pane was still unlocked, which meant my parents hadn't gotten up in my room. *Good.* One less punishment to worry about.

Ignoring the rising panic that tried to overwhelm me as soon as my feet hit the floor, I scooted to the side to let Hunter in.

My parents were high functioning addicts; they stayed sober for work, and no one suspected anything. The mornings were rarely peaceful in our household, yet the house was eerily quiet.

Have they already left for work? All the better for me. I would quickly put on some makeup, change, grab my bag, and we'd be ready to go.

I didn't linger in my room, but headed straight for the main bedroom.

Hunter followed close behind me. "Lyra, I think it's best we left now," he said, but the words didn't register.

My attention was already elsewhere, on the bedroom door that was closed. They always left it open because they wanted to catch me if I tried to sneak out.

The ringing in my head ratcheted from uncomfortable to painful. I had to push down the lump rising in my throat and take a few deep breaths.

Fingers squeezed my shoulder, somehow lowering the torturous noise to bearable levels. "Thank you," I whispered, and pressed my ear to the wood, listening for my father's snores. I was met with silence.

Just get it over with Lyra; you don't have all day. I wiped my clammy hands on my pants, then grabbed and slowly turned the knob. A screechy noise grated my ears, but when no one stirred from inside, I opened the door wide and stopped in my tracks…not comprehending the image that greeted me.

Judy and Michael were lying on the bed, facing each other and embracing affectionately—each had one arm wrapped around the other. One would think we'd caught them during an intimate moment, but their color was all wrong.

"Mom…Dad?" I stepped closer, and my blood turned to ice.

Syringes were hanging from their bare arms, still half full of whatever poison they'd chosen to inject their bodies with. Poison they'd bought with the money I was saving for college.

Hunter approached them. "Mrs. McWilliams? Mr. McWilliams?" He received no answer, and he tentatively reached out to check the spot under my mother's chin. Then he did the same to my father, and his shoulders sagged.

No, no, no. It can't be.

My heart stuttered in my chest, and black spots filled the edges of my vision. Paralysis struck, and I no longer had control of my muscles. When I started to crumble, my best friend lifted me in his arms and carried me out of the room into the living room, where he set me on the couch before crouching in front of me—those turbulent eyes trained on mine.

"I'm sorry, Ly."

A keening sound drowned out the words. Normally, I would have acted, tried to help whoever was hurt, but I was too numb to move.

"Lyra!"

That voice was familiar, safe…but its authoritarian tone was new and it pulled me back from the precipice. "I wasn't enough for them," I whispered the shameful truth, laying my broken soul bare to the figure who'd become a permanent fixture in my life since the moment he'd entered it.

"They were sick," he contradicted, coming to their defense.

Through grinding teeth, I yelled, "They chose their drugs over me, their own flesh and blood." But I didn't stop there. I thumped my chest with my fist. "I was not enough." The confession robbed me of breath. The reality of the situation slowly sinking in.

Their careless action didn't just cost me my parents; it would soon cost me the one person who mattered the most. How would I survive without Hunter?

He grabbed my shoulders and shook me, bringing me out of the stupor that kept drawing me in. "You are enough. More than enough for me, and I will never let you go. I'll never leave you—"

His words were a balm to my wounded soul, but I interrupted him because they were also empty promises. "I only just turned fifteen, Hunt. They'll take me away from you. We can't stop them." My voice cracked at the helplessness that threatened to overwhelm me.

Leaning closer, invading my personal space, his alert gaze zeroed in on mine. "They can't take you away, if they can't find you," he said, his jaw set as he hauled me up. "Let's go gather your stuff. You're staying with me."

I pulled back slightly, stopping him, then opened my mouth to argue because his idea was ridiculous, but nothing came out.

"I've got a plan. Trust me," he insisted, and I shook my head.

A burden. That is what I'd be if I stayed with him. Leaving would be my final gift to him.

Abruptly, as if he'd heard my thoughts, he rounded on me, and I had to step back. "I'm not willing to lose you, so get over the idea of striking out on your own," he growled, then drew me in a back-breaking embrace.

"Okay," I said, and the tears I had managed to keep at bay earlier burst free and spilled down my cheeks.

Hunter let me get it all out. His silent presence—the steady pillar holding me up—allowed me to start processing, for my life was forever altered.

Two duffel bags filled to the brim later, we stood side by side at the entrance of my room.

My limbs were heavy; it had nothing to do with the work it took to gather my things, and everything with the shocking revelation. "It's like I was never here. Look around us, Hunter." Little proof remained that a teenager lived in this house.

"Neither of us has much, Ly...that's all right. We'll make do as long as we have each other," he said, and picked up my bags. "It's time to go."

It took a lot of effort to will my feet to work, to stiffly walk all the way to Hunter's house while one question overshadowed all the rest in my head.

How long would it take before I destroyed his life, too?

A KILLER JUST LIKE HIM

HUNTER—18 YEARS OLD

Fuck, I'm late. Ly will be worried.

I increased my pace, knowing it'd be awhile before my lungs screamed for me to stop running. My feet hit the ground harder, the ferocious winds taking the sound away. Not a soul was in sight as I raced toward our house; everyone was huddled inside this unusually cold summer night.

Today marked two years since Lyra's parents overdosed, and I was determined to replace the awful memory with a good one. The time that'd passed hadn't been easy. She had to witness my utter shame and nurse me back to health every time my father released his wrath on me.

No more, I told myself.

My body was no longer lanky—a boy's coming into his own. Muscles honed by hours of backbreaking work at the local warehouse covered my frame. Everything I went through paid off financially as well, and that money had brought my slightly altered plan to fruition.

My mother had discovered Lyra was staying in my room on the first anniversary of her parent's death. Ly had an uncanny inner warning system—much like I had a healing gift—and she always knew when she was in danger, but that day, she'd been off her game, and my mom had caught us.

After threatening to run away from home, she'd begrudgingly agreed to keep my girl a secret. Besides, she'd already been living with us for a whole year and no one was the wiser.

The last conversation I had with my mother swirled in my memory.

'I'll leave him. Come with you and Lyra,' she'd said, rendering me speechless.

The number of times I had asked her to run away together had been in the thousands, and every time I'd received a resounding no. What had changed?

Answering my unasked question, she'd said, *'Seeing you taking care of your girl reminded me how love should be.'* Then she'd hugged me tight and buried her face in my chest. *'I'm sorry it took me so long.'*

My parent's house loomed ahead, bringing my focus back to now. Light flooded the ground floor, so I skipped the main entrance and climbed up the sidewall to the dark attic.

Lyra would never venture downstairs when my parents were home, so I knew she was in there, even if I couldn't see her.

Moving aside the blackout curtain, I slipped in through the window and found her curled on our bed.

I tiptoed to her side. It was late, and she might have fallen asleep, but I couldn't resist giving her a goodnight kiss when it was the only type of affection she allowed me.

God! A kiss wasn't enough. It'd never be enough, but if she rejected me, I'd lose her forever and that outcome was unacceptable.

When my lips touched the supple skin on her cheek, she sighed.

"You're late. I was worried." Accusation colored her words, and pain put a strain on her voice.

I winced. Lyra wasn't a fan of surprises, but this one wouldn't disappoint...hopefully. Making sure we wouldn't be interrupted by locking the door and pushing the dresser in front of it, I switched on the light and leaned my back against the wall.

My stomach churned.

In the mood she was in, I wasn't sure my slight alteration of our plan would be welcomed.

Time to do something about it.

Making sure to look appropriately chastised, I spoke the words that would ruffle her feathers, "I'm sorry, baby gir—"

"Lyra," she interrupted me, and I chuckled.

"It's so easy to get a rise out of you," I admitted, making her smile, then continued, "I've got a surprise." She frowned, and I couldn't hold my laughter in. "You're the only person I know who hates surprises. It's a good one, I promise."

She tilted her head—like an adorable puppy—thinking about it, before coming to a decision and thrusting her hand out palm up. "Gimme, gimme, gimme."

I loved teasing her and seeing her cheeks flush a lovely rose color with excitement. "So impatient..." I drawled, and she pouted. My lips tugged up in a smile and I handed the papers to her.

The small box burning a hole in my back pocket felt heavier than it should be. "Go on, read them," I encouraged when an emotion I couldn't decipher played across her face.

She lowered her eyes and started reading. A big smile stretched her lips, lighting up the room.

"You got them," she whispered reverently, "we're free."

My heartbeat sped up. The anticipation killing me. Out of all the papers in her hands, the last one mattered the most. I reached backward and clenched in my fist the small rectangle while shifting from one foot to the other.

Lyra turned the page to the last document. "Affidavit of parental advice on…marriage," she whispered, then froze.

My nerves got the better of me. "I know we haven't really talked about it, but this is the best solution, Ly."

Fuck.

I saw the tear sliding down her cheek.

This was bad.

She never cried.

"Why would you have us married to others, Hunter? They will separate us. How is that the best solution?" Her voice trembled while my knees buckled with relief.

If she'd read further than the title, she'd have seen my name, but my hot-headed angel had just jumped to conclusions and refused to open her eyes to go over the rest of the text.

Kneeling in front of her, I took her hands in mine. "I thought you were mad at me."

"I am! Who is this Hunter Hogan to whom I am married?" Her temper rose in tandem with my desire to capture her lips in a kiss that would sear us both. But if I attempted such a thing now, she'd punch me in the face—she was fucking irresistible.

Instead, I brought her left hand to my lips and kissed her ring finger. "It's me. I didn't want you to have my last name because it's his—my father's—and it's tainted. So instead, I chose a new surname for us with a meaning that'd fit us both," I explained.

Like a cartoon, her hazel orbs widened in surprise, and her jaw hit the floor. "What?"

"It's the anglicized form of the Gaelic name Ó hÓgáin, and it means young warrior," I said and offered her the little black box. She eyed it as if it was a poisonous snake about to strike and not an inanimate object in my hand. I chuckled and opened it to reveal the two black tungsten rings lying next to each other.

My breath lodged in my suddenly dry throat. My stomach roiled at the thought of potential rejection. My muscles tensed as if preparing to stop her in case she fled from me.

"One for you and one for me," I said; my voice steady, unwavering.

"They're beautiful," she whispered, before raising her gaze to me. "Will the affidavit withstand scrutiny?"

Was that a yes, I wondered. "It's backdated to when your parents were alive. We won't have an issue."

I should have been feeling nervous. Instead, peace settled in my soul. This was right. "No one will be able to separate us," I said and picked up the smaller band of the two. "Will you marry me, Ly?"

Her face lit with happiness, but it only lasted a few seconds before she furrowed her brows and lowered her head down. I could sense the wall she was erecting between us. *Fuck, she doesn't want this.*

"Only under one condition, brother." Her voice was devoid of emotion, and I'd only ever heard this tone when she talked about her parents. Putting me in the same league as them fucking hurt, but she had more to say, so I remained silent. "The moment you find someone you truly want, you tell me, and we get a divorce."

Message received. But if she thought I'd make it easy on her, she was sorely mistaken.

She was mine.

Mine alone.

"Of course," I replied not bothering to hide the growl while I lifted her left hand between us and put my ring on her finger, "but know this sister…as long as we're married, if any fucker puts his hands on you, I'll make sure he regrets it."

Her eyes flashed with anger upon hearing my threat, but I didn't give a damn. "So it'll be all right for you to have sex with other women—"

A terrified scream stopped her mid-sentence, stunning both of us. When it was cut abruptly, I wrenched myself out of my stupor, pushed the dresser out of the way and raced downstairs to find my father—his back to me—standing on top of my mother, his shoulders hunched, arms hanging by his sides, shaking.

Black tendrils snaked around my mother's limbs, slowly covering her entire body.

A guttural roar exploded out of me. "What have you done?"

He turned around. Wide eyes showing the whites met mine. Spittle had built up in the corners of his mouth and was now dripping. Nostrils flaring, and fists clenching in preparation for an attack.

In place of Jack—because I'd never call this man a father again—a rabid creature stood. An animal that needed to be put down before it claimed more lives.

"It's all your fault the whore is dead. You and the rest of the world stole her time from me. She should have been mine alone," he said and was on me in the blink of an eye, but I was no longer little, frail, and helpless. I met him fist for fist until I gave more than he could take.

The evil bastard crumbled on the floor sooner than I liked, and I followed, pounding his flesh, showing no mercy, as he hadn't shown any to my mother or me.

A punch to his ribs was accompanied by a hollow crack, indicating I'd broken one of them. *Good.* But I wasn't satisfied by his grunt. I'd make him scream, like he made her scream. Two more hooks in succession accomplished my goal, and he cried out in pain.

"How do you like it now, Jack?" I growled and brought my fist down to his face—delighting in the crunching sound of his nose breaking.

He stopped protecting his body and started hitting me, trying to dislodge me.

The fool wouldn't succeed.

Taking advantage of the opening he'd given me, I let the rage boiling under my skin loose on him. My mind was numb. My body on autopilot. Liquid across my eyes obscured my vision. None of it mattered while I finally dispensed the justice the monster that had sired me deserved.

Suddenly, I was knocked off of my target. *Fuck, did he have someone helping him?* I rolled and crouched low; bared my teeth, and raised my fists, trying to clear my vision to see the figure a couple of feet away from me.

"Hunter, stop," a girl's voice pleaded. "This isn't you."

The hell it wasn't. I was a killer, just like him.

"No, I won't let him take you! Hunter, come back to me." Her voice hitched, pulling the knowledge of who she was to the front of my conscience.

"Lyra," I croaked, and she barrelled into me, knocking me on my ass. Her flowery scent cleared the haze in my mind.

She lifted her hands to my face. Slowly.

The hesitation sliced through me like a knife. "I would never hurt you."

"I know." Her instant reply soothed me as nothing else would. "But he hurt you badly. I don't want to make it worse."

He had? I didn't feel it.

"Are they…dead?"

Stars burst behind my eyelids, and nausea washed over me. Turning sideways, I emptied the contents of my stomach. Lyra stroked my back; the smooth circling motion calming. When the cramping eased, I answered her question. "He killed her."

"Did you kill him?" she asked and held her breath.

Shame filled me, for deep inside I knew if Ly hadn't stopped me, I would have. "No. But he needs help."

"So do you. I'll call the police and ask for an ambulance as well."

My hand shot out, blocking her way before she could take another step. The blood that had already dried drew my attention. It felt like a stain I'd never be able to remove. "No. Go to our hide-out. If the police catch you before we're married, they'll take you away from me." As I gave the order, a stark realization hit me. Hadn't Jack done the same thing to my mother? Hid her from the world and demanded all of her time and attention? Was I bound to smother Lyra with my possessiveness, too?

Her voice called me back from the downward spiral that my thoughts had entered. "Okay, I will, but the moment they release you, come back to me." She grasped my shoulders and shook me gently. "You hear me?"

"Yeah."

"Don't do anything stupid. I can't lose you," she punctuated every word. Making it a command that broke through the haze clouding my mind.

"I won't do anything stupid," I told her, and the words seemed to appease her.

She passed the phone to me, then disappeared from sight, leaving me to take care of what needed to be done, fully intending to keep my promise to her.

WE WERE FAILING

BRARN

Two and a half rotations ago.

"The Sirh's ability to bond with its host's genetic code is unlike any I've ever seen before. It's amazing," I said, without taking my eyes off the holo-screen processing the data of the semi-sentient organism reacting to my blood sample.

"Clearly. As this is the tenth time you've said so in the last spire alone," Callibohr drawled.

Since Prince Meskiagkasher became the Second King of Saber, interplanetary trade between Wravuk and Saber had recommenced. And upon Queen Kali's insistence, garments made of this extraordinary plant's fibers were the first item traded. No one had known the reasoning behind her persistence, yet there'd been no disagreements. None from her mates, and none from Callibohr or King Nathraichean. It was comical how easily she'd wrapped these powerful males around her little finger. I hadn't met her yet, but rumors of her powers had already started spreading across our corner of the galaxy.

The Saberian scientists had guaranteed the material would have no ill effects on Wravukians, since the Sirh either bonded with one's genome or didn't. Or so they claimed, but I wasn't willing to risk the future King of Wravuk wearing a suit that had the potential to harm him on a genetic level unless I verified it was safe to do so.

The Royal Arch-healer had attested to its harmlessness but had warned that once the connection between the symbiote organism and a host got established, it was irreversible. So I'd already run a multitude of experiments testing the Saberians' claims using a variety of samples containing mine and Callibohr's, as well as Culhwch and Forsa's genetic codes, and the results had been the same every time. This was the last one. If the bonding was once again a hundred percent successful with no side effects, I'd proceed to the next step of the trial, which was to try on the new uniform made of Sirh fibers and see what happened.

"Not only is he repeating himself, but he's also ignoring my injury," Forsa—Rear Admiral and Third in Command on the Imperial—added, his voice full of mirth.

All Healers had the ability to detect the location and seriousness of a wound as well as to instinctively know a way to treat it—to various degrees, depending on their inherent talent and gained experience. I wouldn't be the Arch-healer of the First Fleet of Wravuk if I didn't have both in abundance, which meant I could sense the superficial cut on his bicep even before they'd stepped into my lab, and it was certainly not life threatening.

Most Wravukians had more than one gift that was strong, and my second ability complemented my strongest perfectly. My touch revealed what the eyes sometimes could not see. Usually, the revelations had to do with the individual's health, but other times one of their truths was shown to me. Most often, these were memories from the past, but there had been a few occasions when what was unveiled to me hadn't happened yet. Unfortunately, it wasn't a gift I could control, so I'd learned early on to avoid touching others unless necessary.

"Are you talking about your bruised ego? Do you need Brarn to kiss it better?" The Second in Command taunted him.

"Fuck off, Culhwch! You got in a lucky hit."

"Yeah, keep telling yourself that."

Both Callibohr and I ignored their banter. When these two started bickering, they acted worse than an old Chosen couple. It was better for everyone involved to let them hash it out by themselves.

The tablet in my hands vibrated, which meant the report from the latest experiment was ready. "A hundred percent compatibility," I mumbled while scanning the rest of the details.

Silence was suddenly too loud in the space. The full attention of the other three males in the lab shifted to me.

"What's the verdict?" Callibohr asked.

"The Sirh is safe to use. It won't harm Wravukians."

"Perfect. I'll try it on first," Callibohr said and went straight to the storage compartment where I'd stored a few of them.

I blocked his way. The hotheaded Prince was always the one to jump head first into a situation, but he was a fool if he thought I'd allow him to do so this time. "That's not happening. I summoned you here because I'll be the one to try it first."

"I'm your Admiral," he growled, stepping into my personal space —a great intimidation tactic that didn't work on me. "It's not up to you."

This was the same old argument. "I'm your Arch-healer and when it comes to your health, my decision overrides yours." The other two snickered, enjoying the show a tad too much. "All of yours," I added, my words wiping the grins from their faces. "So sit tight and let me do this. If there are no adverse effects—which I don't expect any—tomorrow, you'll all get yours."

Callibohr bared his teeth at me but acquiesced, retreating toward the others. Before I had a chance to take a step further, the overhead lights in my lab flashed red.

"Hostile crafts are approaching fast. The Imperial will soon be within firing range," Axr—the ship's AI—warned, and the three males rushed out of the chamber.

They had their hands full, but so did I. The Sirh suit would have to wait for later. I raced out of my lab and headed to Healers' Bay. The Healers under my command had already started preparing the space by activating the extra healing pods we had and gathering surgical supplies in case a battle broke out. I had trust in the Wravukian warriors' abilities, but it was better to be prepared for different scenarios.

Suddenly, the ship tilted on its axis, then righted abruptly, and the lights flashed orange. It was a color we'd only ever seen once in the past, but we hadn't forgotten its meaning. The Imperial had been breached.

Everyone froze, and for a few ticks, silence reigned before a cacophony of sounds erupted inside my Bay. Wide-eyed adult males momentarily forgot themselves, behaving like scared offspring—speaking all at once and rushing this way and that, unsure what to do now that it wasn't a drill.

On top of the disarray, my gut was screaming at me to head over to where the Wravukian soldiers had formed the first line of defense. Hopefully, Callibohr would direct everyone's movements from the safety of the Bridge to minimize casualties. Unfortunately, I wouldn't place a wager on that.

"Quiet! Our warriors are going to need our help. Collect yourselves." My authoritative tone—one I rarely used—was enough to snap them to attention. "Taran, Huon, you're with me. We'll head toward the breach and offer first-aid. Ferchar, Daman, Halwn, and Remux stay here. Prepare for the worst—the Zeta protocol."

Their replies came in the form of grim nods. Picking up an emergency kit and a portable stretcher that wasn't bigger than a small wand in its deactivated form, I raced outside with the other two Healers at my heels.

By the time we reached a safe area near the point of breach, the battle was well underway, and over the commotion of yells, screeches, and laser blasts, Culhwch yelled, "Damn it, Callibohr—we can't risk you. The Order wants the Prince. You're the target. Fall back."

"I wasn't asking for your permission," the Admiral growled, dashing my hopes that he'd stay behind where he'd be safe. "The Trojan is mine."

Damn the male and his stubbornness, I cursed inwardly and lifted my fist, signaling the Healers behind me to stop.

No one knew the Order of the Prime's agenda or the identity of its members yet, but it was quickly becoming obvious they had set Wravuk in their sights. They'd started with attacking the Wravukian citizens, but if Culhwch's assumption was correct and they were targeting the first-born Prince, their actions were escalating.

Peeking around the corner, I took stock of the situation. Only a dozen Pawn invaders were standing, the rest had already fallen. It wasn't the first time we'd fought the insect-like creatures, but we were presented with a great opportunity to capture one and study it, to develop weapons that would be effective against them, because at the moment we knew of only one weak point—the neck. An impenetrable carapace covered their thick bodies that rendered our ammunition useless against them. The four eyes on their round heads gave them the advantage of three sixty vision, and their four legs allowed them easy maneuverability. The way they behaved during battle revealed they were a hive mind species, making them a force to be reckoned with when they were in great numbers.

In their midst three Wravukian soldiers lay on the floor, their bodies cut, dismembered, and scattered. My hearts squeezed in a vise, but there was nothing we could do to help them. They'd already crossed the Vaults of No Return.

Risking another look, I scanned those who were still holding their positions. Five of them were injured but remained on their feet while the rest seemed unharmed.

"Healers arrived at the scene," Taran announced through the comms, letting our fighters know, at the same time steps thundered from behind us.

More warriors had arrived to help fend off the intruders, but the stubborn Admiral had already engaged in a one-on-one battle with the Trojan, who looked like a bigger distorted version of an Osaaj. But even though he was towering over Callibohr, and his multiple arms gave him an obvious advantage, the Prince didn't hesitate, parrying every strike while delivering some of his own.

The six-armed species were known for their ability to invent, take apart, and rebuild all types of creations. Their technological innovations were sought after across the galaxies. Typically a peaceful race unless one threatened their females, which was not the case here and couldn't be the reason for the hostility this one was displaying.

Had whatever caused his gnarled appearance somehow induced aggression? I needed to get my hands on some of his blood.

A howl of rage cut my retrospection short and made my ears ring.

That can't be good. I stole another glance.

Callibohr had sliced off his opponent's lower left forearm. The blood flowing out of the limb was all wrong—yellow instead of dark blue.

The Trojan doubled down and escalated his attack, causing the Admiral to backtrack a couple of steps. He fought as if the blood loss didn't affect him at all; as if pain didn't hinder his movements. He was relentless in pursuing his opponent, using both blades and his natural weapons—his clawed hands—all the while uncaring about the damage he was receiving.

Why isn't he retreating? His behavior didn't make sense, unless… he wasn't planning to escape, which made him even more dangerous. *Fuck, I need to warn Cal.*

The thought hadn't fully formed in my mind when the Trojan presented Callibohr with an opening that'd end the fight, but would also place the Admiral in a more vulnerable position.

"Don't," I yelled a tick too late.

Callibohr grabbed the opportunity by stepping closer; without a doubt knowing such a move would leave his back exposed to the longer limbed creature. He thrust both of his swords into the enemy's abdomen and pushed outward and to the sides in opposite directions, nearly slashing the being in half, but not before the Trojan raked his dagger-like claws diagonally across the

Wravukian's back—tearing his armored uniform, flesh and muscles with little effort.

The enemy fell to his knees before landing with a loud thud on his back while the Admiral swayed, then staggered on his feet.

"Callibohr! He needs a healer. Now," Forsa, who was closest to him, yelled while fighting off a pawn.

Ignoring the battle still raging, I rushed to the Prince. "We have to get you to Healers' Bay." Shudders racked his body, making him waver on the spot. He was fading fast. "You need to walk, soldier!"

My bark accomplished its goal of jarring his hazy mind enough to keep him conscious for a few more steps towards the rest of my team. But as I wrapped my arm around his waist, mindful of his injury, a vision obscured my eyesight and I let go lest I brought both of us down.

A single image was revealed to me, and as it dissolved, my surroundings came into focus once again.

Callibohr started collapsing, and I managed to stop him from face-planting.

The position, though, offered me an unobstructed view of the damage the Trojan had inflicted. His claws hadn't just torn through skin and muscles, but had damaged Callibohr's spinal cord.

My breath caught in my lungs at the enormity of the injury. "Huon, bring the portable stretcher. Taran, race back to our Bay—prepare for surgery."

Both obeyed immediately, and within a few ticks we had the Admiral ready for transport, but before I evacuated with the precious cargo, there was one more thing left to do. Huon would stay back to provide care to the injured troopers, but I needed to make an unusual request.

"Vice Admiral," I called out, and he retreated toward us. "Prince

Meskiagkasher must be summoned immediately. Callibohr's life depends on it."

For the vision had revealed it was his own brother that would save him, not I.

"I'll contact the Nur. You keep him alive, Brarn," he said without questioning my demand and stormed away from the fight that had just ended with us victorious.

In less than a quarter of a spire, we had Callibohr stretched out on the med-pod, prepped for operation.

"Taran, I need the blood analysis."

"I'm on it," he mumbled as he scanned the data. "Only Veran poison has been detected."

"Damn it. It's enough to wreak havoc by itself. Add it to an open wound of this size and it can become life-threatening," I said, gathering the ingredients for the antidote.

I heard the characteristic whooshing sound of the disinfectant chamber working. Then a few ticks later the Second Prince of Wravuk burst through the doors. His gold orbs took everything in with a single perusal before they landed on the unconscious male.

Mes approached the med-pod, lifted his hand and gently caressed his brother's head. "Damn it, Callibohr! You stubborn ass." His voice hitched at the end, and he took a deep breath before raising his eyes to mine. "What do you need?"

No preamble. No hesitation. His royal blood didn't matter. His rank didn't matter. Just like his brother, this male was worth his weight in precious ore, and it saddened me to hear what some of the Wravukian Nobles thought of him since he'd become a hybrid.

Pushing everything aside, I cleared my mind and informed the Arch-healer of what we knew so far. Then we started the arduous task of saving my Admiral.

I'd lost track of how many spires had passed while working to save Callibohr. What I did know for sure, though, was that we were failing.

"We need more plasma and blood. Brarn, the anticoagulant poison has been neutralized...he shouldn't still be losing so much blood." Meskiagkasher said, worry creeping into his voice.

Ferchar gave me the vials, and I connected the new lines. "The Order of the Prime are proving to be more daring than we'd anticipated and are quickly becoming a formidable enemy." Anger deepened my voice. "I swear next time I'll be the one to fulfill Cal's death wish and be done with it," I growled, although I doubted I fooled his brother.

Even though I wasn't that much older than the Royals, and while most of the time it felt as if I was the Admiral's father instead of his friend, I cared deeply for Callibohr.

I needed him alive.

Mes, who'd gone eerily quiet, suddenly barked, "Everyone out!"

"Out," I reinforced his order when my Healers took too long to obey, and ushered everyone out, closing the door behind me because he hadn't asked me to stay either.

This Arch-healer had a gift unparalleled to others, and in this case I knew I'd only hinder him if I insisted on staying. So I left and prayed to the Creator to spare Cal's life.

YOU HAVE THREE ROTATIONS

CALLIBOHR

Two rotations ago.

My gait was heavier than usual as I walked toward the Bridge of the Imperial. Beads of sweat trickled down my spine. Every step engaged the muscles in my body, causing the scarred tissue across my back to stretch.

According to Wravuk's best Healers, I was fine, and the pain that currently ebbed and flowed in tandem with my movements should have dulled. I shouldn't feel fire spreading from my left shoulder diagonally to my right hip, the same kind of heat that seared my flesh when the Trojan struck me down with one of the serrated daggers he was holding, tearing through my uniform, skin and muscles with ease.

Alas, every time my eyes closed my mind seemed to enjoy replaying the fight with the six-armed soldier of the Order of the Prime. But I hadn't let the fucker beat me then and I wouldn't do so now. Clenching my teeth and burying the pain at the back of my conscious, I carried on to my destination.

All eyes snapped to me the moment I entered the Bridge, followed by my soldiers' respectful salutes on my way to the Admiral's Stateroom. Their vibrations battered the protective walls I'd erected, and a few managed to slip in. My soldiers deserved their privacy, so I ignored them as best I could.

The moment I closed the door behind me, the Second in Command of my ship, sitting behind my desk, asked in a daunting tone, "Should you be up?"

Leaning my shoulder on the wall, and donning a smirk just to annoy him, I ignored the question he already knew the answer to and posed one of mine. "Someone has been enjoying the benefits of my absence a bit too much, hasn't he, Forsa? Thinking he can lead the First Fleet by himself."

"You're not pulling me into the middle of your dick measuring contest, Callibohr." Pops sounded as he flexed his legs, stretching his joints. "Last time, I was the one having to listen to both of you whine like meek females," the Third in Command huffed, then on a more serious note added, "Why are you up?"

I'd never allow anyone else to speak to me that way, but Culhwch and Forsa, who were the Vice Admiral and Rear Admiral respectively on the Imperial and under my command, were like brothers to me. We met while at the Wravukian Fleet Boarding Academy and formed a bond that held strong through many rotations and numerous battles. They were worried, and that didn't sit well with me. The responsibility for their protection fell on me when one wrong decision could cost my soldiers' lives.

"I'm fine. Fill me in," I ordered, and their shoulders fell in defeat. It wasn't often that I pulled rank, but I needed them to let it go, and they knew me well enough by now to know not even torture would make me speak of the matter.

"When the Imperial was attacked, we hadn't been the original target, just a diversion." Culhwch pushed the words through clenched teeth. If he pressed any further, he'd break something. "Axr recovered some of their ship's AI's data before it self-destructed...exterminating our females had been their objective."

Forsa picked up from where our friend left off. "Any details regarding how they'd bring their plan to fruition were already destroyed, but the Royal Committee of Scientists has their members working on the issue from dusk to dawn—they'll find a solution."

"We can't do anything for the Wravukian females." We'd failed to protect them...I'd failed. Anger that seemed to simmer right below the surface since the last fight against this enemy bubbled up, and the urge to pound those responsible with my bare hands until nothing but an amorphous mass of bones and tissue remained rose sharply. "We need to fucking destroy the Order of the Prime before they do more damage."

The two Wravukians started coughing, and I noticed the room was suddenly darker than mere moments ago, the atmosphere having turned oppressive. Shadowy tendrils extended from my shadow, taking up room as if they were tangible entities with a mind of their own.

Fuck! What made this injury different, that my inner darkness had become so difficult to control? I let the anger dissipate and focused on pulling the tendrils back to me while turning the puzzle over in my head. The last time I'd had trouble containing it, I'd been a youngling. A consultation with my brother would provide me with answers. Maybe it was time to pay them a visit and meet his mate—my new sister. With a plan in place, and the leash on my dark side secured tightly, I turned to my friends. "I'm sorry—"

The holo-projector on the desk lit up, and the Commander's voice sounded from the speaker, interrupting me. "Admiral, King Nathraichean requests a meeting. Shall I transfer the connection?"

After our last discussion when he chewed me out about my reckless—according to his idea of how a prince should act—behavior, my father was the last person I wanted to talk to, but both Culhwch and Forsa exited the Stateroom, leaving me no excuse to deny. "Put him through, Llyr," I ordered, then moved behind the desk, straightened my shoulders and clasped my hands behind my back. The shifting and bunching of my muscles caused a burning sensation to flare across the scar that should have been healed by now. I let the sensation wash over me until it dissipated.

My father's figure appeared in front of me. Yellow-gold eyes—the color mirroring mine—swept over me from top to bottom before he greeted me.

I bowed. "King."

"I'm glad to see you're better."

Cocking my head to the side, I waited for him to reveal the reason for this call because based on his previous words, the King of Wravuk didn't have the time to deal with a wayward son. No, his Right Hand, Arwium, usually did the checking for everything relating to the First Fleet.

"Your Vice Admiral did a great job as your replacement. He intercepted two Crootan ships and returned thirty-five females to their planets." He was procrastinating, and that didn't bode well for me.

"Skip the pleasantries, Father," I snapped, annoyed; his

narrowed eyes flashed fire at me—an intimidating look that made those on the receiving end cower without fail.

Tough luck. This wasn't the first time I was the recipient of his displeasure, nor would it be the last, and I'd become immune.

"You are to return to Wravuk. It is high time you chose a female. I discussed the issue with the Council. All of their daughters have expressed their interest in you, but Councillor Caelestis, being the highest ranking member, will be considered first. He has three female offspring. Whoever you choose, she will be a good match for you."

I resisted the urge to cringe in disgust and kept my face blank. There was nothing wrong with the Councillors' daughters, they just weren't for me. I had yet to meet a female whose vibrations didn't drive me to the brink of insanity after spending more than a few spires in her company with lowered shields. I wanted my mate to provide solace; I didn't want to have to protect myself from her. "We just learned that Wravuk was infiltrated; that our people were attacked under our noses, and you want me to stop hunting the Order of the Prime in favor of picking a female that won't be my Fated Mate?"

"There will always be a new enemy, threatening our way of life. I won't lose you!" His words took me by surprise and, for an instant, his impeccable composure broke down, fear clouding his eyes. But in the next tick, he regained it and continued. "It's more important than ever to choose the future Queen and show our people we're not giving up…Fated or Chosen doesn't make a difference." His authoritative tone brooked no argument. He believed this was the course we needed to take.

My throat closed up. *Fated or Chosen doesn't make a difference?* I knew that my father ignored anything and everything that had to do with my mother, including the gift we'd inherited from her, but he couldn't possibly be serious. It wouldn't be just my future on the line, but the poor female's as well. "Meskiagkasher is mated now. He can take the throne."

He shut me down immediately. "Meskiagkasher is the Second King of Saber. But even if he wasn't, he's a hybrid now. You're well aware that the Wravukians would never accept him as their ruler."

Funny. Mes had said the same thing. *Time to change strategies and take the spotlight off me.*

"In a rush to step down, father? Don't tell me old age has started impeding your ability to rule already," I taunted with my signature smirk in place, knowing that this type of attitude would get into his nerves and hopefully derail his train of thought. "Have any deaths been recorded? Are males affected or only females?" I asked, not so subtly changing the subject and hoping he'd go for it.

He didn't. My father had a one track mind, and while a useful attribute when solving issues, it only caused me frustration in instances like this one. "I'm calling the First Fleet home." His tone had a finality that looped around my neck, the noose tightening with every passing tick.

Damn it. Like a harvak with a bone, he won't relent. Well, two can play the game. Stubbornness runs in the family, after all. I felt a headache coming on while mulling over what I could possibly say to sway him from his decision. I had to convince him to let me see this mission through even at the cost of my own life. An alternative much preferable to a dark future with an incompatible female that would slowly drive me insane until I ended up dishonoring my name.

"What if the Scientists don't find an antidote in time?" I insisted, not ready to give up just yet. "The Saberians paid the price with their females' lives. Are you willing to take the same risk by calling me back?" The King clenched his jaw, and his frown turned into a scowl, but I continued. "We need a back-up plan, and Meskiagkasher is our most talented Healer."

He held his hand up, warding off my tangent. "What do you propose?"

"Mes needs to examine the data the Scientists have gathered so far, and a discussion with King Arana will further shed light on our predicament and what the best course of action is."

My father pressed his lips together in a slight grimace, then started pacing in and out of view. I waited, knowing that an interruption wouldn't be welcome. The position he was in was difficult; asking for help didn't come easy to Wravukians, but lives were at stake. He came to a stop in front of me once again, the bright color of his eyes obscured by his furrowed brows. "I have faith in our specialists, but we'll need all the help we can get. You have three rotations. Once they pass—whether you've succeeded or failed—you will return to choose a female, and your mission will be passed on to Culhwch."

Three rotations before my life as I knew it ended.... The thought left a sour taste in my mouth, and my hearts thudded dully in my chest, yet I nodded for I had no choice but to acknowledge defeat and show my capitulation to his ultimatum.

"Report your findings once you've convened with the Royals of Saber," he ordered, and disconnected.

Suddenly, my lungs couldn't expand to take in enough air, and my body could no longer hold my weight. My control slipped, and the darkness that always lurked under the surface of the civilized mask I wore swirled and pushed at the edges of its confinement as I slumped into the chair. Needing to center myself, I closed my eyes and pictured the vast space surrounding the Imperial, the celestial bodies orbiting around their stars in the Pyxis System, and the wandering asteroids traveling the cosmos drawn by forces unseen, then let the harmony of the universe sink into me.

It took all my concentration to pull the shadows that filled my office back to me, but I managed, and soon everything returned to normal. Back in control, it was time for the next step. I got up and strode into the Bridge for the passing of time seemed accelerated when it had been inconsequential before, and I no longer had the privilege to waste even a single tick.

Both Culhwch and Forsa raised a single eyebrow in a silent inquiry, asking if everything was fine. It wasn't, but I gave them a sharp nod and ordered, "Set course to Saber, and inform the Royals we're visiting."

WELCOME TO SABER

CALLIBOHR

Following the Royal Guard into the palace, amusement warred with indignity at the welcome I'd just received. The Royals of Saber had recently returned from a trip that Mes had informed me was called a honeymoon, an Earthling habit for newly mated pairs. But that didn't justify whatever had them so preoccupied now that not even my brother could come greet me upon my arrival.

Was their female keeping them busy? I wondered, and a snicker escaped.

The King of Wravuk had spoken highly of her. She'd managed to impress him, and that wasn't an easy feat by any means. While Saberians were a tight-lipped species, news of the hybrid Queen's prowess and strength had spread wide already, effectively directing a spotlight upon Earth, as well as piquing my curiosity about the one who had captured my brother's heart and my father's respect.

Suddenly, an unbidden thought crept into my mind. *How long would it be before the Order of the Prime decided to investigate what this planet was all about?* The notion alone had my body tensing, reading to fight to protect the defenseless species.

The Intergalactic Enosis had added Earth to their Primitive Directive because they hadn't achieved space travel yet. That categorization, though, meant contact was forbidden, which placed their populace in a vulnerable position.

The last fight against the Order's army flashed in my mind's eye, and as if triggered by the memory, the scar in my back burned painfully. When I killed their captain, the Trojan, who'd almost sent me to the Vaults of No Return, the Pawns had scattered as if without direction, and my troops had captured three of them alive. Our Scientists had run tests on them until they'd learned all they could before creating weapons that not even their naturally indestructible armors could protect them from. The Order's soldiers seemed to be more brawn than brains, but what had come as a shock was the discovery that these beings were genetically modified Rohachets, a hive-mind species that thrived underground. Further tests on the Trojan yielded similar results—he'd been a genetically modified Osaaj. The fearsome warrior species had a knack for technology, and their ships were some of the best in the known universe.

Whether the modifications were voluntary was still a mystery, and I had a hunch that it was a bigger issue than what everyone assumed. If they'd indeed started with the attack on Saber more than a hundred rotations ago, our enemy was evolving and their aggression escalating.

We needed to act before it was too late. When we presented the Delegation Committee of the Intergalactic Enosis with the evidence regarding Wravuk's attack, they'd deemed it insubstantial, claiming the Order was not an immediate threat due to lack of solid proof.

I flattened my lips to hide the instinctual reaction at the bureaucratic ways of the Enosis, though a growl still escaped.

The guard accompanying me didn't take offense but remained calm, not missing a beat despite my slip.

"Prince of Wravuk. Welcome." My brother's calm vibrations washed over me, bringing relief when I didn't know I needed it, before his warm voice reached my ears.

Still a little bit miffed, I turned and said, "Second King of Saber." Before giving him my best impression of a flourish bow.

Mes was good at shielding his energy from me, but I felt his intention to charge me a second before he was on me. His speed, way faster than before, took me by surprise, but I was still the oldest of the two and knew all his tells. We had been playing this game since we could walk—always trying to outmaneuver one another.

This time, though, the moment he was on me, the ghost pain in my back flared, the impact taking my breath away. He instantly pulled back. *Big mistake.* He gave me the opening I needed to grab him under the arms, and I used his momentum to throw him across the room.

I didn't see what hit me, not until I was slammed against the wall.

The claws of two giant paws on my shoulders tore my armor like it was the soft underbelly of a domesticated torsek, instead of a Wravukian uniform that was nearly indestructible, and pierced my skin. The silver sabertooth was smaller than the others I had encountered in the past. *Is this Rorc?* I wondered. Would he commit such a crime as to attack his prince or was it the infamous Queen? Surely females differed from males, but the Saberian didn't give an inch, and I couldn't look down to check.

Either way, I kept my posture relaxed and non-threatening, an amiable smile plastered on my face, but fuck the claws hurt something fierce. Then suddenly a quake rocked my body, and if the sabertooth hadn't been on me, I'd have fallen on my ass. My eyes worriedly snapped to my brother, but he was standing at a distance as if nothing had happened.

Then, as soon as Mes started speaking, the jarring sensation disappeared, and I felt nothing. The realization that the vibrations had ceased completely hit me, rocking me to my core. I could always sense the inner strengths and weaknesses of sentient beings as well as their intentions. They came to me as waves or ripples—it was an especially handy gift in battles while a curse the rest of the time. But I had never, in my whole life, sensed a being as powerful as this one.

"My love, let my hotheaded brother go. We were just messing around," he said, his voice gentle but firm. Then it turned mocking, and even though he was addressing his mate, the jab was for me if the smirk on his face was anything to go by. "Besides it will be bad for his reputation to have his ass whipped by a female."

I was about to give him a witty reply when a wet, gritty tongue licked the side of my face from chin to forehead, effectively silencing me.

"Oh Mate, you just earned yourself a punishment." Mes's usual light-hearted intonation lost its mirth. "No," he continued.

A wide smile broke on my lips when I tried and failed to hide my mirth at witnessing this one-sided conversation with his mate, who was still on me. A fact that was clearly frustrating my younger brother.

"Kali." My brother's growl was immediately followed by his mate's snarl. But then she released me and sauntered away.

"Your mate is something else," I commented as I watched her turn a corner.

"She's a handful, that's for sure. She's been driving Arana and Rorc crazy." He laughed and clapped me on the back. "Welcome to Saber, Callibohr."

I pulled him in for a one-armed hug. "It's good to see you, Mes. I'm truly happy for you. Father talks highly of you and your mates."

He lifted his eyebrows and looked at me doubtfully. Understandable. If I hadn't heard the King of Wravuk with my own ears, I'd have doubted my statement too.

"He does. You know I'm not lying. Feel me, brother."

The corners of his lips lifted in a soft smile. "I believe you, Callibohr, Kali seems to win everyone over. Follow me, and I'll introduce you to everyone," he said, and I really wanted to meet his Sacred Mates, but couldn't hold back the question that was slowly eating away at me: Was he still my brother or a stranger?

"So how is it?" I asked, hoping I sounded nonchalant enough.

Mes stopped in his tracks and looked straight into my eyes.

Shit, I hadn't.

My brother was born a natural Healer, who had tremendous powers to be exact, and an empath. I sensed him releasing his feelers—at least that was how I always pictured it when he used his gifts to feel others' emotions—and braced myself. The sensation at the moment of the contact was not exactly unpleasant, but it still felt like an intrusion, even if I knew we were of the same blood.

He closed his eyes and rubbed at the middle of his forehead

before making a hmmm noise in his throat. Then he focused on me once again. "It's been hard. Having a sabertooth can be a constant battle for some, and mine is difficult to control at times." My protective instincts rioted inside me, but how could I protect him from a part of himself? "You've seen both the light and the darkness that reside in me," he continued, "It seems I retained most of the light when he kept most of the darkness. My need to heal is even more powerful now, whilst his need to eliminate is equally strong." It didn't matter that he was a warrior in his own right, capable of dealing with whatever came his way. Shame still filled me because of my inability to help him. "To have my mate, though, I'll gladly endure that and so much more. She calms both of us. She quiets the noise," he finished, and his demeanor changed into a peaceful one.

My eyebrows shoot to the sky. "Is she a Shield?" I asked. It was such a rare gift. On Wravuk there were maybe a handful of them alive.

"She is so much more. How was she to you?"

Everyone on Wravuk was gifted, but talking about it was an intrusion of privacy. It wasn't done lightly, not even between family members. Mes and I, though, found solace in sharing the burden of our abilities. They took a toll on us when we were little, and we had no one else to share our struggles with but each other. So I answered without hesitation. "She is the most powerful being I've ever met. Her energy brought on a quake, rocking me. That has never happened before." I didn't try to hide the depth of the awe I already felt for his female.

His booming laugh took me by surprise. "She was holding back. The offspring make it harder, but she manages," he said.

My jaw must have hit the floor, and I gaped at him like a fish out of the water. *That was her holding back?* My Creator, she was a formidable being. I wouldn't want to get on the bad side of such a powerful female. Ever.

We resumed our walk toward my brother's mates, and all the while I tried to wrap my head around what I'd seen and been told. I tried to imagine Kali in her Earthling form and failed. Was she bigger than the males? Her energy sure felt like it. So when Mes opened the door to let me in, what I saw floored me. She was having an argument with Rorc, who was almost two heads taller than her and had at least a hundred scaths of muscle on her. He'd invaded her personal space, yet she didn't back down. A few paces away, Arana stood, looking at his mates. One corner of his lips lifted, amusement written all over his face.

My attention was drawn to the Queen. Although round-bellied, she held her chin high and had a warrior's stance. Saberian females had once been the most formidable warriors in the Pyxis System. Were humans like that too, or was King Arana training her?

"Do you think you know better, you stubborn pig?" Fury rang clear in her voice and ripples surged from her body like a tidal wave, crashing on me. Her displeasure was sharp little pinpricks jabbing all over my body. But just as suddenly as the sensation had come, it disappeared, stunning me with its intensity and swiftness.

Then her words registered. *Pig?* A laugh burst out of me, drawing everyone's eyes; I coughed to cover my blunder, but barely managed to display a neutral expression.

Rorc took her chin in his hand, his fingers long enough to have engulfed her face, but instead they caressed her cheeks before he lifted her gaze back to his.

"You will not risk yourself or our offspring ever again. Mes could have handled the situation, and you were ordered to stand down. Your disrespect, little one, earned you a spanking. I'll make sure that for the next few days you'll be reminded of your decision every time you sit down," he growled with barely contained anger, before he let her gaze drop and moved away from her.

"That is the second punishment you've earned today, Love." Mes's cheery voice belied his words and drew everyone's attention toward us, but it seemed their argument wasn't over yet.

"You all know I was safe. He couldn't have hurt me or the babies. Arana, tell them," she pleaded with the Saberian King.

"Tsk, tsk, tsk."

The Queen spun and walked away. "Argh…you stupid hussy, why did you need three men? Wasn't one enough?" she asked, mumbling to herself—her voice fading when she entered the adjoining room.

Pregnant females should be handled with utmost care, not get chastised and threatened to be punished. "Is she okay?" I asked no one in particular, worried about her mental state.

"She is, and if you want to stay intact, you will stop your train of —" Her disembodied voice sounded not too far off.

"Kali," Arana admonished, and I could feel the room's energy vibrate. Their Sacred Union allowed them to communicate with each other telepathically.

Not a minute passed before the Queen reappeared and walked purposefully towards me. She stopped a pace away and thrust her hand out. I looked at it and wondered what I should do. It must have been Earthling etiquette.

"You shake it," Mes whisper-shouted in my ear—he was enjoying this.

Vackal, I inwardly cussed my brother, then enveloped her hand in mine. She felt so fragile with her soft skin and tender bones, I was afraid of breaking something, so I carefully—and quite awkwardly—shook hers, left to right, but I must have done something wrong based on the snickers coming from the males. The female just smiled.

"Welcome to Saber. I'm sorry I attacked you earlier. I didn't mean to offend you," she apologized sincerely, but I couldn't focus on her words. Her light gray eyes, pools reflecting the moonlight and highlighting the way into her soul, held all my attention.

Out of nowhere, a hand clapped me hard on the shoulder, managing to bring me out of the stupor I'd fallen. *What the fuck?*

The female minx winked at me and went to Mes. He wrapped his arm around her and held her tightly to his side.

"What are you?" I hadn't meant to let the words escape.

"I'm human, er, human-Saberian hybrid."

And incredibly gifted, I added to myself because, for the second time when we touched, I wasn't being battered by the energy of those around me.

Arana approached me and grabbed my forearm. "Welcome to Saber, Prince Callibohr," he said, then moved aside for Rorc to greet the same way.

"King Arana, King Rorc," I respectfully replied.

"I've just met my new brother. We're family, there's no need for formalities," Kali said, and I inclined my head in acknowledgment. "Let's grab a bite first," she added and headed toward the dining area near the floor to ceiling windows.

Reflexively, I scouted the chamber. The parts of the Saberian palace I'd seen so far were considerably less ostentatious than in the Wravukian palatial manor, but no less regal or posh. The white sofas and chairs taking up the side of the room that led to the terrace looked plush, soft, and inviting. Opposite the veranda, the long wooden table, with two cushioned benches on each side that seated a company of at least twenty, was filled with local delicacies that made my mouth water. A pang of longing zinged through me when the room's warmth seeped through my pores, soothing me from the inside out. The last time our home felt like this had been when my mother was still alive.

YOU HAVE MY SUPPORT

CALLIBOHR

"We have a lot to talk about," my brother said and followed the others, a predatory elegance that hadn't been present before emanating from him as he moved, his steps no longer producing a sound.

Witnessing first-hand evidence that validated the fact that he was no longer the same was jarring, to say the least. Same could be said for Rorc, too. But it wasn't just that. I couldn't really put my finger on it, other than that the distinctive energy around them differentiated them from the rest of the Saberians. Did they feel like they didn't belong? They were no longer Wravukians, neither were they Saberians, but something in between. Hybrids.

On the other hand, the vibrations emanating from the King were stealthy, low-key, until they came into contact with my flesh. Then they burned and pounded every single fingerbreadth of it.

Wary, I looked around, belatedly realizing my feet had moved of their own accord and taken me to the bench closer to the exit. I barely managed to stay upright as I dropped to the seat. Maybe I should have taken my leave and rescheduled for the morning. A good night's sleep would give me time to recuperate and get my head together.

I startled when soft hands cupped my face. *How had I not sensed her approaching?*

Standing in front of me, her gaze was full of worry. "Look into my eyes." The order was unnecessary. Her bottomless gray orbs had captivated me already, but I still had the presence of mind to notice the absolute quiet—no, that wasn't accurate—the absence of vibrations. It was like the world around me had become a blank slate, a haven offering a much needed reprieve, tempting me to lower my shields, to let go and just be. Then in small increments, strength gently flowed into me, her hands the conduit, easing the burden I was destined to carry until the moment I died.

"Your time is coming. Don't give up and don't let anyone's beliefs get in your way," she whispered the cryptic message, and I was at a loss for words—only one thing coming to mind, which I gave to her.

"Thank you," I said, feeling grateful to the Creator for pairing my brother with such a gifted mate.

She held on to me for a tick longer, then bent, kissed my forehead, and let go. The moment the contact was broken, an influx of vibrations assaulted me. I braced myself. No matter how many times I had experienced this sensation in my life, I always found myself unprepared for the initial collision. On this occasion, though, I was able to completely block the ripples of energy so they flowed around me instead of wrecking a path through me.

My eyes snapped toward Kali, and I didn't try to mask the awe and respect radiating from me. Her mates surrounded her, embracing her lovingly when I heard Mes whisper to her, "Thank you, my love, for helping my brother."

"He's my brother, too, sweetheart. He's family." Was her soft reply.

Her actions, protecting my brother earlier, then offering me a cherished respite, along with those words, embedded her firmly in my heart. My new sister was one more person I'd protect with my life.

Arana pulled out the chair at the crown of the table for the Queen to sit, then took his place between her and Rorc. I sat on the opposite side next to my brother, who had just served his female with a plate bursting with food. My eyes widened in surprise when she accepted it without complaint, but I didn't comment as we each followed suit, helping ourselves to a hearty serving. The scents wafting up my nose had me salivating and my stomach rumbling, but I respectfully waited for the Queen to start eating. She rolled her eyes before digging in—she sure had a healthy appetite.

Hmm...maybe the offspring are hungry.

"No, it's all moi." She gestured to herself—the motion exaggerated—then winked playfully at me before putting another bite in her mouth.

Damn. She'd read my mind, and I wasn't sure how the invasion made me feel, especially when I hadn't felt the intrusion. Taking into consideration my gift, such an action should have been impossible.

Mes's brows drew together downward, unease coloring his voice. "What's all you?" he asked, his eyes jumping from his mate to me.

"I'd prefer not to say." Diplomacy was the only way to go when it came to powerful beings who chose to remain silent.

She chuckled upon hearing my answer, then spared me from the inquisition I had coming by saying, “Callibohr doesn’t like me reading his mind.”

Her declaration had an immediate effect on her mates, who all went rigid for a few ticks, as if her reply was news to them. Worry emerged from them in powerful waves that rocked me.

“Isn’t it getting better, little one?” Rorc squeezed her knee, his hand lingering affectionately.

“Monakrivimou.” One word was all that escaped Arana’s mouth, his pain too intense to allow him to continue. But what he didn’t utter, his touch on her arm conveyed, although, whether it was to console her or himself, I couldn’t tell.

My brother cupped her cheek, and she leaned into his touch.

Kali’s skin turned a rosy color before she closed her eyes and mumbled, “I’m getting better at blocking it, and it doesn’t hurt as much anymore. You all help me.”

Realization that this was a new gift for her, one that caused her pain, made me curse under my breath because I had no way of helping.

“Callibohr, you must keep this knowledge to yourself,” Arana warned, a threat hidden underneath the request.

He didn’t need to threaten me or worry, though. I’d never compromise their mate…my new sister. “I’ll take it to the Creator, brother.” My swift answer and the sincerity in my voice were enough to appease him.

The rest of our meal was consumed in silence, and once we were done, we moved to the ample sitting area. The cool breeze drifting in from the open doors—a soft caress on my skin—soothed me further as I made myself comfortable on the deep sofa, but it didn't help alleviate the stress riddling my every waking spire as of late.

Once again, Arana and Rorc occupied Kali's sides, whereas my brother took the seat next to me. He bent forward and rested his elbows on his knees, gazing somewhere on the floor. The news I had to share was bad, but Mes's stiff body and the fact that he avoided making eye contact were indications that his was worse, so I waited.

"During our honeymoon we happened upon a gravely injured and unconscious Keon," he started—as always straightforward and to the point. "With no time to spare without endangering his life further and without a way to verify whether he was a Thirev, I decided to help him…only for his Iski'os to attack me the moment I approached him, or more accurately attack my darkness, which rose and exploded to face the threat head on before I could control it."

"Fuck." The curse slipped through my lips. I knew all too well the kind of havoc his darkness could cause—because mine was equally powerful and volatile—but to go against one of the renowned assassins with the perfect kill records was madness. "I'm glad you won."

The scraping noise coming from the grinding of his teeth had the hair at the nape of my neck rising. "I didn't," he said, and I gaped at him, sure that my jaw had cracked the floor with the speed it dropped, but he wasn't finished. "Kali did."

"Honey, I don't think that's the important part of the story," she interjected, and my brother clenched his fists—the skin on his knuckles turning pink from the pressure.

"You could have been killed!" The twin growls of his Pair-bonds accompanied his outburst.

In all our lives, the times I'd heard him raise his voice could be counted in the digits of one hand. For Mes to lose his composure now—after the fact—showed me he'd been terrified.

Kali went to him, pushed his shoulders back until he straightened, then plopped on his lap, wrapping her arms around him and burying her face in his neck. "So could you, but we're both alive, and so is Alaric. You did the right thing," she said, and I saw the fight drain out of my brother as he pulled her tighter to his body. "My life isn't worth more than yours."

"Of course it is," he denied, echoing my thoughts.

She gave him a peck on the lips. "Silly man, it isn't."

He didn't continue arguing with her, and I assumed it was a discussion they often had by the way he closed his eyes in defeat, buried his nose in her hair, then sighed, before picking up his story from where he'd left off, "The Keon revealed symbiotes don't attack without reason. They only go after their targets or—like in our case —another Iski'os to establish dominance."

Why would they target an Arch-healer? I wondered. Did the Order of the Prime consider him such a threat that they'd put a price on his head?

I must have spoken aloud, though, because Mes called out my name to draw my attention and locked his gaze with mine. "His Iski'os fought mine to establish dominance before Kali stepped in. The symbiote recognized her, and he bowed to his Queen before withdrawing and thus allowing me to save Alaric."

"Fought your…Iski'os?" I parroted, incapable of anything more complex than that because blank thoughts filled my mind as if my brain had stopped working. "I don't understand, we're Wravukians not…hybrids."

Once the words slipped from my mouth, I realized my blunder, but my brother ignored that part. "When Keons mate with other species that have a dominant genetic code, it's uncertain whether the offspring will inherit powers that will allow them to bond with a symbiote. So his theory was that an ancestor of ours had mated with a Keon and their offspring was powerful enough that an Iski'os had chosen them."

While my brother was talking the dam holding memories I'd long suppressed burst, and I heard the voice of our father in my head—loud and clear as if he was standing beside me—yelling, '*The Queen was one of the most skilled assassins in the Intergalactic Enosis.*' Then images of our mother training us on how to shield ourselves, how to control our darkness filled my vision, transporting me to a past era when things had been simple…when I'd been happy.

Mes continued, "Our mother had red eyes. It's such a rare coloring that only three Wravukians had had it in the past two millennia, whereas it's one of the definable characteristics of Alaric's species." The room was overly quiet, as if everyone held their breaths; even the slight breeze that'd been wafting around the chamber ceased. "I'd never paid attention to it when she was alive, but I've got stilted memories from the times we argued and ended up fighting when we were little, of dark shadows clashing around us until our mother would come and separate them and us. Do you remember during training how her shadow would cocoon us before reining in our darkness when we lost control? She was a hybrid. I was one even before I found my Sacred Mates…and so are you."

I dragged my palm over my face, then shot upward and started pacing along the terrace in an effort to de-escalate the storm brewing inside me. A mix of emotions warred within me, and I tried to make sense of them.

Initially, what my brother had shared took me by surprise, rendering me speechless. That feeling soon morphed into disbelief, and a part of me wanted to drop everything else and race to our Scientists; to have them run a molecular genetic test to verify the fact. But then an insipid idea snaked its way into my thoughts, filling me with apprehension because our puritan society would never accept a hybrid King. In the blink of an eye, though, the uneasiness transformed into anger at my father, for he must have known; our mother wouldn't have kept it a secret, whereas he had. With that realization, everything clicked into place and my body sagged in relief because for the first time the pieces that made up "me" fit just right.

My darkness—no, my Iski'os—stirred, and I ruthlessly pushed it down, unwilling to lose even a smidgen of control and risk hurting my family. Drawing in slow steady breaths and exhaling, I said in a measured tone, "But we don't have red eyes."

"Our Keon genes are weak. We don't exactly have our own symbiotes, rather a piece of our mother's Iski'os—it gifted us parts of itself so that when the time came to bond with our own, we'd be strong enough," he explained, and for the second time in less than a spire my mouth fell open as if I had no command over the movements of my jaw.

Although the knowledge I still had a piece of my mother with me warmed my hearts, the news was too much to take in. "How do you know that?"

"Keons can communicate with their symbiotes, and Alaric told us my darkness conversed with his. Iski'os share collective intelligence, but because mine—and I'm guessing yours as well—isn't wholly formed, it isn't able to access it like a fully fledged one can."

"Our father's entire speech about you not being able to take the throne because you're a hybrid...and I'm a hybrid too," I harrumphed before stomping toward the couch and plopping my ass on the empty seat next to my brother.

The careless action jarred my spine, and fire raced across my scar, setting my nerves aflame while stealing my breath. Before I had time to blink, Mes hovered his left palm over my back, easing the pain so that sweet air entered my lungs.

"Why didn't you tell me your injury is still giving you trouble?" Was that hurt in my brother's voice?

Heat suffused my face. I was the older offspring, the one who should worry and care for the younger one. "It seems my recovery is slower than usual, but I'm fine. Father made sure his Healers hadn't left a fingerbreadth unchecked on my body by the time I returned to duty."

My answer didn't seem to appease him, but before he could say anything else, Arana spoke. "Your visit was unexpected, although not unwelcome. What brought you here?"

"I fear nothing good, although I wanted to meet you, sister—the infamous Saberian Queen." I inclined my head toward her with respect, and a flush crept across her cheeks. "Attacking the Imperial had been a diversion. The Order of the Prime's true target had been the Wravukian females in a similar fashion the Saberian ones had been in Yenoctonia." Kali's soft gasp along with the guttural growls emanating from the males accompanied my grim news. "Our Scientists are working on an antidote, but we couldn't recover the details of their plan from their ship, and until they're successful lives will be lost."

"We need to head back to the palace. I'll need to check those infected myself and collect samples—" my brother started and was interrupted by both of his Pair-bonds who unanimously uttered, "No."

Mes's eyebrows shot upward. "Just because my sabertooth lost the dominance battle to yours doesn't mean you get to boss me around." He glared at Arana, then turned his grim stare to Rorc. "You couldn't possibly stand by and do nothing while females are being harmed, even if it is by an invisible enemy."

"No, I don't get to boss you around," the Saberian King took the reprimand in stride before he smiled and gestured at their mate. "She does."

She chuckled, and the sound of her laughter seemed to alleviate some of the tension in the room.

Rorc pressed his lips into a fine line. Head tilted and finger tapping against the arm of the sofa, he seemed lost in thought, but after a heavy sigh, he said, "You're right. It kills me to know that our people are in danger and I can do nothing to help them right now, but you can't go there. Our blood has altered Kali. We can't risk you transferring whatever disease is plaguing Wravukians to our mate."

Between Mes and the Third King of Wravuk—and Wravukian Admiral because my father hadn't stripped him of the title as was the custom with hybrids yet—the latter male had always been the hotheaded one, so it was surprising to hear reason come from Rorc instead the other way around.

"I've received a copy of the data the Scientists gathered so far to pass on to you, and as for a sample, I'm sure we can arrange for one to be delivered here if it's safe to do so," I said as a middle ground solution, and Mes nodded his assent.

The Queen rose to her feet, then silently padded to the terrace.

Looking at her back, one couldn't tell she was carrying precious offspring. While gazing at the golden dunes, she said in a low voice I had no trouble hearing, "I really hope that you won't need them, Callibohr, but now more than ever we need to establish a path between Earth and our planets. Human females are compatible with both Saberians and Wravukians." The gentle breeze, like an affectionate lover, played with her hair before carrying the scents of the evening, now mixed with hers, inside the chamber. Kali's entire demeanor changed to one of alertness, and a few ticks later, a vibration brimming with hostility reached me. I easily blocked the weak sensation; it had already been widely dispersed, which meant whoever it was coming from was somewhere far away.

What worried me, though, was that she'd reacted to it—which meant she'd felt it. I couldn't tell if she was in pain, and I was about to ask when she nodded to herself. "We have to approach them with an official request. We can't wait too much longer." She was blocking her energy, and I couldn't read her, but her clipped tone and rigid posture clued me in as to what she was feeling—she was expecting a rejection.

Rorc leaned forward and rested his elbows on his knees. "Little one, we've—" he started, but didn't get to finish because his mate interrupted him.

"You know I'm right. The more we wait, the more warriors we'll lose." She was adamant. It seemed this wasn't the first time they'd had this discussion.

I held my tongue and thought through her request. Her idea had merit. Hopefully, the Wravukian Scientists developed the antidote before the situation turned dire, but just in case, having access to compatible females was an excellent plan B. "I agree. Saberians need females, and even though I have faith in my people to countermeasure the Order's attack, it is wise to have other options available."

The Queen turned around and gifted me with one of her smiles, brightening the room and lifting the heaviness that had settled over us.

"We need permission from the Cardinal Prime to make contact with a primitive planet," Arana said dejectedly, probably recognizing he was about to lose this argument.

"That will draw more attention to you, little one. I don't like it," Rorc added, not ready to give up yet. "Lord Mo'dta has already promised to visit to meet you specifically."

I jerked backward upon hearing his words—a sudden coldness hit my gut. The Cardinal Prime was the busiest being on our side of the galaxy. He rarely—if ever—left the Intergalactic Enosis quadrant...and yet, he would take time to come here? I didn't like it at all and was about to say so when I noticed the change in her stance.

Maybe it'd be wiser to keep my mouth shut.

The Queen lifted her chin, a defiant glimmer in her eyes. "Let him come. I'm not afraid." Three snarls followed swiftly after her declaration, and Kali huffed in exasperation. "It's amusing—NOT—how you three think I'm a weak, defenseless person. You know one-on-one Dawn could take you on...and win."

"You have my support." My sister was something else, nothing like the Wravukian females I was used to, and I briefly wondered whether the other humans were like that too. "I will stand beside you when it's time to deal with the Cardinal."

"Vackal, don't encourage her," my brother swore at me, whereas the other two males growled. I snorted in an effort to confine my laugh, but if the males' death glares were anything to go by, they weren't amused.

Too bad.

"I really appreciate it, Cal," Kali said, gifting me with another one of her bright smiles that I returned. "Now let's get down to business."

The males groaned.

This was going to be fun.

WHEN HAD I STOPPED?

KALI

Back on Earth—One year ago.

The negotiations and planning with the Intergalactic Enosis to obtain permission to approach my home planet with an initial proposal for Earth to potentially join the Intergalactic Enosis had lasted a whole year, during which Lethe had claimed the lives of a few warriors. Most of the Saberians were older than me, but I'd 'adopted' them and having to put down my own family when there was an easy solution to our problem was taking a toll on Dawn and me.

But we are finally here, I reminded myself.

And we're not going to take no for an answer, Dawn warned.

My sabertooth preferred to settle things using teeth and claws instead of words. *Bloodthirsty kitty,* I said affectionately. *Of course, we won't accept anything less than what we came here to accomplish, but it might take a while.* I'd only had her for the last two years, but I couldn't imagine my life without her in it besides her sometimes feral manners.

Mes squeezed my hand, pulling my focus back to our mission, and I scanned the surrounding area…or as much as I could see because my overprotective mates along with my 'brother-in-law' had boxed me in the middle, and they themselves were encircled—much to their dismay—by the Royal Guards that would accompany us into the building. Callibohr's soldiers remained on standby inside our transport from the Imperial.

Not wanting to draw attention to us before we had a chance to talk with the President, we activated stealth mode and headed toward the entrance of the White House. A few moments after we revealed ourselves—the whole convoy appearing out of thin air inside the Grand Foyer—armed men burst forth from all directions, rushing towards us with guns raised and effectively fencing us in.

Yelling, growls, and a few choice words uttered in both languages were all I could discern, but one thing was clear, the volume was increasing by the second.

Uh-oh.

With the situation escalating rapidly, unless I did something, things would spiral downward faster than one could say Jack Robinson. None of my men could pass for human, but maybe the sight of one would help the security guards calm down enough to make our request.

At least I hoped it did. So I carefully inched my way out of the protective circle, or so I thought when Arana roared—the chilling sound revealing the predator hiding in plain sight.

Everyone froze, and you could hear a pin drop. Not only had I angered my mates with my little stunt, but the rest of my companions as well—their displeasure thick in the air. Fuck, I was in trouble.

'Oh you bet, Mate! That wasn't our plan,' he said, and the gravelly tone of his voice full of dark promises slithered around my body, making me shiver.

Sensing my resolve to ignore his silent order through our Sacred Bond to return to safety, Arana, Rorc, and Mes formed a wall in front of me. Callibohr moved as one with them too, surprising me. I was keeping the mental pathway open enabling all of us to communicate telepathically, but I hadn't conveyed my plan. Hiding my intentions from my mates was extremely difficult and I could only get away with it for a few minutes tops, so I'd expected their reaction. How had Cal known, though, I pondered; but this wasn't the time for speculations because my plan had worked, and even though the guards didn't lower their guns, they'd started asking questions.

"Miss, are you in danger?" one of them asked, and a giggle escaped my lips before I schooled my expression.

Dammit! River was rubbing off on me because I didn't giggle. "No," I said out loud. "We need to speak to the President. Take us to him," I ordered, hoping against hope that my austere tone would be obeyed.

"We cannot do that," someone else replied, irritating me. What did he think they could do, I wondered.

'My loves, let me pass,' I implored my mates.

'No.' Mes was absolute. When any of the three of them got like that, none of the others would budge.

I leaned forward and rested my forehead against Rorc's back. The reason why we were here was important, and their stubbornness was making the situation harder than it should be, leaving me with no other choice.

Rorc reached backward and pulled me closer to his body when a tremble rocked mine.

The first time this gift manifested it had been after a heated disagreement with my mates. In the midst of my frustration, I'd accidentally compelled five warriors to face me in the Pit simultaneously. That move, though, had been more than my males could handle, and they intervened, taking their fury out on the warriors who'd dared attack the pregnant Queen, sending them straight to the infirmary.

Another shudder raced down my spine.

That whole incident had left me feeling grimy…tainted somehow; I couldn't think of a more despicable action than robbing someone of their free will, but in this instance, I couldn't let the Secret Service guards divert us from our goal.

Dawn, who'd been quietly observing from the recesses of my mind, came forth and joined her power with mine. We inhaled deeply, cataloging the plethora of information the scents provided, then exhaled slowly. Centered and in control, my sabertooth joined her voice with mine when I said, "Take us to him now." The lower pitch carried an alpha command that would haze their minds, rendering them unable to disobey.

The humans turned around as one—like puppets manipulated by the string master—and led us farther into the White House. They stopped once we arrived outside the Oval office, and knocked on the door.

Someone opened it and sucked in a deep breath when he noticed their men's blank faces, along with the alien crowd behind them. My warriors with their imposing figures and their Sirhs imitating their colorful skins were a sight to behold.

I released the Secret Service agents from my hold only for the yelling to begin again. Wanting to show them we meant no harm, none of us reacted. We only needed to warn the president and form an alliance. *Easy-peasy.* Or so I thought, when the muzzle of a gun pressed against my temple. The next instant, it was gone, and a furious Callibohr, who'd been standing next to me, had grabbed the agent by his neck and lifted him off the ground.

The poor guy was futilely trying to pry the Wravukian's fingers open, turning bluer by the second.

"Stop," I shouted. "You maybe have five seconds to lower your weapons before you have a bloodbath in your hands, and trust me when I say, you won't be the ones left standing in the end."

Finally, the president, who'd probably recognized how dire the situation had quickly become, put an end to it. "Let them in," he ordered, and his men obeyed.

Every single person who was standing outside entered the Oval room, and suddenly we were packed in like sardines. Too many aliens, who took up a lot of space anyway due to their size, and too many humans.

My Kings, send the Royal Guards back to the ship. They aren't needed here. The humans aren't a match for one of you, let alone three of you. Keeping myself out of the equation would appease their overprotective nature and appeal to their egos. I snickered inwardly. That tactic seemed to work more often than not.

Comparing notes with Tris and River, I'd realized that every male—no matter the species—had one, and with the right kind of stroking, a woman could get much accomplished.

'Don't think I don't know what you're doing. That's a second punishment earned in just a short while.' Mes's smooth voice caressed my mind. Its seductive timbre pulled a physical reaction from me as goosebumps rose on my skin, but when he shared images of what he was planning to do once we were in our quarters, my core quivered in anticipation. A punishment, especially accompanied by their brand of pleasure, was not bad, not bad at all.

When some of the warriors stole glances my way, I realized my mistake—everyone had heard my mate's comment—and my cheeks burned from embarrassment. *'Focus,'* I chastised, but only managed to make everyone laugh, although outwardly their stern expressions betrayed nothing.

"Aux and Dagoner, stay. The rest of you go back to the ship. Use stealth and do not engage with the humans." Rorc gave the order in Saberian. By now we could all speak English, Saberian, and Wravukian, but we had agreed to let the humans know as little as possible.

Funny how I didn't identify myself as human anymore. *When had I stopped?*

You are not one anymore. Dawn, who was once again curled in a corner of my mind, lifted her head and put in her two cents.

I'm half human, kitty cat, I told her, but she'd already gone back to sleep.

When my mates were present, and my little beastie didn't feel a threat around us, she would trust them to take care of us—and so far they'd always done so.

The Royal Guards obeyed their Third King's order and silently slipped out of the room.

"Where are they going?" a Secret Service agent asked.

"Back to our ship."

"Call them back immediately," he ordered and pointed his gun at me. "There is no ship. We'd have seen it."

I immediately spread my arms wide, stopping my two mates closest to me from attacking the not-so-bright man. "Really? How do you think we got here? We drove?" My sarcasm was obvious, but I could feel the situation escalating again. So I told Admiral Culhwch to uncloak the transport ship only. Pasting a saccharine smile on my face, I said, "You might want to take a look out the window."

Gasps and awed murmurs filled the otherwise quiet space as the reflection of the sun on the shiny chrome of the exterior of the ship lit up the room, but once their attention diverted back to us, it was time to get to the point.

"Now that we've got the subject of our transportation out of the way, how about we get back to business? We are here to talk to you, Mr. President, preferably with a smaller audience than the one that is here now."

Ruckus followed my statement, but the president kept his composure. He gestured for us to sit, then followed suit himself, ignoring my request. "Who are you?"

'These humans are testing my patience,' Rorc grumbled, and I heard Cal's snicker in my head.

I gestured at each person before introducing them, leaving myself for last.

"You're human, they aren't," he pointed out, and I was about to say thanks genius for the observation, but held my tongue.

Sarcasm would not help in this tense situation, so instead, I went with honesty…or more accurately, semi-honesty. "Yes, before

I became the Queen of Saber by marriage, I was a Brigadier General serving as a Deputy Commander to the commanding General of the First Armored Division," I said, sticking as close to the truth as possible.

He narrowed his eyes at me—and it was as if I could see the wheels in his head turning—before locking eyes with one of the Secret Service agents, some kind of signal passing between them. "How did they get you?"

The president was sharp, but the moment he uttered those words, the guards raised their guns, pointing them at the alien males this time.

Dawn's reaction to the perceived infraction was swift, but I managed to push her back and swallow down the growl. Revealing secrets would hurt us more than help us. The rest of my company, though, was quite vocal in their displeasure over the treatment. Neither species would behave this way toward an official representing the Intergalactic Enosis.

"Mr. President, we're here on official business. I give you my word. We pose no harm to you or to another human. Please tell your guards to lower the weapons and leave the room."

A phone beeped, and the agent closest to the politician looked at its screen before leaning over and whispering to the man's ear, unaware our hearing was superior to theirs—my little beastie came with cool new abilities, which by now I had learned to utilize to full capacity. The guy had just relayed the news of my death.

Even though this information wasn't new to me, my muscles still went numb upon hearing it. Instantly, warmth overflowed from the mental pathway I'd been maintaining, filling me and lifting my spirits. I was blessed to call these males family.

“I'm afraid I cannot do that,” the politician replied with an air of authority.

And I'd had enough. “If you keep pushing, you'll soon discover our patience has its limits, Mr. President,” I growled, dropping the friendly pretense. “Our word stands. You think if we meant you harm, you'd still be standing?” I scoffed, then added, “Maybe a demonstration of power will convince you.”

NOTHING ELSE TO ACCOMPLISH

CALLIBOHR

I couldn't feel more proud watching my new sister handle the situation. Not only was she dealing with the human nuisances, but she was shielding us from their aggressively volatile energies, too.

'Callibohr, I need you to give the order, and I'll channel the command through you.' Kali had manifested mind control abilities—an extremely rare gift that took a toll on the bearer, yet she seemed to be getting stronger the more she used her powers. Still, I kept my eyes open for any signs showing she was getting overwhelmed.

"Guards, leave us, but you four can stay," I ordered in Wravukian. We'd anticipated and prepared for several contingencies on our way here, and the leadership of this species was proving to be quite predictable.

A buzz-like vibration spread in the air—the signature of telepathic communication—and Kali's cheeks turned a light pink.

'Mind out of the gutter, Kali,' she said, earning side-glances from all of us; immediately her eyes widened and her face flushed a deeper shade upon realizing she'd broadcast her thoughts.

Her mates smirked, and Rorc remarked, amused, *'You're adorable when you talk to yourself, little one.'*

I snorted out loud, having never expected the big, stern Admiral's vocabulary to include such words as 'adorable'.

Under Kali's influence, all the guards but the four I pointed out ignored our interaction and, one by one, left the chamber. The unoccupied space made breathing a little easier. The three floor to ceiling windows and the three glass entrance doors let plenty of light in, but they were also points of tactical vulnerability. What were the humans thinking, placing their leader's seat in front of the clear panels? Why hadn't he rearranged it? Didn't he care about his safety?

Although, a quick glance told me that said leader, who was looking askance at his people walking out of the chamber, as well as his baffled advisers, seemed to be more afraid of us than what could potentially be outside. "How did he do that?" he asked, the tremble in his voice overtly pronounced.

"They differ from humans." She left it at that, not wanting him to know more than absolutely necessary. "Now, can we sit down and discuss matters like civilized people?"

"Of course," he stuttered, and we gave him a few moments to compose himself. When he next spoke, his voice was calm and steady. "How did they get you?"

Straight to the point. At last.

"I was abducted, and the Kings saved me. I'm sure the government is aware of the existence of extraterrestrial species and understands that, like all living beings, some of them are good whereas others are bad." She let him digest her words before adding, "One of them is coming straight to Earth...unfortunately they're deadly, and you'll need our hel—"

The leader slapped his palm on the desk, interrupting Kali. "We can stop them."

Was it ambition or his ego driving him to make such a statement?

"How will you do that, Mr. President?" Sarcasm colored her words. "We entered Earth undetected. We landed in your own backyard and no one was the wiser. We walked into your house unseen. Your security realized the threat after we revealed ourselves."

The more we conversed with the arrogant beings, the more my opinion of them worsened. "Those species are technologically more advanced than Earthlings. You will need our help," I added, steering the conversation back to the main point.

And even though they didn't understand my words—not until Kali translated—my regal tone brooked no argument. Witnessing the war waging behind his eyes was satisfying. He should be afraid.

My comm unit buzzed in my ear before Culhwch's disgruntled voice reached me. "The aliens are trying to breach our ship. What do you want me to do, Admiral?"

One demonstration hadn't been enough for them? Well, the humans' behavior was just plain insulting. I shot off my seat and prowled toward the leader. The temperature of the room cooled in proportion to my soured mood. The human guards tried to block my path and failed. They raised their weapons, trying to intimidate me. They failed at that too, but they were tenacious. I'd give them that. "I suggest you call off your soldiers trying to infiltrate our ship, otherwise this discussion will take a turn for the worse, and I'm not sure you are going to like the outcome." All politeness stripped from my voice. Speaking English hadn't been in the plan, but they were about to cross a line that would have dire consequences.

No one threatened my brother's offspring, who were on the ship, and lived. My troops knew their safety was a top priority. Not that I worried humans could threaten the integrity of our ship, but if the Vice Admiral considered this species a threat, he'd retaliate with lethal force.

Mes's amusement rippled through the mental path connecting us all. *Here we are, being friendly and willing to save their asses, and they're trying to take over our ship. Hmph! Humans.* The mirth along with the tranquil quality of his voice helped dissipate the anger rising in me at the blatant disrespect shown to us.

The President paled, but he didn't call them off.

Fine. If he wanted another show of power, we'd grant his wish.

Speaking the Earthlings' language so they understood, I ordered, "Activate the shield, Culhwch."

A few ticks later, screams echoed around us. The energy field had flung those who were trying to break into the ship a good distance away, where they writhed on the ground. They wouldn't die, but they'd hurt for circles.

The humans inside the chamber once again rushed to the windows and watched their troops contort in pain as they thrashed on the ground.

Lips forming a tight line and shoulders almost reaching his ears, the leader plopped down on the chair behind his desk, then spoke into a handheld device. "Okay, enough. Everyone stand down." Then he turned his narrowed eyes our way and said, "What are you proposing?"

I scoffed internally. His suspicions were misplaced. We had already declared our intentions, and our word was law.

"We'll offer protection and technology. In return, we'll have access to Earth." Arana's deep voice was void of emotions, but the gravel underlining his tone warned everyone that Beast was near. Not that the Earthlings could possibly understand what that meant, but a displeased sabertooth was the last thing we needed.

Kali threw a pointed look his way before translating what he'd said.

"What do you mean, access?"

"Your planet makes for a beautiful vacation destination. When visiting, our species will be free to interact if they choose to do so," my brother replied calmly, not allowing the tension I could feel running through him to show, and his female interpreted his words. The message didn't even come close to conveying the importance of this request, but nonetheless revealed the reason for our coming here.

"If the masses find out extraterrestrials exist, there will be chaos."

"I'm sure the government's PR team will adequately handle the situation," was Kali's swift reply.

We could practically hear the wheels turning in his head. The deal we were offering was great. Humans would greatly benefit from our technology, and with having both Saberian and Wravukian sentinels, this planet would become the safest destination on this side of the galaxy.

"This isn't my decision alone to make. I'll schedule an assembly, but they'll want to meet with you, too, as well as see proof of the existence of this alien threat."

Upon Kali's insistence, I'd already agreed to stay behind for the negotiations. "We have recorded the destruction they caused on the last planet they invaded. I'll share the footage during your conference. Until then, I'll remain within the solar system, and you can contact me through this device," I said and placed the holo-projector on his desk.

Knowing nothing else would be gained from this meeting, the rest of my company stood, intending to leave. A knock at the door halted our progress, then it slid open and revealed more Earthlings.

A tall male for a human, with a commanding presence and an air of authority, entered the chamber flanked by two others. Their dark blue uniforms signified their warrior status. Broad chests and fit statures showcased their strength, but their rigid postures gave away the tension they felt. They posed a threat we could handle but should not underestimate.

Suddenly, Kali gasped, throwing everyone into action. The newcomer stepped toward the Queen, but before he could get to her, Rorc and Mes blocked his way. Arana pushed her behind him while Aux and Dagoner covered her back. I stepped in front of them, adding another sentry between them and danger. The move earned me a growl from the King, who didn't seem to appreciate the protective gesture.

The picture of a mental eye roll flashed in my mind—Kali didn't appreciate the overprotectiveness, either.

'Tough luck, sister.' I grinned inwardly, but quickly sobered up.

So far, this species had exhibited a volatile emotional behavior, which meant what I was about to do wouldn't be fun at all, but it was necessary. Taking a deep breath, I lowered my shields. Intense vibrations assaulted me from all sides, but thanks to whatever magic Kali possessed, I was able to let the vibes pass through me, releasing their energy whilst absorbing the intel they carried in the process. Information that helped me gain insight into these beings' intentions.

Facing off, everyone stood still. Anticipation, satisfaction, grief, and denial were the most prominent emotions of those around us.

'They think you lied. They called...a General to identify you.' Disbelief colored Rorc's mental voice, who was familiar with the Earthlings' ranking system and was faster to classify the officer whose way he was blocking.

Waves of distress emanated from behind me, nearly driving me to my knees. Kali's anguish overshadowed everything else as she whispered, *'They called my father.'*

At her admission, Arana stepped aggressively toward the President. A deep, blood-curling growl rumbled through his clenched teeth, the sound bringing everyone to a standstill. His murderous intent leaked into the mental path connecting us all.

Shit. The last thing we needed was an enraged sabertooth on the loose.

My brother seemed to agree because he reached out and stopped his Pair-bond's progress before the King could put his hands on the Earthling.

'It's all right, Arana. This was bound to happen. Rorc, Callibohr, let him pass.' Kali's soft voice dispersed the fury that had started clouding our minds. But while easing our tension, she erected shields around her and schooled her expression, so when she next spoke aloud, her authoritative tone was void of warmth. "General Foster."

I could taste the anger coming from my brother and his Pair-bonds even though they tried to rein in their emotions for the Queen's sake. There was history there, but it wasn't my place to ask questions, so I followed Rorc's example and moved aside.

When her sire's gaze met hers, his light gray eyes—the same color as Kali's—widened and his breathing ceased. Even though

Kali's DNA wasn't just human anymore, and her appearance had been altered by the Wravukian and Saberian genes she now carried, the resemblance between them was still there, indicating they were related.

Suddenly, as if waking from a hazy dream, the General exploded into action, launching himself at her, but instead of taking her down, he enveloped her in his arms and squeezed tight. "I thought I lost you," he gasped.

"Dad…it's okay, I'm here," she said and gently extricated herself from his embrace, and wiped away the tears streaking down her cheeks.

The President cleared his throat. "General Foster, is this your daughter?"

"Yes."

"Can you prove it?"

Now the Earthling was starting to piss me off, too. They didn't even trust their own kind. Why would her sire lie? *Freaking humans.*

The male in question didn't hesitate before replying. "She has a scar across her back that runs from her right shoulder to her midriff."

The humans looked pointedly at her.

My eyebrows shot upward. "What the hell? They want you to show them?" I asked Kali in Wravukian, but her mates' snarls were enough of an answer, and I was in agreement.

We boxed her in, pushing the terrestrials—who'd raised their pathetic weapons once again—out of the way, and headed toward the door.

The Queen put her foot down, halting us. *'It needs to be done. It's all right,'* she sent mentally.

'It's not all right.'

'No fucking way!'

'No.'

Her mates' voices boomed in my head, disorienting me for a tick.

The stubborn female, though, didn't give them a choice. She pulled Arana flush in front of her, whilst she projected to the rest of us what she planned to do. Mes and Rorc immediately covered her sides, and I, along with Aux and Dagoner, moved out of the way, leaving her back visible.

"I'll open my suit now, but I'd appreciate it if you lowered your weapons first," she said, and as soon as the humans obeyed, she revealed her bare flesh and the scar that proved she was whom she claimed to be.

The height of everyone's emotions skyrocketed upon witnessing this act of utter humiliation Kali had to endure. And even her tremendous power wasn't enough to keep the vibrations circulating around me from piercing my shields. The darkness inside me, that had been dormant so far, unfurled its feelers and pushed against the boundaries I'd set. I ground my teeth and pushed back. Now was not the time to lose control because the Queen's mates were hanging by a thread.

"Thank you," the president said, breaking the silence when she turned after having covered her exposed skin.

Kali nodded in acknowledgment, but that expression of false gratitude wasn't nearly enough for the rest of us.

"You will regret shaming our Queen this way," the King growled in Saberian, keeping up the charade.

When she stayed silent, he reprimanded her.

"Look at his face, Arana. He might have not understood your words, but your tone said it all," I replied in my mother tongue, knowing he'd understand me. Then I turned toward the president and spoke in English. "Mr. President, I'll expect the meeting's details soon…and if you try anything funny, we won't be as forgiving the next time." The threat rang loud and clear in my voice —I wanted no misunderstandings.

There was nothing else to accomplish here today, so we turned, dismissing the humans, and marched out of the chamber. On the periphery of my vision, I saw Kali's sire following suit. Hm, I guess he was coming along.

I HAD TO LET HIM GO

LYRA—27 YEARS OLD

Earth—Present day.

"He's been tracking you all night. Lyra, I said I'd help, but you're making a mistake," my former co-pilot and good friend warned, but didn't stop dancing with me on Dark Angel's small dance floor.

"I have to do this, Dylan," I insisted, hoping he didn't back out now.

Tomorrow night, I was set to take the TR-3 Alpha—the newest US manufactured stealth spacecraft—to space. My mission was simple really. Find proof of the alien threat, record it and then return to Earth—easy peasy…although, my gut churned every time I thought of what might await me out there. Something told me my life would forever be altered…but maybe that was nerves, for what I was about to do tonight would break the heart of the one person who'd stood by me my whole life.

Exactly why I have to do this. It's better this way, the soft voice of my conscience reiterated. This incessant inner war had been waging for a while. It was exhausting, and, for the sake of my sanity, needed to end.

"Why?" Dylan insisted as he pulled me flush to his muscular body, and now even I could feel Hunter's gaze burning a hole in my back.

"Because I might not come back." I realized the mistake the moment the words slipped from my lips, but it was too late to take them back.

His fingers flexed on my hips, painfully tight. "What the hell?" he growled in my ear.

Instinctively, a plan of attack formed in my head, the reel playing in my mind's eye, showing me the most efficient way of taking my opponent down. I could squeeze my bicep and forearm closed and wrap my other arm around his neck, then pull his head forward and block his airway. It would take ten, twenty seconds tops to get him off me. But this was Dylan, not an enemy, so I ruthlessly suppressed my desire to fight back and remained still.

"Lyra."

His persistent growl coupled with the feel of his taut body and his masculine scent would have melted the panties off any hot-blooded woman, but it did nothing for me. It would have them giving him anything he requested, but my mission was highly classified. It was a topic I couldn't discuss even if I wanted to—which I didn't. Luckily for me, though, there was a course of action that would shut him up while setting the wheels in motion.

Turning sideways, I locked my lips with his, stunning him, if his frozen body was any indication.

Oh my God!—It felt like kissing a family member in the mouth —*Just a few seconds longer, Lyra,* I thought to myself.

Suddenly, I was wrenched from his arms.

"What the hell, man?" Hunter snarled before he punched my co-pilot in the face, causing him to stagger backwards—his cheek already turning a deeper shade of chocolate brown.

I slammed my hands on Hunt's chest, trying to push him backward and failing miserably. Instead, he maneuvered me with his arm, and I had to step sideways or lose my balance. Damn it, I hadn't expected violence. They were good friends, so I'd assumed my husband, for all intents and purposes, would get mad and yell at us, not hit him.

But he didn't yell. Instead, his body vibrated with menace, and even though he'd never hurt me, I couldn't guarantee the same for anyone else.

Realizing he was on thin ice, Dylan raised his arms, palms out. "Sorry, bro," he said, going along with my plan, "I got carried away." Then he spun around and walked out of the pub.

The loud music and the people surrounding us disappeared as my world shrank to a small bubble that contained only Hunter and I. He turned toward me, and silence descended between us. His furrowed brows obscured the pain clouding his vivid blue eyes, but I'd seen it and could no longer maintain eye contact, so I lowered mine to the floor. Resentment filled every crevice of my essence, for I was hurting the one person I loved with my whole being.

For a few tense seconds, he didn't speak, nor did he touch me. But I could feel the heat emanating from him—Hunter was fuming and rightfully so. It seared my soul, and I welcomed the pain, allowing it to recalibrate me and strengthen my resolve, for he was a great man and I needed to set him free before I dragged him down with me…like my mother had done to my father.

Suddenly memories of the past surfaced, and like a black hole consuming everything in close proximity, sucked me in. My vision turned hazy. Raised voices reached my ears first, then the nerve endings along my back burned as if set on fire, and images of my parents on top of a child's curled body—on top of my body—lying on the floor replaced the dimly lit dance floor.

My whole body trembled. My teeth chattered and a metallic taste filled my mouth. *Fuck, I bit my tongue.* In the back of my mind, I knew what was happening…I was having a panic attack. It'd been years since the last time one had me in its grips, but I couldn't shake it off. Not until a hand on my shoulder jolted me back to the present.

"Is everything all right, Lyra?" Daemon, the pub's bouncer, asked, seemingly nonchalant, but the low, even tone of his voice carried an undercurrent of menace. He—like Hunter—was the type of man who didn't get riled up easily; who didn't raise his voice when angered, but got quieter, like an undertow building in strength with none the wiser, not until you were in it, being pulled under the surface.

Clearing my throat, I stole another moment to compose myself. "Yes…it was just a misunderstanding."

"Is that so?" He directed his question toward Hunter this time, and I sighed.

The situation had the potential to quickly get out of hand. They both were of similar size, around six seven, with broad shoulders, and not an ounce of fat. Daemon was bulkier than Hunter, but I'd seen the latter take down bigger men than him while defending us during the time we'd been homeless.

They seemed to converse in silence, their bodies slowly tensing, and I was about to put a stop to whatever was churning when Hunter spoke.

"No one touches my wife."

The answer seemed to pacify Daemon, who gave him a sharp nod and left.

Without another word, Hunter spun around and strode out of Dark Angel. This wasn't over. He definitely had things to say to me, but he'd always been the type to keep our matters private, regardless of the issue. So I followed him out to our car. The moment I put my seatbelt on, he drove off toward our home.

We didn't live on base. After our childhood, we both cherished secluded spaces. So the moment our salaries allowed, we got a one-story house further away from the rest, near the edge of a forest, with a lot of land surrounding the structure.

Suddenly, the constant buzzing in my head that usually calmed whenever I was with him intensified, making the confined space feel even more constricting. As I grew older, my internal warning system evolved. It warned me not only of danger but it often showed me the best strategy to deal with any situation. It was what kept me and my teammates alive during missions that went downhill in the blink of an eye, and now it was telling me to let him put his thoughts in order. So I remained silent during the ride.

The door holding all my nightmarish childhood memories locked away creaked and groaned. They wanted out tonight, but I couldn't deal with them and do what I had to do…I wasn't strong enough to face both.

My mother's voice, demanding I give her the pocket money I'd gathered from selling lemonade or else, filled the interior of the car.

She's not here anymore, I reminded myself as I pushed against the memory, burying it where it belonged…in the past.

Alas, it didn't stay there.

My hand flew to my neck when fingers wrapped around my

throat, closing off my airway, choking me, only for my nails to scratch the sensitive skin there in my desperation to free myself. *It's not real...just a memory.* I repeated the mantra that usually snapped me out of it.

The dull thud of the garage door closing brought a cold splash of reality with it, startling me but also effectively rooting me to the present.

This was it.

The beginning of the end.

A squeaking sound pierced the silence as the leather on the steering wheel protested under Hunter's death grip. Unable to stand the oppressive air filling the space, I opened my mouth to speak, but he got out of the car before I had a chance to utter anything.

So this is how it's going to be, I sighed. He'd only ever been in this state of mind a handful of times under extenuating circumstances, but even then, I'd never been the recipient of his anger. *This sucks.*

I followed him inside, noticing he didn't turn on any lights. The skylights above the kitchen as well as the floor-to-ceiling windows taking up the entire side of the living room allowed the moonlight in. The open floor plan of the main area of our house, with the uninterrupted views of the tall trees surrounding the structure, made it seem like the forest was an extension of our home. I'd never felt the walls closing in on me until now.

Suddenly, Hunter spun around. The icy flames dancing in his blue eyes stopping me in my tracks. He didn't immediately speak, and beads of sweat gathered at the back of my neck, the cool air in the room making me shiver. "What the hell was that, Lyra?" he asked, his emotions spilling into his voice, adding a grittiness that had never been there before.

An invisible hand squeezed my heart painfully at the same time his tone sent a bolt of electricity straight to my core. My clit throbbed in tandem with my rising heartbeat. God, no one could evoke such reactions from my body without even touching me. Deep down, I was afraid that Hunter had forever ruined me for all other men…and we hadn't even had sex.

"Don't you think it's time we dropped the charade?" Even though we often ended up sleeping in each other's arms because it kept the nightmares at bay, for those nights that we needed some alone time, we each had our own space. So I marched into my room and grabbed the manila folder sitting on my desk. Turning around, I bumped Hunter's abs, and electricity sizzled at the point of contact, making my pulse spike. Startled, I jumped backward, barely avoiding the corner of my desk. *Geesh.* He was lethal to my libido. Plus, he could be eerily silent when he wanted, and I hadn't realized he'd followed me, but I seized the opportunity and pressed the envelope to his chest.

He grabbed it without paying attention to its contents, then stepped closer to me, making me step backward only to have the wall block my retreat. "Charade?" He repeated, his low timbre sounding more menacing than if he'd been yelling, and yet no alarm bells rang in my head. Hunter was losing his patience, but he'd never hurt me…that I was willing to bet my life on.

I looked pointedly at the buff colored envelope before lifting my eyes to his and raising an eyebrow questioningly.

Without moving an inch, he tore its edge and took out its contents. As soon as he lowered his gaze to the document and read the title, creases appeared on his forehead as he lifted his brows in surprise.

My hand was already in the air when I realized what I was about to do—smooth them out and tell him that together we could fix whatever troubled him. That couldn't be, though, because I was the reason he was upset, so I dropped my arm. There was no other way to fix this. If I wanted him to find happiness, I had to let him go.

His surprise lasted all of two seconds. His face transformed in front of my eyes, as I witnessed his brows furrow, his jaw clench, and the vein at the base of his neck jump wildly as if trying to escape from his skin.

Uh oh.

He lifted the papers at my eye level, and slowly, oh so slowly ripped them in four pieces—the sound breaking the silence—before he let them drop on the floor.

"Really? What are you, five? I can get more where that came from," I snapped, my tone challenging because once again I hadn't expected such a reaction.

"And I'll rip every single one of them to pieces."

I huffed in frustration at his childish behavior. *Okay, Lyra, if he chooses to behave like a child, you have to remain the adult,* I told myself and tried again. "Hunter, we had an agreement. When either one of us would be ready to have a family, we'd get a divorce." My voice hitched on the last word, and I closed my eyes in an effort to center myself and push the pain away. *Why is this so painful?* I asked myself, but got no answer in return. It didn't matter, though. I had to push through. "I'm not blind. I've seen all those women who fawn over you…I know you've been discrete, and I thank you for that, but—"

His whole body tensed so much that if I poked him with a finger, he'd break into a hundred pieces. "You think I've been fucking other women?"

The crude words made me flinch. I had expected the night to evolve differently, but three times in a row his reactions caught me by surprise, sending flushes of adrenaline tingling through my body.

Careless, go for careless.

"You've never brought another woman home, but then again, I'd never bring a man here, either. You have plenty of time and space at the hospital, the same as I have at the base." Looking at a spot over his shoulder because it was too painful to look at his eyes, I lifted my shoulders as if to say each of these words that slipped from my lips didn't feel like a dagger being plunged repeatedly into my heart.

YOU. ARE. MINE

HUNTER—28 YEARS OLD

Now, she's gone and done it! I was a doctor, sworn to save lives…but if another man dared touch what belonged to me, I'd kill them and not lose an iota of sleep.

Pulling my arm back and punching Dylan was as instinctive as breathing, and it brought the memory of the first time I saw that ten year old girl with eyes too big for her face being bullied all those years ago to the forefront of my mind.

I'd known then that she was mine, the same way I knew now exactly what she was doing; I'd witnessed time and again Lyra push away anyone that came too close to her heart. She guarded the damn organ with a vengeance, but I'd never expected her to include me with all those other people.

Yet…she hadn't pushed him away…she'd kissed him back.

Was she in love with him? Being co-pilots, they had developed a closer relationship than most colleagues since their lives depended on trusting each other implicitly. Spending a lot of time together up in the air and on land seemed logical, and I thought nothing of it. I'd even been glad she had someone to keep her company during the long hours I'd been working since my last promotion.

Lyra was the type of person who had backup plans for her backup plans. She left nothing to chance. So did the little minx know what she was doing right now? Was this her roundabout way to let me know I'd neglected her? If she was testing my patience, she would end up biting off more than she could chew this time, though.

Or has my absence led her into the arms of another man? The thought alone was too painful to even consider, but the insidious whispers swirled in my head, planting seeds of doubt. They drowned out the constant chatter of people shouting to be heard over the music, yet seemed to amplify my other senses. A mix of woody, green, and smokey scents tinged with the stench of hops and barley overwhelmed my sense of smell. Lyra's touch on my chest seared my skin, even though my shirt should have provided a barrier.

Unable to stand the contact, I eased her to the side, then locked my muscles in place in an effort to calm the red haze threatening to overpower the logical part of my brain. My nails dug into my skin —the sting a welcome distraction—but I didn't dare loosen my fists. Not when I wasn't sure whether I'd stop from pounding a retreating Dylan into pulp this time. I jerked my eyes away from him and zeroed in on Lyra.

Mad didn't even come close to describing my inner turmoil. *'How could you do this?'* Was on the tip of my tongue, but pain had momentarily stolen my voice. My breathing was overly loud in my ears as I inhaled and exhaled through clenched teeth. My first instinct was to protect her from everything that would distress her, but this time I allowed her to see the anguish she caused with her action. In the next few seconds, though, I regretted it as I watched her eyes turn glassy.

Fuck! She was about to have a panic attack. She hadn't had one in years, yet the signs of an oncoming one were etched in my mind forever. Before I could react, Daemon's voice brought her out of whichever hellish memory her mind had taken her to and back to the present. "Is everything all right, Lyra?"

"Yes," she stuttered, "it was just a misunderstanding."

His narrowed eyes locked on mine. "Is that so?" He widened his stance and turned sideways, presenting a smaller target.

He was ready to fight me.

"No one touches my wife," I growled, hoping it'd be enough.

He seemed to understand what I had left unsaid—that I'd rather cut my own arm off with a blunt knife than hurt her—because he nodded and left.

Suddenly, I could no longer stand the bodies shifting around me, nor all those men accidentally coming into contact with her lithe form as they danced too damn near us. Home. We needed to get home and talk without distractions, so I spun around and headed to our car, knowing she'd follow.

A bitter tang filled my mouth, and just the idea made my skin crawl, but damn it, I was turning into a possessive demon...into my father. I didn't deserve her. God! I'd even punched our friend.

He dared to kiss my woman, the little devil on my shoulder reminded me, but that didn't justify my reaction or the lengths I was willing to go to for her.

The ride should have helped me calm down, but the closer we got to our house, the hotter my anger burned, and I had half a mind to turn around and go hunt Dylan.

I managed to resist.

Barely.

But when we stepped into our living room, I couldn't hold back any longer—I needed answers. "What the hell was that, Lyra?" Not the most eloquent way I could phrase the question, but frustration tied my tongue.

"Don't you think it's time we dropped the charade?" she asked, then walked away.

Oh no. This wasn't a discussion she'd avoid by hiding in her room. I was on her heels and ready to drag her back to the living room when she spun around, her hands grazing my lower abs and the top of my cock over my jeans. Heat flared outward from the point contact, enveloping my whole body as blood pooled south in a rush, waking up the damn organ. Had she done that on purpose? Suddenly unable to tolerate anything between us, I grabbed whatever she'd picked up and stepped into her personal space. "Charade?" I growled—she couldn't be serious.

She ignored my outburst and instead looked at my hand before raising her eyes to mine, the challenge clear in their hazel depths. She was as stubborn as a mule when she wanted something.

Fine, I'd play along. I tore the envelope and pulled out papers. The first thing I noticed was the title in bold lettering: *'Petition for Divorce',* then I did a double take and blinked a few times for good measure, to make sure I wasn't seeing things, because surely Lyra wasn't asking for a divorce.

When the writing didn't change, but remained the same, mocking me, my surprise turned to anger. If she thought that I'd let her push me away just like that, she was sorely mistaken. So I made sure to get my message across by ripping the papers in front of her.

"Really? What are you, five? I can get more where that came from."

My body had a visceral reaction to her words. My muscles tensed and my heart pumped faster, as if in preparation for an attack. If she kept the attitude up, I'd turn her over my knee and punish her like the five-year-old she accused me of being. "And I'll rip every single one of them to pieces."

"Hunter, we had an agreement. When either one of us would be ready to have a family, we'd get a divorce. I'm not blind. I've seen all those women who fawn over you—" she sounded resigned, but her tone had a bite to it "—I know you've been discrete, and I thank you for that, but..."

Confusion broke through the red haze that clouded my mind. Without conscious thought, I brought my hand up, and my gaze dropped to the luscious flesh as I ran my thumb across her bottom lip—its soft texture distracting me further. Then her lips parted as her breath caught, and I realized what I was doing. Slowly, I braced both my fists on the wall, caging her in my arms. "You think I've been...fucking other women?" I raised an eyebrow as the tips of my mouth lifted in a pleased smirk, even though what she thought was preposterous.

She didn't look at me, but focused on a spot above my shoulder, when she answered, "You've never brought another woman home, but then again, I'd never bring a man here either. You have plenty of time and space at the hospital, the same as I have at the base." The careless words she threw at me were fucking daggers in the heart.

"Wrong answer, baby girl."

Her eyes snapped to mine, then narrowed, concealing their beautiful colors. She was getting mad.

Good. Now she'd know how she made me feel.

Closing the meager distance between us, I let my anger show.

She squared her shoulders and lifted her chin at me.

My smile widened, but it was more a show of teeth rather than an expression of joy. *Wrong choice, darling. You should have submitted.* But it wouldn't be Lyra if she had.

I grabbed the hair at the base of her neck and clenched my fist, bunching the strands.

An angry hiss slipped from her tight lips, but her body…her body told a different story. Her pupils dilated, and the pulse at the base of her neck jumped in quick succession. My girl found the bite of pain arousing.

"Let go," she snarled.

I did not relent, instead I reminded her of the pact we had made when we were little. "No lies." Using my bulk, I blocked her limbs. Ly was lethal, but we'd trained together since we were teenagers and I knew her moves. She couldn't use her legs effectively the way I'd trapped her, so she brought her palms to my chest, readying to push back. Faster than she'd expected, I captured her hands and pulled them over her head, trapping both under one of mine. The other returned to her hair.

"Hunter, don't make me hurt you."

I laughed at her threat. "You're welcome to try, baby girl."

This was a fight she wasn't going to win.

"Lyra," she growled, correcting me.

Feisty.

Perfect.

We'd been together through her lowest lows and her highest highs, and this side of hers was one of my favorites—even if most times it made me want to turn her over my knee or fuck her brains out to make her see what was in front of her. Most certainly, though, I'd take this behavior any day over her feeling ready to give up because the shitstorm that had been our life had knocked her down one time too many.

The scent wafting from her skin was mouth-watering. It always drove me crazy, instantly turning my cock rock-hard. "Are you jealous, love…of those hypothetical women of mine?" I taunted her before allowing myself a little taste for the first time.

No more holding back.

I kissed the side of the column of her neck, and added, "Or maybe you have an itch you want scratched." Before grazing the vulnerable flesh with my teeth.

The sweetest moan escaped her pursed lips, and satisfaction warmed me from the inside out.

She burned for me like I burned for her. Was she ready to admit it, though?

"Why would I ever be jealous?" she asked, her tone all prim and proper—albeit a little breathless—while doing her best to look down her nose at me.

I raised an eyebrow. We'd both heard the lie, and a smile tugged the sides of my mouth upward, but what came out of hers next, wiped it from my face.

"You had no right to interfere with Dylan. You have no right to interfere with my sex life."

Fuck that. "I have every right," I growled.

She knew how to push every single button I had—and she often did, but listening to her saying she was interested sexually in another broke the dam I had so carefully constructed. The one that was keeping all my feelings for her behind its high wall…and she'd demolished it with a few words.

"This is not just about sex, Hunter. I'm ready to have a romantic relationship. An exclusive one, and I can't do that if we're married."

At work, I was renowned for my control under pressure, but at the moment, she had me holding on by a thread. Then she tried to use her upper chest to shove me off her, only managing to squish her breasts against my pecs, making me groan. The bodycon dress she had on failed to cover the fact that her nipples had turned into two hard peaks. A second later, her heat on my thigh registered. The flimsy fabric covering her pussy failing to act as a barrier. Her warmth spread slow as molasses, igniting an inferno that would consume both of us.

And just like that, the civil mask—the controlled one I wore at all times—masquerading the monster I'd unwillingly inherited from my father, shattered.

I leaned closer, looming over her. Her breath tickled my cheeks, her sweet lips a hair's breadth away from mine, tantalizing me.

"If you've let other men touch your body, you better pray I don't find out their names, baby girl," I let the threat hang in the air, while I trailed the tips of my fingers across her ribs, grazing the side of her breast. "This body is mine," I said, my voice huskier than usual, before I dragged the back of my nail beds across the top of her breast, until I pressed my palm flat in the middle of the two globes, my thumb strumming over her nipple, making it harden even more under my touch. "Your heart is mine." Her gulp was audible in the silence of the room, and I could see the trepidation in her eyes.

"Do you think, after all this time, I'd let you go just like that?" Anger kept my tone low while darkness swirled around me. Its seductive whispers trying to ensnare me, demanding I punish her for giving herself to another, but I'd fucking kill myself before I laid a finger on her. I closed my eyes and breathed through my nose, taking Lyra's scent deep into my lungs. It was enough to center me, and bring back a modicum of control, but I needed to make something very, very clear. "You. Are. Mine." I punctuated my words with a press of my covered cock against her pussy.

The contact was electrifying. An involuntary shudder racked my body, and my control snapped. I crashed my lips to hers.

She froze, like a deer caught in the headlights, but I was determined. I pushed my body flush against hers at the same time I licked the seam of her lips. Electricity sizzled between us, and she gasped.

Seizing the chance, I delved into her mouth, and miraculously her tongue started dancing with mine. Ly squirmed against me, creating sweet friction, rubbing my cock, and inflaming my hunger. She tugged her hands, but I held firm. If I released them and they started exploring my body, I wouldn't be able to last.

In the sanctuary of our home, the rest of the world disappeared, only we remained. Every point that was in contact with her felt on fire, injecting heat into my veins that traveled through my bloodstream only to pool low. My cock was stretched to its limit like never before. I might have been ravaging her lips for minutes or for hours when I felt as if I was about to break apart at the seams. This wasn't enough. I wanted, no…I needed more. I broke the kiss, but she chased my lips, making me chuckle before pulling her bottom lip into my mouth. I glided my tongue along the curve of the soft flesh, then nipped it with my teeth. She rose on her tiptoes, a low moan interrupting the silence, before she turned the tables on me and attacked my mouth with fervor.

Fuck, Lyra—my love—was kissing me back.

The sensation was out of this world, but the insidious thought that someone else also knew how she tasted probed and teased the monster inside me until its roars overshadowed the pleasure, and I had to know. I couldn't simply let it go.

I broke our kiss, took a small step backward, and rested my forehead against hers. Our panting breaths mixed and we shared the same air, but it wasn't enough. She would become mine tonight, but first she'd give me the names I wanted.

"Baby girl," I whispered, and she stiffened as if she'd sensed, with that sixth sense of hers the change in my mood.

She tugged her hands, and this time I released them. She brought them to her lips and mumbled, "What have we done?" A tremor ran through her body, and I would have missed it if I hadn't been paying attention to her subtle nuances for most of my life.

"What we should have done years ago." My tone was firm and authoritative. I didn't want her to have a single doubt about my intentions. "No more games, Ly. I love you." I hated myself for chickening out years ago, but I wasn't about to repeat the same mistake. "You're mine, and mine alone." She lowered her gaze to the floor, but I wouldn't let her hide from me, from us. I lifted my hand and wrapped it loosely around her neck, letting her feel the weight there before applying pressure with my knuckles under her chin until she lifted her eyes to mine.

"I will ask once and never bring it up again…but you need to answer honestly." I waited for her nod, then added, "Who have you let inside your body?"

Her throat worked under my palm as she swallowed, and the pulse at the base of her neck twitched under my little finger. Her nervousness was contagious, and suddenly my stomach rolled a warning as nausea gripped my middle. *Fuck, is it that bad?*

I growled her name when she remained silent for far too long.

"Love destroys everything and everyone in its path. Look at what happened to our parents, Hunter."

"Look at what happened to us, Ly. Love helped us overcome all the obstacles thrown our way. Love has held us together for all these years," I contradicted, without missing a beat.

"Brotherly and sisterly love! Not—" she yelled, stopping mid-sentence and inhaling sharply through clenched teeth in an effort to calm down. The space I'd allowed between us gave her the opportunity to slam her palms under my collarbone and push hard. She failed, though, to move me a single inch.

I had at least fifty pounds on her; if I didn't want to move, she couldn't make me. And this time, I wasn't going to give her time to process her feelings. I couldn't allow doubt to enter her mind because she'd end up talking herself out of what she was truly feeling. I shook my head, both disagreeing with her admission and denying her the distance she wanted to put between us.

Upon realizing her efforts were fruitless, she continued, her voice subdued, "Look at how you're reacting now."

"I know what you're afraid of, baby girl. But you're not her. You aren't your mother, and I'm not your father." My words seemed to appease her.

Triumph warmed my chest, and I pushed further. "Our love was never brotherly and sisterly. I knew you were mine the moment I laid my eyes on you." Slowly, I lifted the hem of her dress, giving her every opportunity to stop me, but she didn't. Instead, she allowed me to bunch the fabric at her waist, putting her smooth creamy skin on display. I drank in the sight.

She was perfection. A panting mess in my arms, I could no longer resist…nor did I want to.

As I lowered my head, her lips parted slightly and she nibbled the bottom one, pulling another groan from me as the image of Ly on her knees—her teeth gently biting into my length—made my cock jerk within my painfully constricting pants. My fingers tightened around her waist on reflex, and before I knew what I was doing, I'd closed the gap between us and kissed her. Every emotion I'd ever felt, every desire I'd ever had, went into that single action. So when she clasped her hands behind my neck, responding to my touch, delight filled me. Her sweet surrender would be forever etched in my memory, but before we moved further, I had to know. "Tell me who they are, baby girl."

Lyra furrowed her brows, confusion clouding the lust darkening her hazel eyes.

I dragged my palm from her hip to the middle of her thighs, then slid my finger along one edge of her silky thong's gusset before gliding my finger between the fabric and her pussy...only to find both soaking wet. Fuck, I had to taste her. I dropped to my knees, wrenching her panties downward at the same time.

The sudden move must have startled her because she grabbed my head to stop me and stuttered, "What are you doing?"

The musky scent of her arousal filled my nostrils, and my eyes closed on their own accord as I inhaled deeply.

"Hunter!" she admonished, making me look up. Her cheeks were tinged with pink, her lips parted, and images of her mouth stretched around my length flooded my mind.

But my cock would have to wait because I needed to taste her first. I let my eyes drop to her heaving chest, then to her taut tummy that trembled the moment my gaze fell on it. My baby girl was nervous, but she didn't need to be. Leaning forward, I placed a gentle kiss above her belly button, before I finally allowed myself to feast on the glorious sight of her pussy, which was slick with her juices—the shaved mound hiding nothing.

She wanted me—her body betrayed her desire, yet her hands were pushing my head away from where she needed me the most.

Anger broke through my lust-filled mind. Why was she stopping me? *Is there another man in her life?* I instantly dismissed that thought because she wouldn't have kissed me.

Lyra wasn't the type one could force. She'd stopped being helpless when we were teenagers and had to live on the streets until we had found jobs that'd afforded us a dingy place to rent. No, she was lethal, and I'd given her plenty of openings to stop me if she wanted to. So did she push away all the men who tried to go down on her or was it just me?

A snarl rumbled in my throat. The thought of other men reminded me she hadn't given me their names.

Looking into her eyes, I repeated the question that would torture me until she answered. "Who has touched you before me?"

She dropped her hands from my head as her lips flattened into a thin line and she shifted her weight. She was pulling away from me, and that was the last thing I wanted. So I did what always pacified her when she was cornered—I gave her a piece of myself I'd kept hidden.

"I've loved you from the first moment I saw you. You ruined me for all other women and I hadn't even felt your body surrounding mine yet." Slowly, so she had every chance to stop me if she wanted to, I placed a gentle kiss on her smooth mons. Her breath caught, but she didn't push me away. "Other women don't hold a candle to you. I've always been faithful, waiting for the moment you were ready."

An expression crossed her face but was gone too fast. Had I seen regret mar her beautiful features?

"No one."

The nagging feeling tugging at my insides had me lost in thought, and her reply didn't register. "What?"

"I've never been with anyone else," she clarified. "My heart chose you a long time ago, and I could never..." Her voice trailed off, but I'd heard enough. I didn't need more words.

THAT'S WHAT LOVE DOES

LYRA

I hadn't expected his confession, but hearing there'd never been another woman who knew his body intimately appeased the green monster floundering inside me—the one I'd tried to suffocate multiple times and failed miserably at each and every one.

So I blurted my true feelings, and a weight lifted off my shoulders, making me feel lighter…not for long, though, because another much heavier one settled on top of me, grounding me abruptly.

Come morning, I'd go on a mission I might not return from. Did I really want to leave without having felt what truly belonging to Hunter was like?

No, dammit. That'd be a regret I'd carry with me to the afterlife, I thought, even though a voice at the back of my head insisted that there was something missing.

I hushed it.

Tonight would be perfect, and I wouldn't let anything spoil it.

"Hunt, I need you." Any other time, I'd have cringed upon hearing the whimper in my voice, but not on this occasion.

Thankfully, he didn't make me wait. Holding my eyes captive, he brought his left hand to my waist, whereas his right one landed on my ankle, but it didn't remain there.

His touch left goosebumps in its wake as he dragged his palm upward, and when it hooked behind my knee, I braced myself against the wall behind me.

"You're so soft," he whispered, and lifting my leg over his shoulder leaned forward and inhaled deeply, before pulling back slightly to peer up at me. "You smell fucking amazing, baby girl, and now—at last—I get to taste you."

Oh, Lord! My face heated from embarrassment, but that didn't deter him in the slightest. When he closed the distance, I thought he'd go straight for my pussy, but boy was I wrong because instead, he placed an open-mouthed kiss above my hipbone, then slid the flat of his tongue over my skin.

My breath hitched as he nibbled his way toward my navel. My muscles clenched in anticipation while he swirled the tip of his tongue around the orifice, making me giggle.

But he didn't linger; instead, he used light pecks and tiny nips to draw a downward path.

A whimper—or three—slipped through my lips when he continued past the spot I wanted him at the most. He went down my calves, to the side of the shallow depression at the back of my knee, which he then sucked roughly.

Out of the blue, electricity zinged from the point of contact, straight toward my pussy, making my legs shake.

Damn, I didn't know that was an erogenous zone, I thought, but couldn't stay focused on that little fact because the anticipation was killing me.

Hunter had always been a quick study, but more importantly…

he could read me like an open book. So it would only take him a few minutes of fumbling before he discovered, then zeroed in on, what I liked.

And while I was quite familiar with how my orgasms felt when induced by my hand or by the delicious pressure the showerhead sprays exerted, I didn't know how one would feel at Hunter's hands and mouth. And at the moment? It was the only secret I cared to uncover.

It seemed my not-so-silent mewls told him as much because he chuckled while his lips traced a path up my other leg. I raked my hands through his hair, gently scratching his scalp with the tips of my fingers, before I fisted the dark strands, threatening to pull unless he picked up speed.

"So impatient..." He tsk-tsked, then grabbed my waist, and pulled my body up against his face. He drew another deep breath, but I didn't even care anymore.

Finally, my inner voice sang, and my soul echoed the sentiment.

A ghost of a touch tickled my senses when I felt a featherlight caress over the spot I was aching the most.

"Hunter, stop teasing me," I pleaded, and maybe that was what he'd been waiting for because suddenly he thrust his tongue outward, the tip breeching my opening and drawing a high-pitched moan from me. Needing more, I pressed down on his face...but went nowhere—his hands were keeping me locked in place.

This was his non-verbal way of showing me he was in control. He'd often use this tactic during our boxing sessions, and the fastest way to get him moving was to acknowledge my defeat. So I let my body turn into a pliable mass in his hands, ready to be moved and handled as he pleased, and that did the trick. His tongue resumed its wandering ways and drew an invisible line from my entrance to my clit, parting my nether lips in the middle and gathering my essence in his mouth.

A desperate, filthy sound burst from his lips, startling me with its intensity, and I lost my balance. On reflex, the fingers circling my waist clenched, securing me in place. His firm grip caused indentations to form on my skin around the outline of his palm. But instead of feeling pain, his possessive touch excited me, and I already knew he'd never let me fall, so I surrendered to his will, thrilled to reap the rewards.

My loud moans and his guttural grunts were the only sounds interrupting the peaceful night, but there was no way I could keep them in.

Whatever he might have lacked in skill initially, he more than made up for it with eagerness. Hunter was eating me out with the hunger of a starving man…he was eating my pussy like it was the best freaking dessert in the entire world—not that I was complaining.

I'd never complain again if that meant I'd get to experience this over and over again. "I'm so close, Hunt," I said, and too soon, or maybe not soon enough, he amped up his efforts by bringing his fingers into play.

He swirled a digit in my juices, then positioned it at my opening. His clever tongue, playing with my clit, working me higher the whole time.

"Ooo…Oh! Yes, like that," I encouraged him while trying to grind my pussy on his face, but he pulled back, taking his magic touch away from me. "Noooo," I cried.

He arched an eyebrow, and the tips of his lips lifted. "Will you be a good girl and let me give you what you need, or will you keep trying to take over?"

"I'll stop," I said, but silently vowed to make him pay when my turn came—delayed gratification was a bitch.

As if reading my thoughts, he laughed heartily. "I'm big, baby. I need to get you all slick and ready for me because I don't want to hurt you."

Oh.

His explanation made sense, but a slither of fear crept down my spine. How big were we talking about? Not that I had a 'real life' point of reference, even so, that'd sounded ominous. I was about to ask him when he sucked my little nub hard, then flicked it with some kind of short and fast taps, completely derailing my mind from my worries.

I'd been sitting at the precipice already, and the abrupt change in motion sent me spinning out of control, distorting my reality and erasing any doubts from my mind.

For a moment, the world around me disappeared, and I felt weightless, as if I was on a parabolic flight, training for zero gravity conditions, but that sensation didn't last long. My core muscles contracted, and waves of pleasure exploded out of me while I screamed Hunter's name.

Expecting him to slow down and gently ease me back into my body, I wasn't prepared for the sudden pressure I felt at my opening. My eyes snapped open, and I gasped—it was too much.

But Hunter apparently thought it wasn't enough. He continued sucking my little nub, varying the pressure and speed with which his tongue moved, but this time he brought his fingers into play.

I was already soaking wet, so when he pushed the first one in, there was no resistance. The unfamiliar sensation sent my heart soaring. If this was a precursor of how it'd feel when he entered me, I wanted more. "Hurry, Hunt. Please," I begged.

He nipped my clit, the sharp sting making me jolt, reprimanding me, but fuck if it didn't turn me on even more. I doubted that had been his intention, but my juices flowed out of me.

Oopsie.

"Fuck, Ly. You're so wet for me," he breathed in a reverent tone before screwing a second finger inside me, stretching me.

The slight burn of being filled for the first time with something thicker than my fingers wasn't enough to keep me from bucking. "Oh my God."

I couldn't hold back my moans any longer. The assault on my special spots had me hurtling dangerously fast toward the edge, and the intensity was scary. "Hunter?" My voice shook.

Understanding what I couldn't yet, he took his lips off my nub, but kept pumping his digits in and out of me, making sure the pads of his fingers rubbed a spot inside of me that made black spots dance at the edges of my vision. I'd never found my G spot, yet he had just like that.

I'd also never cum more than once, but I was ready to go again, and so soon after my previous orgasm—another first.

The Cheshire cat-like smile adorning his face told me he knew he was rocking my world.

I wanted to tease him about it, but couldn't form words, and when a third finger joined the other two, I was hurled over the precipice I was standing on and into the abyss. My knees went weak and my mind turned fuzzy as I soared high into another dimension, but then I felt liquid squirting out of me.

It took a few seconds for my vision to clear, and when I looked down, my eyes nearly fell out of their sockets. My cheeks heated, and I bet even my ears had turned red from embarrassment.

I'd made a mess of Hunter's clothes, but he didn't seem to care, grinning like a maniac. "I'm so—" I started but was cut off.

"That was un-fucking-believable, baby girl!" Awe mixed with smugness colored his voice. "Never apologize for showing me you enjoy what I do to you."

He placed a gentle kiss on my mons and rose to his feet, lifting me in his arms bridal style at the same time.

"Let me down, you doofus." I laughed.

"Never," he vowed, and laid me on the bed.

Before he could escape, I wrapped my arms around his neck and fused my mouth with his. I licked the seam of his lips and he parted them to let me in. My taste mixed with his was an even headier aphrodisiac, and suddenly I couldn't wait any longer.

I untangled my fingers from his hair and began unbuttoning his shirt. I was down two buttons when he straightened and reached behind his back to pull it off in one motion.

"I want to do it." I said and moved to grab his belt buckle, but he stepped out of my reach. "Hunt, I need to touch you," I whined.

"Sorry, baby girl, but if you do, I'll explode, and I can't have that. When I come, it'll be inside you."

I whimpered. I fucking whimpered.

He shushed me gently, then said, "Next time, I promise to let you play."

"Fine." I pulled my dress the rest of the way off, then crossed my arms over my boobs and my legs at the ankles.

Noticing my antics, he chuckled and continued undressing.

I'll just admire the show, I thought to myself and wiggled into a more comfortable position.

In the past, when living with a Greek God personified became too much, I'd let myself fantasize about us like this...but none of those fantasies held a candle to reality.

Sleeve tattoos with the story of our life decorated his arms, but his chest was bare. Well...bare besides the two nipple piercings. Oh, how I had longed to use my tongue to play with them, but they were a forbidden fruit.

Not anymore.

Slowly, I let my eyes trail lower. At the sight, my pussy clenched on air of its own accord. If our washing machine broke, I could always use his abs for a washing board.

A metallic clunk drew me out of my reverie. Hunter had just dropped his belt on the floor. He'd already removed his shirt, shoes and socks, and his fingers were now at the top button of his jeans.

"Show me how you play with yourself," he ordered, and I might have gushed a little upon hearing the need in his gravelly tone.

I untangled my limbs and bent my legs before dropping them to the sides.

This was another new experience. Another new first he was claiming, but I didn't mind at all because I wanted all his firsts, too. So I gave him a show while he unbuttoned his jeans. But as he pulled them downward, taking his boxer shorts with them, I got my first peek of his cock.

My fingers stilled, and my breath caught in my throat. He was easily eight or maybe nine inches, and as if that wasn't enough for a girl, he was thick, too.

"Um...Hunter, you're too big." My voice shook with trepidation.

He crawled over me, then grabbed the hand I had between my legs and licked my fingers clean. Carefully, he let me take more of his weight as he lowered his body onto mine, trapping his monster cock between us. "I'll take it slow, baby girl, and if you need me to stop, all you have to do is say so, and I will." He punctuated his words with sweet pecks all over my face. "Please, let us try."

Hunter was never afraid of being vulnerable with me. And it was his vulnerability when he pleaded with me that pushed my fears away. He'd never hurt me intentionally. I was safe with him.

"I've fantasized about us together…an embarrassing amount of times, Hunt. I want us to try."

His smile lit up his face, and I was sure mine matched it. Having been given the green light, he transferred his weight to his left elbow and used his right hand to lead his cock to my opening. I was so slick the head eased right in, but then he met resistance.

"Fuck! You're so tight," he groaned. "Take a breath for me, love." He brought his hand back up and caressed my face before closing the distance between us and locking his lips to mine in a sweet kiss. "You feel amazing."

His ministrations took my mind off where a certain body part of his was, and I relaxed under him.

Delicious pressure sent my senses haywire as he slowly pushed deeper until he had to stop once again because my hymen was blocking the way.

He leaned his forehead against mine and closed his eyes. Slight tremors rocked his body, and his shuddering breaths tingled my nose. "Am I hurting you?" I asked, confused.

"No, baby girl. But I'm afraid I'll be the one hurting you."

I threaded my fingers through his hair and massaged gently, trying to comfort him. "It's all right, Hunt. You know I can handle pain. I'm not fragile, and this will only be a pinch."

He lifted his head, and the action caused his cock to push against my membrane, making me wince. His bright blue eyes searched mine, and he must have found what he was looking for because in quick succession he pulled out, then pushed back in, taking my virginity and filling me to the hilt before freezing in place.

Hunter grunted in pain, then groaned as his breathing turned ragged.

Fuck. That hurt, I thought, but pinched my lips together to keep a whimper of pain from escaping. I didn't want him to feel bad over something he had no control over.

"I'm sorry, baby girl," he said and ran his thumbs over my cheeks, wiping the tears that had escaped.

Not trusting my voice, I shook my head, but he cradled my face in his palms and stopped the motion. "Don't move. Let me set the pace because I don't know how long I'll manage to last. You feel like heaven, but I want to feel your pussy choking my cock. I want to feel it squirt on me."

He wanted to set the tempo, but I couldn't stay still anymore. The pressure was getting too much to handle, and I needed friction. So I took the matter in my own hands.

A wiggle earned me a groan.

Pulling my pelvis backward as much as the bed would allow earned me a growl.

Thrusting forward, impaling myself on him, earned me what I was craving: Hunter out of control.

He drew out of me, leaving only the tip of his cock at my opening, then lunged forward.

My inner walls clenched around him, and I screamed, but not from pain. Although there was some mild discomfort, the euphoria coursing through my veins overpowered it, for Hunter had hit my G spot.

Encouraged by my reaction, he started pistoning in and out of me, slow at first, then as he sensed I was no longer aching, faster.

Long moans and hoarse screams were interspersed with guttural grunts and gravelly groans. The symphony we were creating was beautiful.

"Tell me you're close, baby girl," he said through clenched teeth.

Making love with Hunter would never be a drawn-out affair. Hitting that magic spot every time he moved his hips meant I'd always be done for within the first ten minutes.

And right now, I wasn't just close. I was teetering on the ledge while looking down at the abyss, and seeing him barely holding on did it for me.

My pussy clenched around his thick girth, and I almost fainted. Then I remembered to breathe, and the black spots that had entered my vision disappeared.

Hunter's thrusts turned erratic, and with a full-body shudder, he cried out my name.

I felt his cock swell even more, right before he erupted inside me. Hot jet after jet filled my womb, and for a microsecond there I felt sad that our union wouldn't lead to a pregnancy. Then I remembered who I was, and who my parents had been, and I snapped out of it. I wouldn't curse a child with my DNA.

My man, overcome by his explosion, gave me all of his weight, pulling me out of my head. Thankful for that, I gave him a bear hug, wrapping both my hands and legs around him, holding him close, until both our breathing returned to a somewhat normal level.

"I love you, Ly," he said, while pressing soft kisses to the nook of my neck.

I debated withholding the enormity of my feelings, to make tomorrow's separation easier, but it wouldn't be fair to him. "I love you, too, Hunt." Sadness had crept in, marring the post-orgasmic bliss flowing in rivulets inside me.

Suddenly, he pulled me flush to his body, then threw his weight sideways, taking me with him.

When we stopped rolling, I ended up sitting astride him, the new angle making me realize he was still hard.

"Don't you need time to recover?" I gasped when he thrust upward, going deeper than the first time and hitting spots I didn't know I had.

"No. I have a lifetime to make up for." He brought his hands to my hips and applied pressure until I lifted higher but not off him. "Ride me, baby girl," he said and slammed me downward, making me see stars.

Our first time had been amazing and Earth shattering, and I'd thought nothing could top it.

Hunter proved me wrong.

I had lost count of how many times he'd filled me with his cum and how many orgasms he'd drawn from me, and been pleasantly surprised that our bodies could actually perform like that.

Claiming that tomorrow I'd be sore was the understatement of the year.

But it was worth it because tomorrow, once I exited the atmosphere and left Earth behind, I'd have a tangible reminder of our first night together.

Lying sideways, nestled in his embrace, I tried to push the sad thoughts out of my mind. Then another one crept in, and even though Hunter's breathing had evened out, this needed to be addressed. "Um, Hunt? Aren't you worried I might get pregnant?"

"Fuck, Ly," he exclaimed with joy. "I can't wait for the day you'll swell with our child."

My jaw smacked the floor. Had he lost his fucking mind?

I'd obviously said that out loud because next thing I knew, he'd maneuvered my body like I was a rag doll and not a full-grown woman, and pinned me under him.

Stormy blue eyes warned of the turbulence brewing underneath the surface. "You. Are. Mine. And any children you have will be mine too."

"You're not thinking clearly, Hunter. Thankfully, I've got the issue covered."

"Covered?" he asked, his voice dropping lower.

"I've got an implant."

His fingers went unerringly to the little bump on my arm as if he'd been the one to put it there.

"Who the fuck put this in you?"

Uh oh. I pinched my lips tight to keep from blurting out Dr. Drew's name. Even though they'd been working together for the last couple of years, they didn't get along. But he was one of the two gynecologists at the hospital on the base, and Dr. Wirkam—the other gyno—was a bit too handsy for taste during examinations. So I didn't have a choice, really.

Hunter was like a dog with a bone when he wanted something, and he didn't like me withholding information. "I only need to look into your file to find out, baby girl. The fucker who agreed to put it in you behind my back will pay."

"My body, my choice," I snarled at him and tried to push him off me.

He clamped down harder. Grabbing my wrists and trapping them above my head. "Wrong, sweetheart—"

Most times I secretly loved his pet names for me, but not this time. "Lyra," I corrected him, yet he went on as if I hadn't spoken.

"You belong to me, the same way I belong to you. Your body belongs to me. And all the children we'll have will belong to me, too." His gravelly tone meant business. He believed every single word he uttered. "If you weren't going on a mission, I would remove it right this second."

"You wouldn't dare!"

He snickered. "Dare I would, baby girl…but I'll let you keep it for now."

I tried to wriggle free, but he just pressed his bulk against me, blocking my exit. "Thank you very much, your Highness." My voice dripped with sarcasm.

His hand gripped my throat, and his fingers nearly wrapped around the delicate column, not squeezing, just laying there for me to feel their weight. "The moment you return, though," he added, "I'll fucking get it out of you."

Something must have been seriously wrong with me because when his digits squeezed, threatening to constrict my airways, my body's first reaction was to lean into his touch, not defend myself. And when he delivered his threat in that gravelly tone, my pussy clenched on air.

My contrasting emotions were just too much. I couldn't handle the conflicted feelings without losing it and bawling like a baby, so I pushed them to the side to take out and examine later, under the cover of darkness, when the world was quiet. Only then would I try to untangle the mess inside me.

Feeling like I carried the weight of the world on my shoulders, I sighed, and I could have sworn the otherworldly sound coming out of my mouth was my soul sighing with me. He needed to hear the truth about why we needed to get a divorce.

"Hunter, I love you, and not just like my brother, so I can't drag you down, too…I wouldn't be able to live with myself." Uttering these words felt like I was thrusting a serrated knife into my gut, over and over and over again. It was one of the hardest things I'd ever done, and I half hoped he was asleep already and he wouldn't hear me.

His arms, though, tightened around me, and he placed a kiss on the crown of my head. "You're the one for me. You always have been, and I love you, too. But that's just bullshit, Ly," he said, cutting through the chase and going straight to the heart of the problem. "You're nothing like your mom. Sleep, angel. Everything will look brighter in the morning, and you'll remember there's nothing we can't solve together," he said, and soon after his breathing evened out once again.

That's what love does. It blinds you, Hunt, I thought, and the words followed me deep into my restless dreams.

THE ALIEN HADN'T LIED

LYRA

Why had I accepted this mission again? I thought as I executed another systems check.

The instrument panel of the TR-3 Alpha looked like something that would belong to an alien spaceship and not a man-made craft...and I guess part of it actually was, at least, a reverse engineered version of one. It even came with an AI co-pilot, AJ-R379, or AJ for short.

With the safety shutters currently retracted, the bleak black of space bled through the flight deck windows, threatening to swallow me whole.

"Elevated heartbeat detected," AJ's female voice reported. "The suit's cursory check reported functions are normal. Shall I do an in-depth check, Captain?"

"No need," I said and shook my limbs to disperse the sudden claustrophobic feeling that threatened to overwhelm me. My ship was quite spacious and nothing like the traditional spaceships that had been built so far. "But I need the hull's check report. Display on screen," I added, and within seconds watched the data flashing on the holo-screen in front of me.

When nothing was amiss, my gaze was once again drawn outside. I'd gotten over my fear of the dark around the age of ten, but…the dark vastness surrounding me was daunting. At times, it felt as if a gigantic mouth was about to swallow me whole, and I'd never be seen again.

Shake it off, Lyra. It's all in your head, I told myself, and focused on the route marked on the holo-screen.

During the briefing, General Foster had announced that an alien species—the Wravukians—had made contact, informing us that a threat unlike any humans had faced before was fast approaching Earth, and we'd need their help to fend them off.

Their fleet was supposed to be orbiting Earth, but I was outside of Earth's gravitational force, way past the moon, heading to Mars, and I'd yet to see another spacecraft.

My mission was to document proof of the alien threat and gather intel, but if friends or foes were out there, I had yet to see any. The radars were picking up traffic, but so far it'd been space junk, meteors, or other aerial bodies rather than aliens.

"You've got an incoming video call, Captain."

I wiped my suddenly sweaty palms on my uniform because I knew it wasn't my superiors at the other end of the line. Being by myself had never been an issue, so loneliness was the last worry on my mind when I accepted this mission, but the truth was…I already missed my best friend and wished he were here with me.

The whole operation was highly classified, and even though Hunter had a high clearance himself—he'd been part of the team monitoring my vitals and running physical tests during the preparations phase—I hadn't been allowed to divulge specific details, like the not so little fact that I wouldn't only test the craft within Earth's atmosphere but in space as well. At least not until I exited said atmosphere, because then it'd be hard to continue hiding this particular aspect of my assignment from the one family member I was allowed to contact.

Taking into consideration, though, the way I left things between us and the promise that I'd be returning home soon to discuss our relationship, I wasn't sure how the unexpected news would be received.

The situation had disaster written all over it, but I had to be honest with myself. The responsibility lay with me because I ran. I ran scared.

And even if I didn't have the excuse of my current mission for my absence, I'd have found a different reason to run away.

Such a childish way to react…and exactly what I'd done the day after Hunter told me how he truly felt.

How could I dread what I'd been longing to hear since I first met him? The moment he uttered the words *'I've loved you from the first moment I saw you,'* warmth radiated throughout my body, and my heart felt in danger of bursting from happiness.

But then one of the memories I kept locked away escaped from its confinement and a reel of my parents—yelling at each other, fighting, then not speaking to one another for days, until it was time to find their next dose that is—played in my mind's eye, sucking me in, obliterating reality and relegating me to the child version of myself. Helpless. Afraid. Weak.

And the times they weren't fighting weren't great either. My mother wielded her body as if it was a weapon, and sex always got her what she wanted. Father could deny her nothing, and when she started viewing me as competition because I was stealing his time from her, she'd turned him against me.

My role models growing up sucked, and I was afraid that if our relationship changed, I'd mess it up. With Judy and Michael's DNA embedded in mine, our ruin was guaranteed. And I couldn't do that. No matter how much I wanted to be with him. No matter how I'd never feel for another what I felt for him. Because there wasn't a worse sin in my book than destroying the one person you loved the most.

So I fled. I took on a mission that could very easily lead to my demise, if what the president had informed us of was the truth. Aliens were planning to subjugate Earth, and I was on a reckon mission, not allowed to engage unless attacked, which honestly, at that point, I'd be screwed.

The TR-3 Alpha was built for speed and stealth. The craft was beautiful; on the outside, nano-silver agents had been embedded into the hull's alloy, giving it a prismatic-like effect that reflected its surrounding environment. On the inside, the reverse engineered electromagnetic propulsion system—the first of its kind to be tested by humans—allowed flight at breakneck speed, right angle steep turns with zero Gs, and anti-gravity capabilities. But that was not all; its greatest feature was another reverse engineered creation—a cloaking mechanism. Which was a great asset because the craft was armored with a basic level of weaponry since their goal when engineering it had been reconnaissance, not war.

"Captain?" The smooth voice of the AI inquired, pulling me out of my reverie.

I sat on my chair, touched my hair to make sure everything was in place, then chastised myself because this was Hunter. He'd seen me at my worst and knew my every dark secret. There was no need for the anxiety coursing through me. "Yes, AJ. Initiate the call," I ordered, and within a few seconds, the black mop of Hunter's hair filled the screen, blocking out the view of the dark vista.

"Hey, terrestrial," I said and watched his shoulders lifting and dropping as a heavy sigh reverberated around me.

Shit, he knew. The General must have informed the medical team about the second phase of the mission.

Hunter lifted his narrowed eyes to mine and shook his head.

From his pinched lips and tension-filled expression, I knew he'd been informed of my whereabouts, and he didn't approve. "Hi, extraterrestrial," he replied, with that smooth tone of his that always put me at ease. "How are you, Lyra? Are you feeling well?" His voice cracked at the last word, but he covered it with a cough.

He forgot to fix his stiff posture, though. His shoulders were tense, and I could hear the *tap, tap, tap* rhythm his fingers were beating on the table. Hunter was always the zen one of the two of us. A rock. He was always so quick to keep in check his reactions and hide his emotions that these outward signs spoke volumes about his true feelings of anxiety and fear for me.

Would the same emotions underline my voice, too? We'd spent almost every waking moment together since we were teenagers. It was ingrained in us to worry about the other person if we were apart. *Why had I done this to us?* My subconscious butted in again, dousing me with guilt. Had I accepted this mission for the wrong reasons?

"You tell me. You're monitoring my vitals. How am I doing?" My flippant answer was meant to be a distraction, but he didn't bite—he knew me too well.

"Cut the snark, Ly," he ordered, and I lowered my gaze to the floor in shame.

He didn't deserve my attitude. Hunt hadn't done anything wrong.

Inhaling through my nose, then exhaling through my mouth, I tried to expel the temper that I could feel rising. When I gathered the courage to look at the screen again, I noticed the dark circles under his blue eyes. He was rubbing his jaw with his thumb, back and forth. The gesture told me he'd had a tough day.

"I'm feeling all right, Hunter. Following your schedule to the letter, eating and exercising in intervals," I replied in a subdued tone—a lame peace offering.

"Good."

A curt answer. Dammit, I wasn't forgiven. "How was your day?" I asked, hoping a discussion would calm him down eventually.

"It was okay."

"You know I can tell when you're lying to me, right?"

Hypocrite. A little voice echoed in my head.

Shut up, consciousness.

Momentarily, I wondered if having a conversation with one's self was a bad sign or not. Was I going to go mad out in space? Well, nothing to do about that now, but I could help Hunter.

"Today was…hard. I lost a soldier. He was only eighteen, Lyra. A stray bullet had pierced his chest. We managed to stop the bleeding in time, but his heart stopped beating." His shoulders slumped forward and he ran his hand over his face. "I saw the shadows gathering, the dark tendrils slithering toward his body, and when the defibrillator failed to do its job, I pumped his heart with my hands, hoping…but I failed, too."

I reached out and touched the screen where his cheek was, wishing like hell I were next to him to comfort him. Hunter's gift —the ability to see death approaching—would break lesser men, but not him. He was down but not out, and I hated I couldn't be there.

"You did all you could. May God rest his soul and ease your pain, Hunter. But it was not your fault he didn't survive." I emphasized the last part, hoping it would get into his thick head that he was not responsible for every living soul on Earth, and knowing that it probably wouldn't.

He shivered, and it was as if his entire being was trying to dislodge the painful memory from his brain. "I know that, but enough about me. How is it out there?"

"I see what you did there, changing the subject, little monster." I laughed in an effort to lighten the mood and got a small smile in return with the use of the inaccurate pet name. But then the image of Hunter in all his naked glory appeared in my mind's eye, making me blush—there was nothing little about Hunter. I cleared my throat, and his grin widened, but I ignored him and instead answered his question. "It's vast and dark for the most part, and a great way to make a person feel small and insignificant."

"Well, it won't be that long before you get back, right? You just have to be patient for a while longer and you'll be en route to home before you know it."

Lights started blinking on my right, drawing my attention. At once, I turned to check both ranging instruments—the RADAR and the LiDAR. "Hm." Something big was moving towards me. Fast. It could be an asteroid, but I didn't think so if the sudden buzzing in my brain was any indication.

"Muting video call. Incoming vessel, Captain. Scanning showed their weapons are disengaged," AJ reported, confirming my suspicion.

I needed to wrap our session short. "AJ unmute Hunter."

"What's going on Lyra? Is everything all right?"

My heart skipped a beat and sweat trickled down between my breasts. On reflex, I lifted my hand to swipe the gathering moisture but hit the obnoxious, stiff suit that hindered my every movement.

"Lyra," he demanded and got up—head jerking left and right, fists clenched and muscles coiled tight. Wanting to do something, to act, needing to protect me from the threat he couldn't see, but knew was there because he could read my body language even when I tried to hide things from him.

I was certain he wasn't privy to this part of my mission, so I'd have to lie to him. Again. A vise squeezed my heart and it hurt.

"Sorry, a notification distracted me. I'm approaching…a meteor shower, and I need to navigate. We'll talk soon. I love you, Hunter. Always." His eyes widened, but before he could speak, I terminated the video call.

My heart was breaking, but at least he knew now how I felt, too. He'd be mad that I had hung up without giving him a chance to reply, but I'd deal with it later. First, I had to live through this. Taking over the controls of the TR-3 Alpha, I adjusted my course to get out of their way. The moment I left Earth, I activated my ship's cloaking mechanism, so they wouldn't be able to detect me. "AJ, track the alien craft's movements because given its size, I don't think we'd survive a collision."

"My sensors are picking up magnetic waves. They sent a message."

"They shouldn't be able to pick up our position. Are they fishing AJ?" I questioned, while considering what our best options were.

The ship's cameras were continuously recording, so proof would have already been documented. But that was only the first part of my mission fulfilled. Opening a communication channel between us would allow me to gather intel. That might mean I'd get to go home to Hunter sooner rather than later. But not knowing whether they were friendlies amped up the risk. Would I manage to evade them if the latter was true?

Well, there's an easy way to find out.

My internal alarm system wasn't screaming at me, which was a good sign. "AJ take over the steering. Change positions every five seconds," I ordered, then took a deep breath as I strapped in and armed TR-3's weapons—my hands steady on the controls even though on the inside I was a quivering mess.

At the base, the feeds from all the cameras had gotten corrupted during the aliens' visit, so I had no idea what they'd look like. Would they be humanoid or completely foreign? I wondered and hoped that we'd be able to communicate effectively.

"Have you managed to decrypt their message?"

"Still processing, Captain."

"Open communications, limit vision to my face alone. Do not open my mic yet," I ordered and waited.

A deep, throaty voice reached me first. The words unintelligible, but their effect on me was intense, nonetheless. A sudden flush of warmth spread from my core outward, and my heart started pounding as if the damn organ was determined to escape from my chest.

Then his face appeared on the screen in front of me, and my breath left my lungs in a loud whoosh. My jaw might have dropped on the floor, but I was quick to recover my composure. This humanoid alien with piercing gold eyes that seemed to penetrate my soul, and rich, deep red-colored skin was striking. He repeated something in his language and waited.

"AJ, can you translate?" I inquired, but already knew the answer. If the AI could, it would have done so by now.

"Negative."

"Open my mic then," I ordered, and cleared my throat before addressing the male before me. "Hello. I come in peace." Declaring my intentions seemed the safest bet to avoid any unnecessary discord. Even if they couldn't grasp the meaning of my words, hopefully, they'd at least understand my motives based on the inflection of my voice and softness of my tone.

The image on my holo-screen widened, and the rest of the huge male took up the space on my screen. He was wearing a dark, skin tight uniform that outlined every hill and valley on his body, leaving little to the imagination. And even though I was used to being around Hunter, who didn't have an ounce of fat on his body, and around my brothers-in-arms who all had sculpted bodies, his was on another level. *Oh, my...somebody fan me.*

"Captain, they just armed their weapons," My AI informed me at the same time the alien broke eye contact and barked orders to his crew.

The small flame of hope I'd been fostering inside me was snuffed out in an instant, and all thoughts of arousal disappeared. "AJ, get us out of range," I said and steered the laser, getting a lock on the target.

"Earthling, we will not harm you." Even though his accent was strange, the meaning was clear. Then it hit me he'd spoken in English, not his language. *What the hell?* That meant he either spent a lot of time on Earth or he had a human on his ship—neither scenario reassuring, really.

"They disarmed their weapons," my digital companion reported, right after his declaration.

The alien on the screen stood still, his entire focus on me. The way he was looking at me—unblinking—was unnerving. It felt like he was trying to reach my soul in an effort to uncover my deep, dark secrets. If my past had been different, if I hadn't been through what I'd gone through, I might have fidgeted, but as it was, I mimicked his posture, putting on a brave face.

"Has the human leader sent you here to negotiate?"

So these were the aliens that had met with the President, to warn humans of a new threat. Which meant he knew the answer to that question already, and he was just testing me. But he'd said negotiate—that was a detail my superior officers had conveniently forgotten to mention.

This male was waiting for an answer, though, and I didn't want to outright lie. But telling the truth would get me in trouble, so I settled for something in between. "No. I'm here to test my ship, not act as a mediator in any official capacity."

He nodded. Something in his expression, though, was off, but I didn't know him well enough to tell what exactly. "Then, as a gesture of good faith, allow us to update your language database."

Before I had a chance to accept or decline, my holo-screen blurred. AJ had blocked the communications channel to speak to me. "Their AI initiated contact. Do I accept the file it's transmitting?"

My gut told me yes, but if I was wrong, it would cost me dearly. I wasn't one to give in to fear, though. "Scan the data."

"No known viruses or malware detected, Captain."

"Then accept the file and unblock the comms." A moment later, his pixelated image cleared again. "Thank you for the update. Much appreciated." Fuck. Was there a protocol I needed to adhere to? I didn't want to piss them off and jeopardize whatever had been negotiated between our species, so I added, "Is there anything I can offer in return?"

His lips tilted upward into a Cheshire cat's smile that transformed his face, taking my breath away. He was hot when he was serious, but like this? He was drop-dead gorgeous. "I wish a meeting with you. Direct your ship to the planet side Docking Bay. Directions will be forwarded to you shortly," he said and ended the broadcast.

The damn alien hadn't waited for an answer. If he thought he could order me around, he had another thing coming. But on the other hand, one of my mission's objectives was to gather intel. What better way to do it than meet them?

Worrying my lip—a nervous habit of mine I thought I'd gotten over a while ago—would accomplish nothing. It was now or never, and I wasn't a quitter. Decision made, I accepted the co-ordinates the alien sent, deactivated the cloaking mechanism—it had proven useless anyway—and navigated toward their ship.

"AJ, send the footage from this meeting back to base and open the recorder."

I looked at my reflection on the screen. My eyes shone bright with excitement, for I was about to do what no other had done before me, but my face had lost its color as fear suddenly settled in the pit of my stomach. There was an actual possibility that I might not make it out of there alive no matter what the alien had promised, and I couldn't leave Hunter wondering for the rest of his life.

He deserved to know the truth.

"Hunt, this might be my last message. I just want you to know, I got scared..." I choked on the last word and had to pause to compose myself—it wasn't easy, but he was worth it, so I pressed on. "The only example I have is of my parents and it's a bad one. I got scared that I'd end up like them. I'd end up destroying what we have and…the truth is I cannot live without you in my life. I need you like I need air to breathe. I love you and not just like a brother. I'm sorry"—my image blurred, but wiping the tears didn't stop them from falling—"that I won't be there for the rest of your life. Please, please find the strength to move on…to find happiness again."

"AJ, terminate message and store. If I die, send it directly to Hunter and delete the archive."

"Affirmative, Captain."

That was all I needed. Now I had to get myself together before I met the aliens, for I had a hunch that my life would forever be altered after this meeting. "How did they detect us? What did you gather from the scan?" I thought out loud.

"Axr, their ship's artificial intelligence, blocked me. It only allowed me to read their disengaged weaponry…their technology is vastly superior to ours." Was there a wistful tone in AJ's voice?

"Has the green monster of jealousy gotten you, too?"

"I do not feel emotions, Captain," my ship's AI said in a monotone, and I laughed out loud but sobered up quickly because the alien spacecraft was getting bigger by the second and the open gate was now visible.

God! The size of their spacecraft is humongous, here's to hoping this isn't the biggest mistake of my short life, I thought as I piloted my vessel through the opening.

After docking the TR-3 safely, I got up and dragged my feet toward the hatch. It would be stupid to meet them unarmed, but I suspected they would remove any weapons in my possession the moment I stepped foot on their property. Nonetheless, I strapped a gun on each side of my waist and stashed two knives in the suit's hidden compartments along my thighs, then locked my helmet in place. I double-checked the oxygen level and pressed the lever that would lower the ramp.

As it slid downward, more and more of the spacecraft's brightly lit interior was revealed, making me squint my eyes, as they'd gotten used to TR-3's dim lighting. I descended to the platform and was surprised to find I was the only one there. The bay could easily fit another five ships, but mine was the only one occupying space.

No faith in my piloting skills, I see. I chuckled at the thought when a door to my right swished open, revealing three males marching toward me.

Instinctively, my hand dropped to my gun, but I didn't remove it from its holster. I didn't know what I'd been expecting, but it definitely wasn't what was swiftly approaching me.

The red-skinned alien I'd talked to was at the helm, flanked by two others that had blue skin, and together they formed a formidable sight.

Standing at six-one, I wasn't short by any means, but they were enormous, close to seven feet tall if not more. Their dark crimson uniforms were hugging their buff bodies like a second skin, highlighting their broad shoulders, cut abs and narrow waists. It took a lot of will-power to stop my eyes from traveling lower, but I managed.

Although, that hadn't stopped my imagination from guessing what they packed, and if the warmth on my face was any indication, my cheeks had just turned a flaming red. Upon closer inspection, I noticed all three of them had what looked like tattoos decorating their skin, but where the blue males' were in a darker shade than their skin, their leader had veins of muted gold forming an intricate design along the sides of his neck that disappeared under his uniform. Their sight was strangely inviting to the eye, and the thought perplexed me. How could I feel anything other than fear when they were standing only a couple of feet away from me?

The blue alien on the left said something in their tongue, and the other blue guy laughed.

Rude much? Internally, I scowled at them, but outwardly, I just focused on the alien I was more familiar with, disregarding the other two as inconsequential on purpose because two could play the game.

The red male was staring at me. For all I knew, gold eyes were common in his species, but the unusual coloring along with his intense gaze made me uncomfortable. It was full of requests I couldn't comprehend.

"Welcome to my ship, Earthling. I'm Callibohr, Admiral of the Imperial, and these are my Second and Third in command, Culhwch and Forsa." He pointed at them as he made the introductions, and once again, I was taken aback by his use of English.

My fingers clenched around my gun's grip. His knowledge of my language was disconcerting—it gave him another advantage over me, and that little fact didn't sit well with me. Yet my inner warning system was silent.

The other two stiffened upon noticing the slight movement; their Admiral, though, seemed unencumbered.

I didn't think it'd be wise to cause an incident before I had the chance to gather more information, so I relaxed my fingers and lowered my hand to my thigh. Assuring myself that if they attacked, I still had easy access to a weapon they didn't know was there—my knife. "I'm Captain Lyra Hogan."

"Please allow Forsa to take your vitals. I believe you can breathe our air, but I want to be one hundred percent positive before you take that bubble off your head," Callibohr said, and the thought of taking off the cumbersome helmet had me grinning enthusiastically.

Even though my spacesuit was slicker than the traditional suits used by the other astronauts back home, it was still too bulky for my liking, and I knew during a fight it would hinder my movements and speed. I nodded and one of the blue aliens, who'd been carrying something that resembled a tablet, stepped forward, leaving less than a foot between us.

I didn't get any malevolent vibes from him, but when he lifted what looked like a wicked tuning fork that had tendrils of light jumping from one rod to the other, I took a step back, unsheathed my gun, and point it at his chest—hopefully where his heart was.

"We are not going to hurt you," Callibohr's deep husky voice wrapped around me like a fuzzy blanket, bringing with it feelings of warmth and security.

When I took too long to lower the gun for the other blue alien's liking, he stepped forward next to Forsa. "Scan me first," he told him, startling me.

"Do you all speak English?" I blurted, and they chuckled.

"Yes. We have a translator embedded in our brains that allows us to understand and speak all known languages," Forsa said while hovering the wicked tuner thingie over Culhwch.

I returned my weapon to its holster, and a minute later, the blue male turned the tablet my way. On the screen, there was an alien diagram with letters I couldn't recognize.

Okay, I was eighty percent convinced the device wasn't a weapon. Just to be sure, though, I took a few seconds to check in with my inner warning system, and when I didn't get the usual buzzing that accompanied danger, I closed the distance between us and allowed him to scan me.

Similarly to how he used the device on the other alien, he formed my outline with the wand, then looked intently at the screen. "We're compatible," he said, looking pointedly at his Admiral, before he focused on me and added, "The air is safe for you to breathe."

What did that look mean? And had I detected excitement in his voice? Were these aliens concerned about my convenience, or did they have an ulterior motive? I guessed I would find out the answers to my questions soon enough, so there wasn't any point in worrying about them, but I did have to make a decision now.

Did I trust their technology or not? We only lived once, and this whole experience was one in a million. I doubted I'd ever get to experience anything even remotely close to this encounter in the future. Plus, I needed to gain their trust, and the easiest way would be by showing faith in them first.

Time to test their theory, I guess.

Slowly, I raised my hands to the mechanism that would release the helmet's lock. From the corner of my eye, I noticed their forms were relaxed, waiting patiently for me to choose. If they were lying, I hedged I'd probably make it back to my ship to get the life-giving oxygen I'd need.

The hiss of the seal breaking was deafening in my ears. I removed the helmet, instinctively holding my breath first, but after a while my lungs complained, and I had to take the breath that could easily lead to my demise.

So I did, and nothing happened.

The alien hadn't lied.

SHE CAN'T BE MINE

CALLIBOHR

I wasn't sure whether I should be insulted or impressed.

After the rotation-long negotiations, the human leader still hadn't signed the Intergalactic Enosis Treaty. Instead, he sent the female Captain on a mission that could have cost her life if we hadn't intercepted her barely armored ship. The solar system wasn't as vacant as we'd initially thought. Earth, we'd come to find out, was a popular destination for pirates. During our stay here, we'd intercepted many of their ships that, had they landed, the scums would have managed to abduct humans that would either end up as slaves or worse, as food.

Neither option an acceptable one, especially when Wravukians might be needing human females sooner rather than later. The Order of the Prime hadn't managed to kill all our females—thanks to our Scientists working endlessly to create a cure in time—but their attack had been successful nonetheless. The same antidote that had saved their lives had caused an unexpected adverse reaction, and now more than half the female population of Wravuk had become infertile.

Hm, maybe I should thank the human leader.

Because the treaty wasn't finalized yet, access to Earth and its citizens was forbidden, thus making the verification of our theory —that reproduction was feasible between our species—impossible.

Kali and River had both graciously volunteered to be tested, but they'd been Changed by their Saberian mates—their DNA altered—before they carried offspring, hence rendering them unsuitable test subjects.

But another human female had just landed in our laps, and we would take advantage of the opportunity presented.

Forsa ran the scanner over her. It would give us an initial assessment of whether her reproductive system was capable of carrying a Wravukian offspring. If it was, we'd follow up with gene testing that would ultimately define this species' ability to procreate with us. Forsa's bouncing vibrations reached me first, and I knew the answer before he looked over his shoulder at me and said, "We're compatible." Then he turned back to the Captain and added, "The air is safe for you to breathe."

Doubt clouded her strange-colored eyes, but determination quickly replaced it, and she unlatched her helmet.

Human technology was primitive compared to ours, and it was a wonder they'd achieved space travel so fast. Although judging from the outdated cloaking mechanism on her ship, they still had a long way to go. Another way her species would benefit from signing the treaty if…. I lost my train of thought the moment she took off her helmet and revealed the exotic beauty hidden within.

Brown hair the color of rich soil was slicked back, highlighting her heart-shaped face. Slender arched eyebrows framed hypnotizing feline-like two-toned eyes unlike any I'd ever seen—a thick green ring formed swirls around a dark-gold one—eyes a male could get lost in. Small light brown spots were scattered around and on top of a dainty nose, giving her an ethereal vibe. My eyes trailed to her mouth, and I had to stop myself from laughing when I noticed that her plump lips had formed a firm line in an effort to hold her breath.

Was her scent as alluring as her looks? Needing it in my lungs more than I needed air, I breathed deeply, but her ship's fumes blocked it from me.

I huffed in annoyance, and let my gaze drop lower. Her bulky suit hid her body from me, and suddenly one thought superseded all others: enough obstacles were hiding her true form from me and that was unacceptable. I had to tear the garment off her. I had to find out how she felt under my palms. My feet of their own accord stepped forward, the movement drawing her attention.

She locked eyes with me, and the vulnerability in them stopped me in my tracks. The haze of lust that had clouded my mind cleared as I watched her exhale slowly, then take a tentative breath in, quickly followed by a small smile upon realizing we hadn't lied.

Culhwch cleared his throat and spoke in our mother tongue, bursting the bubble that had formed around the alien female and me. "She seems harmless, but should I remove her weapons?"

"Really? You think this female could harm you?" Forsa taunted my Second in command.

"You've seen what the Queen of Saber can do. I'm not willing to risk our Prince's safety."

Ignoring the jab he threw my way because we all knew he was intimidated by the little monster I called sister—as he should because she was deadly in either form—I stepped closer and offered her my hand.

Her eyebrows lifted in surprise as she looked at me, then at it, and laughed.

Had I done something wrong?

"Apparently you've met humans before," she said and grasped it with more strength than I'd have thought her capable.

Something in her tone had me thinking this was a trick question, but Culhwch didn't get the hint. "Prince Callibohr is in charge of the negotiations with your leader, Earthling."

The female tugged her hand, giving me no choice but to let go, then inclined her head with respect, putting distance between us.

A growl of displeasure vibrated in my chest, and her eyes snapped to mine. *Fucking Culhwch.* He'd be overseeing the cleaning of the hull for the next three cycles.

The bay stank of engine fuel and metal, yet suddenly the acrid scent of her fear permitted the air, making me wrinkle my nose. I hated it.

"I've met your leader indeed, but that isn't why I'm familiar with humans." She leaned toward me, curiosity getting the better of her. "My brother is mated to one."

A flush of red covered her cheeks and neck. "What does mated mean?"

"It's like they're…married." Marriage didn't really describe mating—when one could be temporary if the pair chose it so, the other was permanent because not even death could keep the mated pairs apart for long—but it was the quickest way to get her to understand the concept.

She blinked slowly, then mumbled something that sounded like *'a human with an alien?'* to herself. Emotions crossed her face too fast for me to decipher, but she was adorable with her guard down, and I wanted more.

"Actually, it's a human and three aliens. My brother is one of the three," I said, wondering how she'd react.

Her mouth fell open, and her breath hitched.

Was she shocked, intrigued, or scandalized by the news? I lowered my shields, needing to learn more about her, only to notice the absence of vibrations.

My world was eerily quiet. Even the pain on my back—a souvenir from my fight against the Order of the Prime's soldier—had turned into a dull ache.

I shifted from foot to foot as I struggled to remain still, to contain my unease, for she wasn't an ordinary human, but a Shield.

In my long life, I'd only ever known two beings having this rare gift. Two beings whose mere presence brought peace if they wished it—my mother and Kali.

And now...Lyra, I thought as I looked at her with fresh eyes.

Her exotic beauty would draw attention wherever she went, but her ability would always set her aside from all other females.

She was special. A female I could see myself spending the rest of my life with without losing my mind, but dammit, she wasn't Wravukian, and my people would never accept an alien for their Queen.

The flicker of hope that sparked a few ticks ago vanished, and my world turned a shade bleaker than before. At least, I had one rotation left before I needed to pick a Chosen Mate, during which I could enjoy this human's company, who was unknowingly offering me a much needed reprieve.

"Captain Lyra Hogan—" I started, but she interrupted me.

"Lyra. You can call me Lyra."

I dipped my head, acknowledging her request, then gestured toward the entrance of the bay. "We have much to discuss. Let's head somewhere we can talk in comfort. Culhwch, Forsa, return to your posts."

Leading the way, I'd already turned my back to them, when she mumbled under her breath, "Hopefully not in the ship's cells."

A grin stretched my lips all the way toward my office, our company attracting all sorts of looks from my warriors. Upon further consideration, though, it wasn't the sight of the three of us that drew their hungry gazes, but hers. That realization caused a pang of jealousy to spear through me, and a warning snarl to rattle in my throat.

Fuck. I wasn't ready to share her attention, so I took a sharp turn, changing course and heading toward my quarters.

Culhwch, picking up on my new destination, stepped forward and blocked my way.

"Move," I snapped.

Ignoring the direct order I'd given him—something he didn't do unless genuinely concerned—he said in our mother tongue, "You're being reckless, Prince Callibohr." My title, a purposeful reminder that royalty could only mate with pure Wravukians. "She is a human. We need to complete the gene testing, and then introduce her to the rest of the warriors to see if she incites a Mating Fever."

My darkness didn't take well to disobedience regardless of the righteousness of the reason, and while a war raged within me—the duty I had to my people versus my wants—shadows slipped through my control and filled the surrounding space. Forsa and Culhwch started coughing, but my second didn't back down. Neither did I. Not until the sound of Lyra's frenzied heartbeat broke through the red haze clouding my mind.

In an effort to calm myself, I turned toward her, and my eyes widened in surprise. The Keon part of me that harmed everything it came into contact with had formed a protective bubble around her.

That had never happened before.

And when I called it back, it didn't fight me. *Odd.*

Forsa—always the voice of reason—spoke in English before Culhwch had a chance to open his mouth again. "Captain, our Healers need to clear you first before you're allowed to explore the Imperial. We need to make sure you don't carry any pathogens that might be harmful to our species. Will you allow them to examine you?"

Her movements were subtle as she leaned sideways, presenting a smaller target. "What kind of examination?"

I couldn't feel her vibrations, but I knew a defensive move when I saw one. Did she think we were dishonorable beasts who'd grab and experiment on her? We'd never stoop so low to such despicable acts.

"The Healers will take a blood sample. That'd be all," he said.

There was another option, and I offered it to her because the thought she might consider us savages didn't sit well with me. "Or we can take you back to your ship."

"Fair enough. If a blood test is all that's required of me, I consent."

Her answer appeased Culhwch, who inclined his head and moved to the side.

"We'll discuss the repercussions of your disobedience later," I growled at him in Wravukian, before moderating my tone and addressing Lyra. "I'll lead the way."

Soft footfalls trailed my own and when she didn't ask any more questions or otherwise engage in conversation, I let my senses expand to take her in. Her heartbeat had settled on its regular rhythm, which showed she somewhat trusted me. Or maybe it was placing myself in a vulnerable position in front of her and presenting her with an easy target—my back—that she found reassuring.

Her scent carried no sour tones that indicated fear or trepidation, but it was still mostly masked by her spaceship's fumes, although this time I could detect a hint of a flowery note underneath. The promise of the seductive aroma made me salivate.

Having taken the fastest route to the Healers' Bay, we arrived shortly. Axr reading my bio-signature allowed me entry, and the female followed without hesitation. When my Second tried to step in too, I blocked his way. "You're pushing it," I warned, no longer in the mood to appease him.

"It's my duty to protect you, especially when you behave so carelessly."

Before he finished speaking, I'd slammed him against the wall, blocking his airway with my forearm. Blatantly provoking me was taking it a step too far. Heat flashed through my body, and I ground my teeth. "You think I can't defend myself against a lone female? Do you have no regard for your life insulting me like that?"

He didn't try to defend himself, seeing death in my eyes, sensing my darkness stirring. I was aware of every kill spot on him. My body coiled tight, ready to explode into action, all it would take was one move—pulling my arm backward, then smashing my elbow to his jugular.

A small hand touched my back and sent a jolt of electricity through me that started at the point of contact and widened like a ripple, engulfing the rest of my body. Along the way, it consumed my anger, then replaced it with a new fire that burned for this female alone.

She'd witnessed my outburst, yet her soft-spoken words held no fear when she said, "Please don't." Her breathy cadence had an immediate effect on me, and my muscles relaxed, obeying her command. Too soon, though, she withdrew her palm, breaking the contact.

I pulled back and off Culhwch, but he wasn't ready to drop the issue. Menace continued to hang heavy in the air.

Nostrils flaring, he squared his shoulders. I could almost see the cogs turning in his head, debating whether to tackle me.

Taunting him, I bared my teeth. If the fool wanted a fight, I'd oblige him, and at the same time, remind him which of the two of us was the dominant one.

Lyra stepped between us, earning a snarl from me for placing herself in the middle of danger. One stray punch would be enough to damage her fragile body, or worse. Ignoring me, she gave me her back and craned her neck to face my Second. "You flatter me."

"Flatter you?" he repeated, confused. "Why?"

A mischievous smile lit her face. "Because you think I could take both of you on," she replied as her gaze slid downward—taking all of him in, then spun around and headed inside the Healers' Bay, stunning us both and effectively diffusing the situation.

Culhwch's mouth fell open in surprise. "If the gene testing confirms our compatibility—"

"If you value your life, you won't finish that sentence," I growled at him, and he wisely shut his mouth, but that didn't stop the anger from blazing through me at the mere suggestion of someone else being interested in her.

She. Was. Mine.

Damn it, she isn't. She can't be mine.

I had to stop this now, before it was too late. Culhwch could make sure she got tested and then coerce her to reveal the true reason she was here. I tried to turn and step away from the Healers' Bay, but my feet had a mind of their own, taking me straight to her side.

Fuck, I'm in trouble.

HELPLESS TO RESIST

CALLIBOHR

The Arch-healer of the Imperial was the only other occupant in the chamber, and he was looking at us—his head cocked to the side, and an inscrutable expression on his face. "To what do I owe the pleasure?" he asked in English, before bowing and scraping with a flourish. "It's not every circle that the Admiral and his Second grace me with their presence." Brarn knew very well why we were here, but I guessed the theatrics were for our guest's benefit. And his trick seemed to be working because Lyra was fighting to keep a straight face.

I made the introductions, then led Lyra to the med-pod he indicated before turning around to gather the needed items. "Prepare a translator for her as well as a tracker," I ordered in our mother tongue, and that earned me another inscrutable look from him.

What was it with my soldiers questioning my decisions this circle? I was about to scold him when he nodded and returned to his task.

"Would you mind if I scanned you once again, Lyra? You see, the med-pod is more accurate than the portable scanner Forsa used earlier," Brarn said as he carried the tray with the supplies.

Faster than I'd have given her credit for, Lyra jumped out of the pod and scampered backward away from the three of us, drawing both weapons and aiming at me and Culhwch.

Suddenly, an influx of vibrations hit me, catching me by surprise and nearly bringing me to my knees, and I realized she had just raised her mental defenses.

Clever female. She'd scoped out the place and pinpointed the bigger threats. "We mean you no harm," Brarn said, and I raised my hands to appease her.

"It's a big ass needle you have there."

"Forgive me. I asked him to give you a translator. We all have one, so I didn't think it'd be a big deal." As I spoke, Culhwch tiptoed toward her.

"Take another step and we'll see if you're faster than a laser beam," she warned, sparing only a glance at him.

A part of me wanted to test her reflexes, to see how good she was with the blaster, but I couldn't risk my Second's safety either. We healed fast, but there were certain injuries we couldn't come back from, and she was aiming at his head.

"It's safe," I said and took a single step toward her. "I promise, Lyra. I'll even let Brarn demonstrate on me first." When she didn't warn me off, I slowly closed the distance between us, leaving only a fingerbreadth between the muzzle of one of her weapons and my chest—the other remained steady on Culhwch. "Do you trust me?"

She tilted her head back; her eyes the only part of her moving as they searched mine. "If I asked you to let me go now, would you?"

Up close, the dark gold ring of her eyes had widened and almost swallowed the green one completely. I felt mesmerized, as if I was sinking into their depth.

"Would you?" she demanded.

"Yes," I said and backed up my word with action by stepping out of her way. "Will you trust me, Lyra?" My voice sounded huskier than usual, revealing the desire she'd awakened in me.

Wravukian females were known for their quiet disposition and coquettish manners. In the past, that was the kind of female I'd always been attracted to, but Lyra portrayed none of those attributes. She was daring, fearless...a fighter. All traits I should find appalling, yet I didn't.

"Okay," she acquiesced, and my hearts rejoiced.

"Please lie down on the med-pod. We'll start with the scan first, which is non-invasive," Brarn instructed, and she put her weapons away before walking—chin lifted high—to do as told.

I followed and stood beside the Healer, when something sharp pressed the spot right between my balls and my cock. My eyebrows reached my hairline at the sight of Lyra's knife in that area.

"Since I'm putting my life in your hands, don't you think it's fair you put yours in mine?" she asked sweetly, and a laugh choked out of me.

"Human, this is an offense punishable by death. You don't threaten the Prince of Wravuk and live," Culhwch's dark tone told me Lyra was about to push him past his limits. His vibrations brimmed with hostility, and that didn't bode well for anyone.

I had to diffuse the situation. "Stand down. It's a fair request," I told him, then knelt, so we were at eye level. My action placed the knife to my jugular, but I trusted she wouldn't hurt me. "The Order of the Prime has targeted Earth. We are here to protect your planet and all its citizens. Our word is our honor," I said, hoping she'd hear the truth in my voice.

"You may start," she told Brarn, her hand steady at my neck.

A quarter of a spire later, he said, "You're all done, the examination is complete. Now, please sit up."

"You're fast," Lyra replied and lowered her armed hand.

"Our methods are more advanced than yours," the Arch-healer said distractedly as he studied the scan data on his holo-screen, but then his eyes widened comically. "Initial findings show ninety-five percent compatibility," he reported, awed, before clearing his throat and assuming his usual demeanor. "You're at optimum health. The implant will alter the Wernicke area with no issues."

Her knuckles around the hilt of the knife turned white, and her shoulders tensed. "Have you done this before?"

"Placed a translator in a human?" he asked, and she nodded. "No, but I'd never let anything happen to you. I've studied your physiology, and there isn't a human ailment that we can't treat. You needn't worry. You won't feel a thing. Now let your hair down. I need to touch your scalp first."

She eyed him suspiciously.

"Lyra, Brarn is one of the best Healers in Wravuk. He has patched me up more times than I can count." She still didn't seem fully convinced. "Do you want him to demonstrate on me? I've already got an implant, so he can't place another one, but he can show you what he needs to do."

She hesitated, but ended up denying my offer.

Brave female.

"Come here," I ordered, and she obeyed without hesitation this time, but stopped too far for my liking.

That wouldn't do.

I reached out and pulled her closer until her body was flush against mine. Her bulky suit was too cumbersome, and I made a mental note to gift her a Wravukian uniform as a reward for her obedience once the process was done.

She huffed in annoyance but didn't step out of my embrace, instead she removed the band from her hair and the luscious strands fell down her shoulders and over my arms.

Brarn approached behind her, and she stiffened. "It will be over before you know it," I said as I lowered one arm and wrapped it around her waist, then lifted the other and curled it around the nape of her delicate neck, effectively immobilizing her.

She was nothing like the tall and willowy females of my kind. She barely reached my chest, but that didn't detract from her appeal. Not one bit, and I couldn't resist caressing her soft skin with my thumb.

She shivered, but then froze when the Healer started feeling her scalp. When he found the spot he was looking for, he picked up the injector—the instrument clinking against the tray.

If her muscles tensed any more, they'd snap. I ran my thumb against her long neck to draw her attention. When she didn't respond, I called out her name. Again, no response.

"Open your eyes and look at me," I growled, letting authority color my tone.

Her eyes snapped open, terror filling them.

"It will only hurt for a heartbeat." I inclined my head to let Brarn know to proceed. "Keep looking at me, Lyra." She tried to nod, but couldn't.

Not until I let go.

Her instant obedience, though, had me hardening.

It had me thinking I should never let her go.

Based on the data the Saberians had given us, the Healers on the Imperial knew how to diagnose, treat, and operate on humans if need be. Brarn had already calculated the anesthetic dosage he needed to administer, and that was the only thing she would feel during the procedure. When he did, she flinched and hid her two-toned eyes from me.

"Lyra," I growled more harshly than necessary. Her exotic name rolled off my tongue as if I'd been using it my entire life. My abrupt tone had the desired effect, though, as she focused on me once again.

Brarn positioned the injector on her scalp, and she tensed in my arms, but I assumed it was due to the foreignness of the experience, not pain. It was over in a flash, and the Arch-healer picked up the wand and hovered it over her head to make sure she was not harmed. "It's done," he reported and gathered the instruments.

The female was heaving, and even through the bulky suit, with every inhale her mounds squashed against my abs, sending bolts of lust straight to my groin.

"How are you feeling, little one?"

"Not sure…," she said and laid her forehead against my chest.

I was about to let her go, to give myself some breathing room, but she sounded so forlorn. So instead, I massaged her neck gently, keeping her in my arms for a bit longer.

"You might feel a little woozy because of the anesthetic. It won't last long," Brarn said in Wravukian, looking at her expectantly.

I felt her nod.

"She understood you."

He furrowed his brows and used the portable scanner to check her once again. "Maybe it'd be best if she lay down to rest for a while. In two spires, she should try to drink and eat something light."

"I can take her to the guest chambers," my Second suggested, reminding me of his earlier comment.

Since the initial gene testing showed ninety-five percent compatibility, this female had just become fair game.

Not if I have anything to do about it.

"Arch-healer, your assistance is required at the Training Bay." Taran summoned Brarn through the comms, and that was our cue to leave.

"Vice Admiral, the Bridge is yours for the rest of this circle. Thank you, Brarn. I'll make sure she gets the nutrients she needs."

The Arch-healer opened his mouth as if to say something, but then thought better of it and gave me a sly smile instead.

I had no idea what that was about, but I was certain he'd let me know at some point because Brarn wasn't shy when it came to telling me how he truly felt about something, so when neither commented, I picked her up in my arms and left the Healers' Bay.

She was safe, had both the translator and tracker implanted, and now she needed rest.

I'd make sure she got it.

"Where are you taking me? I can walk." She complained, but there was no weight behind her argument.

"And I can carry you." The faster she learned I got my way, the better it would be for both of us. "You are lighter than a Saberian cub," I teased.

"Where are you taking me?" she insisted, sounding weaker than a few ticks ago.

"To my chambers, where you can rest. We'll talk after." Because at some point I would have to explain about the tracker, but not yet.

"Bossy." She chuckled and burrowed closer to my body.

The Arch-healer must have given her a bigger dose of sedation than needed. I didn't mind one bit.

The fragile human female was fast asleep in my arms before I entered my personal quarters. She fit perfectly in my embrace, and I could hold her forever, but I didn't think she'll appreciate the gesture when she woke up, plus she stunk of engine fumes.

A shower was in order, then bed. Taking off her bulky suit took some maneuvering, but I managed. Mine took only a thought to recede beneath my skin, leaving me naked.

Since my brother became Saberian Royalty, trade between our two planets recommenced once again. I, along with a select few others, were testing the new Wravukian uniforms created using fibers from a local plant on Saber called Sirh. They wouldn't replace our exosuits, as those were specifically engineered for space travel, but they'd be worn underneath for extra protection.

During testing, we'd discovered that the semi-sentient organism had the ability to bond with the wearer's genome, and enhance their natural defenses. So while a Saberian donning a Sirh uniform was nearly indestructible, the same didn't apply to a Wravukian. It amplified our own defense mechanisms, but although a laser blast wouldn't kill us like before, it'd still wound us.

I wondered whether the Sirh could bond with human DNA, and decided to gift one uniform to Lyra to see what happened, since they wouldn't harm her if they weren't a good match.

My eyes lowered to the naked female in my arms. *Shower or bath?* The water would definitely wake her up, so shower it was. I stepped into the enclosure and once the entrance sealed, a gray mist descended, covering us slowly from head to toe. The moment it came into contact with our skins, it sizzled, and bubbles formed as it burned away whatever waste lay on the surface. The tickling sensation was quite pleasant, but it had a whole different effect on Lyra, who squirmed, then moaned.

The sound startled me. Was it hurting her? I scanned her body. Her skin was flushed, but there were no visible injuries. I was about to wake her up when her scent touched my nostrils and nearly brought me to my knees.

A groan left my lips as I greedily inhaled the heady, sweet-smelling aroma deeper in my lungs.

Fuck. Pain wasn't the cause of the moan, but arousal.

Blood rushed down to my cock, turning it hard as ore, and disorienting me.

As warm air blasted around us, taking with it the last remnants of the gray mist, desire fought with morals, but the latter won. There was no way I'd touch her without her consent.

So with both of us clean, there was nothing else to do but what the Healer had ordered. I returned to the chamber and lowered her on my bed, then turned her to her side, and laid behind her, molding my frame to her smaller body before pulling her flush against me.

Peace settled on me like a warm blanket. The ever present pain across my back should have flared with my previous movements, but I felt nothing.

Lyra was a Shield. Of that I was certain because even in her sleep, she was blocking the vibrations from reaching me, offering me another reprieve from the constant barrage of unwanted sensations.

Shields were famous for their ability to thwart external intangible threats, not internal ones. Arch-healers could, but I'd never heard of a Shield stopping the feeling of pain. Was such a thing possible?

She was a mystery wrapped in a very appealing package. Everything about her drew me in like a super charged magnet, and I was helpless to resist.

But as I lay there, with my arms wrapped around her warm flesh, and the soft floral scent rising from her skin, lulling me to sleep, I couldn't get out of my mind this nagging feeling that insisted an important piece of the puzzle was missing.

IT'S DONE

BRARN

The low whoosh from the Healers' Bay door sliding open alerted me to the presence of others, but I was too absorbed by the latest data Forsa had transmitted to pay attention.

"You're pushing it," a familiar voice growled.

The heavy sigh that accompanied Callibohr's words revealed his companion's identity. "It's my duty to protect you, especially when you behave so carelessly."

Suddenly, a loud thud reverberated in the space followed by a muted 'oomph'.

Those two are a pain in my ass.

This wasn't the first time the hot-headed males ended up fighting to solve their differences, so I didn't bother turning.

A faint alien scent entered the room.

It was delicate, like the blooms of a rare Orad.

It was soft, like the finest fabric made of silky fibers spun by the Araneae.

Craving more, I inhaled the alluring female smell deeper, willingly tantalizing my senses.

I never expected one whiff would be enough to rock my iron clad control when I wasn't one to easily give in to my body's desires. Yet the wisps of her natural aroma curling around me had all my blood rushing to my groin, momentarily leaving me light-headed.

Mine. Whoever she was, she belonged to me. The insidious thought bounced against my mental walls, and it felt like jackhammers pounded inside my brain.

Shaking my head, I tried to will logic back. They'd brought the human here so I could complete her examination, not claim her. Getting a grip over my body's functions—both mental and physical —was imperative because the last thing that broadcast cool, collected, and trustworthy was an erection.

Never mind that the two Wravukians, who'd stopped fighting, would never let me live it down if they noticed.

Taking back command proved harder than I'd expected, but I managed by pushing my mind to focus on the fascinating similarities and differences between our two species, as well as on the fact that I'd soon get an answer to the most important question of all. I'd verify once and for all whether we were compatible enough to procreate.

Adequately composed, I turned to look at her for the first time, but Callibohr's bulk hid her smaller frame.

Too lost in my retrospection, I'd missed part of their conversation, but they had my full attention now.

"Because you think I could take both of you on," the female said, her tone soothing.

I furrowed my brows in confusion, not liking the ambiguous

meaning of her words. *Did she mean sexually?* The thought alone had me clenching my fists.

"If the gene testing confirms our compatibility—" Culhwch said in Wravukian but was interrupted by a furious Callibohr, whose every word felt like the lash of a whip—sharp and leaving quite the impact.

"If you value your life, you won't finish that sentence."

Hm. That's...interesting.

My sire had been the Royal Arch-healer responsible for leading the team tending to the King, Queen and their offspring. Like the rest of the members, we'd been residing at the palatial quarters designated to the Healers' families, and because of that, I'd known Callibohr my whole life. Growing up, we attended the same schools, and the moment he took over the First Fleet's command, I got appointed Arch-healer on the Imperial.

Never had I seen him, though, act proprietarily over a female. His status and accomplishments garnered a lot of attention, and at times, he basked in it while taking advantage of certain perks, but he was always respectful and aloof.

If that wasn't enough of a sign something weird was going on, I'd never heard of Culhwch showing interest. I thought the gruff male wasn't keen on the fairer sex. Yet now, he was butting heads with his Admiral over this human.

Should I let the situation progress just to see where it led, or should I intervene before things got too out of hand? I wondered. *Who was this female that incited such intense reactions from both these males and me?*

While pondering the pros and cons, she put an end to my indecision when she tiptoed away from them, and I got my first glimpse of her.

Though shorter than the average Wravukian female, she was tall for a human according to the data General Thora had gathered when he'd gone to Earth on a mission with the Saberian who was now his Pair-bond.

Her bulky garment hid her figure from my eyes, but the exposed patch of creamy skin across the length of her neck made me salivate. I wanted to bite and lick it, to discover if she tasted as sweet as she smelled.

My fingers itched as the desire to plunge them into the shiny brown strands gathered at the back of her head rose sharply. I might have taken an involuntary step, too, when she trained her eyes on me and took my breath away.

High cheekbones framing a heart-shaped face.

Plump lips made for kissing.

Unusual dual-colored eyes a male could get lost in.

She was ethereal.

All the other females I'd chosen to find temporary solace with—and had found beautiful at the time—paled compared to her.

A memory from long ago came to the forefront of my mind and I heard my sire's voice saying to my twenty rotations old self, *'When I saw your mother for the first time, I was instantly lost. Nothing else mattered but making her mine. As the days passed, my brain could focus on nothing else besides proving to her I was the best mate she'd ever have—no one would provide for her like I would, no one would protect her with his life like I would, no one would love her like I would. If you are ever blessed with a Fated Mate, you'll know exactly what I mean.'*

I hadn't been able to fathom the devotion he'd talked about, not truly. Now, though, as my world narrowed to only this alien female, I got it.

We belonged together.

There would be those who objected to the Arch-healer of

the Imperial mating an alien, but I didn't care. My bloodline would override hers because I was positive the Wravukian genome was superior to that of the Earthlings'. Once we completed the Mating Ritual, my blood would give her longevity, and it'd boost her immune system, helping her body fight off diseases, turning her into a sturdier version of herself.

No, I wouldn't mind having a hybrid mate at all, but first I needed to prove what my instincts were telling me—that we were compatible.

The Admiral moved to her side, and something that I hadn't been aware was coiled tightly in me eased, and realization hit me. I hadn't liked Culhwch—an unmated male—near her, but didn't mind Callibohr…in fact, quite the opposite. If I couldn't be by her side, I preferred him next to her because he'd protect the female with his life.

Examining my feelings carefully, I couldn't find even a smidgen of jealousy toward him. With how possessive I already felt towards her, it made little sense.

But first things first, I thought and asked in her language, "To what do I owe the pleasure?" Then I bowed with a flourish, exaggerating the movement on purpose, hoping my silly gesture would lighten the mood and put her at ease. "It's not every circle that the Admiral and his Second grace me with their presence."

For a moment, the tips of her lips curved upward before she schooled her expression, and satisfaction at being the one who made her want to smile warmed my chest.

"Captain Lyra Hogan, I'd like you to meet the Arch-healer of the First Fleet of Wravuk, Brarn," Callibohr said, and she offered her hand.

Already familiar with basic human customs, I grasped it with mine.

The moment my skin came into contact with hers, my body jolted as if it'd been struck by an electric bolt, and in the blink of an eye, I was sucked out of the chamber, no longer having a corporeal form. A wind was carrying me away, and everything around me was hidden behind a semi-transparent veil. I could see vague shapes and colors but nothing in detail…nothing, except four beings far below me.

Noticing them brought them into focus, and I suddenly found myself lying on the bed next to them, clearly seeing who they were as well as the gold line that united them all, forming a Sacred Union.

The action of my hand being shaken jerked me out of that vision and back into my physical form.

I glanced at Callibohr to see if he was experiencing the same thing I was, but his expression was inscrutable.

What was shown to me would affect both of us. Him being the next in throne more so than me. Did he know already, or should I tell him that we would form a Sacred Union with two Earthlings? How would our Humans react? My eyes quickly riveted back to her…to our mate, and I sucked in a deep breath, taken aback by the euphoria coursing through my veins just by the simple action of holding her hand.

She seemed impervious to what had just happened. Instead, her eyes strayed behind me to the med-pods.

Adorable. There was no need for Lyra to be nervous, though.

And maybe it'd be better to let our bond grow before speaking to Callibohr about our Union. Yes, this decision felt right.

"Nice to meet you, Captain Lyra Hogan," I said and gestured

toward the pod. "The examination isn't painful and it will be over in a few ticks," I added while gathering the instruments I needed.

"Please call me Lyra," she said softly, almost shyly, making me smile.

"Of course, and I must insist you call me Brarn," I replied. There was no need for formalities between mates.

"Prepare a translator for her as well as a tracker," the Admiral said, and I glanced at him over my shoulder.

I doubted she trusted us enough to allow such a procedure performed on her. Callibohr must have known, and that's why he hadn't spoken in her language. I furrowed my brows and considered the options.

On the one hand, the process was unavoidable. I'd end up implanting a translator eventually because she was meant to be ours, and once we completed the Mating Ritual, she'd get responsibilities that would have her meet many other species. She'd need to be able to communicate. A tracker, though…. I understood my Pair-bond's motives for requesting one, and it would ease my mind too, but I had a feeling she wouldn't like it when she found out.

Deciding on a course of action, I nodded at Callibohr, and gathered everything I needed on a tray. "Would you mind if I scanned you once again, Lyra?" Her alien name rolled off my tongue as if I'd been using it my entire life. "You see, the med-pod is more accurate than the portable scanner Forsa used earlier," I said while approaching my mates.

Quick as a flash, she retreated from us and aimed her weapons at the other two. Her face had lost its color, and the acrid scent of fear emanating from her burned my nose.

"We mean you no harm," I said, trying to defuse the situation, not understanding what had scared her.

The need to comfort her rose sharply, but I stayed put because I didn't really know how she'd react, or whether she kept her wits about her under pressure. If Lyra injured or killed her own mate, she'd never be able to get over it. The guilt would drive her insane.

Thankfully, her hands were steady, and her voice calm when she replied, "It's a big ass needle you have there."

"Forgive me. I asked him to give you a translator. We all have one, so I didn't think it'd be a big deal."

Culhwch, the fool, crept towards her, thinking Callibohr was trying to distract her by explaining. He didn't fool her, though, and pride filled me.

"Take another step and we'll see if you're faster than a laser beam." Her sweet voice in contrast to the very real threat she delivered.

She was nothing like the Wravukian females, but I didn't care. She was magnificent.

"It is safe. I promise, Lyra. I'll even let Brarn demonstrate on me first." Callibohr took slow, measured steps toward her. "Do you trust me?" he asked when the tip of her blaster against his sternum stopped him from moving closer.

Soldiers bigger and stronger than her had cowered under his intense gaze, yet she stood her ground. "If I asked you to let me go now, would you?" When he didn't answer quick enough for her liking, she repeated, unyielding, "Would you?"

"Yes," he replied, and I almost protested—there was no way I was letting her go—but he quickly added in a cajoling tone, "Will you trust me, Lyra?"

My eyes were glued to her while I held my breath, waiting for her answer. When she gave us her assent, I didn't hesitate. "Please lie down on the med-pod. We'll start with the scan first, which is non-invasive."

Both Callibohr and I followed her to the pod, then stood on opposite sides. I was programming which exams I wanted done and not paying attention to what the others were doing when our female purred, "Since I'm putting my life in your hands, don't you think it's fair you put yours in mine?"

My Pair-bond laughed whilst Culhwch exploded. "Human, this is an offense punishable by death. You don't threaten the Prince of Wravuk and live,"

On any other occasion, I'd side with the Second in Command, but no one threatened my mate. I picked the micro laser cutter and was about to step in his way when the Admiral ordered him to stand down.

"It's a fair request," he told him, then knelt next to Lyra, so they were at eye level. The new position brought her knife at jugular height. "The Order of the Prime has targeted Earth. We are here to protect your planet and all its citizens. Our word is our honor."

I wasn't sure whether it was his action—placing himself in a vulnerable position—or his explanation that put her at ease, but she allowed me to proceed, and I intended to make this procedure as painless as possible.

A smile played on my lips. The whole time, her hand never wavered from his neck. Life with our mate would never be dull. I wondered if she was as attracted to us as we were to her. Did humans have Fated Mates? Sacred Unions? Had Callibohr figured out what it was he was feeling?

The med-pod spat out the data, interrupting my train of thought. "You're all done. The examination is complete. Now, please sit up."

"You're fast."

"Our methods are more advanced than yours," I mumbled, my attention on the data, looking for a specific number… *Whoa!* "Initial findings show ninety-five percent compatibility." These words meant nothing to her, but to the two males in the room with us, as well as to the rest of my species, they meant everything. I didn't want to scare her, though, for the next part wouldn't be as pleasant as the first portion of the examination. "You're at optimum health. The implant will alter the Wernicke area with no issues."

Like a wire pulled taut, she tensed. "Have you done this before?"

"Placed a translator in a human? No, but I'd never let anything happen to you. I've studied your physiology, and there isn't a human ailment that we can't treat. You needn't worry. You won't feel a thing. Now let your hair down. I need to touch your scalp first."

She didn't believe me, but that was okay. I would prove myself to her soon enough.

Callibohr, sensing that my words hadn't convinced her, added his own. "Lyra, Brarn is one of the best Healers in Wravuk. He has patched me up more times than I can count. Do you want him to demonstrate on me? I've already got an implant, so he can't place another one, but he can show you what he needs to do."

Culhwch opened his mouth to speak, but decided against it. Instead, he crossed his arms over his chest, and continued watching the alien female as if she would suddenly raise the knife she was still holding and stab his Admiral.

Her lips pressed together in a slight grimace, and her brows pulled in as she looked downward. My little biska was on a precipice, and she needed to choose whether she would trust us.

When she lifted her exotic two-toned eyes, they were full of determination. "You don't need to demonstrate."

Our courageous female had put her faith in me, and I couldn't contain my smile as Callibohr positioned her flush against him instead of allowing her to sit on the med-pod and murmured reassuring words to her at the same time he restrained her movements.

Since she had her back to me, I reached out slowly, not wanting to startle her. The soft strands of her hair tingled my skin, and I wondered how they'd feel sliding across my body. Gently, I touched her scalp.

"Open your eyes and look at me," Callibohr growled. "It will only hurt for a heartbeat. Keep looking at me, Lyra."

Her whole body turned rigid, broadcasting her fear.

We weren't barbarians, and I'd make sure she wouldn't feel a thing during the entire procedure. Adding a little more than necessary, I administered the anesthetic agent first, then a few ticks later, proceeded to make an incision with the micro laser cutter directly over where the Wernicke area of her brain was located.

Taking my time, I carefully injected the nanoparticles into one of the sulci, then watched them move to form the implant that would allow her to understand and speak all known languages without hindering her brain's functions. The cessation of movement indicated the process was complete, so I added a sealant agent that would clone bone and skin and make it as if nothing had happened.

One down, one to go...

The tracker had to be placed at the base of the skull because its nanoparticles needed to attach to the bone. It was a fairly standard procedure since all soldiers of the Imperial were required to have one implanted when they got transferred to this fleet, and it was finished shortly after it started.

In the beginning, Lyra's vitals had been elevated because she was stressed, but she shouldn't still be panting heavily in Callibohr's arms.

I broke out in a cold sweat. My hearts started pumping faster. Had I made a mistake? Had I miscalculated the numbing agent's dosage? Had I…hurt her? Those and a hundred other questions terrorized my mind during the few ticks it took for me to snatch the portable scanner and hover the instrument above her head. Not long after, the report flashed on the screen.

All indications showed optimum health. Both implants had integrated successfully and were working properly. But then why was she so scared?

"It's done," I said in English, hoping she'd calm down once she heard the procedure was finished.

Callibohr's arms tightened around her. "How are you feeling, little one?"

"Not sure." Her voice was soft, broadcasting how vulnerable she felt, and a sense of contentment filled me because she felt safe enough with us to lower down her walls.

Even though the report showed everything worked properly, it was time to test the implant. "You might feel a little woozy because of the anesthetic. It won't last long," I said in Wravukian and waited.

"She understood you," Callibohr replied instead of her.

My pulse picked up again, and I used the portable scanner once more on her. A few ticks later, the report came back normal. "Maybe it'd be best if she lay down to rest for a while. In two spires, she should try to drink and eat something light."

"I can take her to the guest chambers," Culhwch said, and everything inside me revolted at the prospect of this unattached male spending alone time with our mate.

I was about to insist she sleep in a med-pod so that I could monitor her further, but my comms sounded. "Arch-healer, your assistance is required at the Training Bay."

Damn it. My whole being rebelled at the idea of leaving the Second in Command in charge of taking her to the guest quarters, but it seemed I had no choice.

Thankfully, Callibohr seemed to echo my sentiments. "Vice Admiral, the Bridge is yours for the rest of this circle," he ordered before turning to me. "Thank you, Brarn. I'll make sure she gets the nutrients she needs."

His words conjured an image that had me hardening in an instant. A picture of Lyra on her knees, her throat working furiously, swallowing Callibohr's cum popped up in my mind's eye, and I couldn't keep the sly grin from forming on my face as I thought that he'd give her the nutrients she needed, indeed.

A GREAT PLAN

LYRA

Consciousness returned slowly and painfully, as if I was waking up from one of those dreams where one feels paralyzed and can't move their limbs to save their life; the one where one screams for help but nothing comes out of their mouth.

"Hunter," I croaked without opening my eyes because I was certain that the light bleeding through the curtains in his room would make the ache worse. "My head is killing me. I need a painkiller."

Where did he go? I remembered his arms around me while I slept. His body was curved around mine, keeping me warm. I called out his name a second time, louder, but he still didn't show.

Think, Lyra. What day is it? Did he have a morning shift? Did he leave for work already?

I tried to remember but couldn't, so I opened my eyes, feeling groggy, and was met with…darkness. I pressed my forefingers on top of my lids and rubbed, then tried again.

Still darkness.

Panic slowly set in, and I started hyperventilating. "Where am I?" I whispered, and sat up on what felt like a very hard mattress—definitely not Hunter's.

The moment I was upright, the room lit up, blinding me, and that was when it all came back to me. My hand shot to the side of my head, searching my scalp for bumps, incisions, stitches... anything. But the surface was smooth, as if nothing had happened, yet I remembered receiving the implant that'd allow me to understand and speak all known-to-Wravukian languages.

Soon my eyes had adjusted to the brightness, and I checked my surroundings. To my right, screens covered the biggest part of the wall, and a freestanding desk-like surface made of a see-through material ran across its length at hip height. *Someone was a bit of a workaholic,* I thought, then noticed the part that wasn't covered by monitors formed a door-sized indentation. *Was that the exit?*

To my left, another door-sized indentation stood out because the rest of the wall on that side was bare. Although, upon a more careful inspection, I saw a few knobs protruding here and there. My mind went straight to hidden storage compartments because there wasn't a closet or cabinet in sight, and he had to store his uniforms along with the rest of his stuff somewhere.

When I focused on the part of the room in front of me, the sight of the red planet right outside the floor-to-ceiling window took my breath away. Our government wanted to establish a colony there, and once I returned to base with more information regarding the alien threat, that was one of the projects the Spaceforce would tackle next. I sat there lost in thought about what a future on Mars would look like, especially if the Wravukians helped us because their technology far surpassed ours.

After a while, I finally managed to pull my gaze back and

noticed the sitting area that occupied the space on that side. *How often had Callibohr sat on the L-shaped couch enjoying the view? Did he often entertain company at the table that sat four?* I wondered, but then shut down that train of thought. His personal life didn't concern me, and since the red-skinned alien wasn't here, I flexed my muscles and stretched my limbs carefully. Everything worked as it should, so I scooted my butt to the side—my legs dangling from the freakishly huge bed—when I did a double take.

Correction. My very naked legs dangling from the freakishly huge bed.

"What the heck?"

I was naked.

I never slept naked.

Jerking this way and that, I caught sight of my discarded spacesuit, and another realization hit me.

It hadn't been Hunter's arms and body around mine, but Callibohr's.

Had he or the doctor undressed me while I'd been out?

Motherfucker.

I knew no 'probing' had taken place because I wasn't sore. But still, I hadn't agreed to having my uniform removed, although...*Had he slept naked too?* The insidious idea crept in, turning my nipples into pebbles, and my core clenched at the thought.

What the hell, Lyra? I chastised myself. Hunter was an amazing guy and the night before I left, he'd rocked my world. I shouldn't be lusting after anyone else, and it was twice now.

First when the gold-skinned Healer with the red markings examined me, all kinds of scenarios of 'let's play doctor. I'm sick and the only medicine that'll cure me is an orgasm' flooded my mind, making it almost impossible to hold in my moan, and now

Callibohr evoked reactions from my body without my permission.

Yet there was something about both that drew me in. And once a mental spotlight fell upon the possibility of the Admiral having slept unclothed beside me, images of his ripped musculature in all its glory took up residence in my head that soon turned even more wicked because the red-skinned alien wasn't the only one next to me…Hunter and Brarn were with us too.

"I'm worse than my mother!" I exclaimed before mumbling in a resigned tone, "At least she had eyes for my father alone. She'd been happy with one man." Then I started toward my suit, not noticing that something was hanging from the edge of the bed. My feet got tangled, and I fell face down on the floor. "Damn it," I cried to no one in particular, then burst into laughter.

If either Hunter or Callibohr had seen that, I'd never live it down. Instinctively, I knew that Brarn wouldn't laugh. He'd kneel next to me to make sure I wasn't hurt, that not a single bruise marred my skin.

Stop thinking about the aliens, I ordered my inner voice, and rolled to the side to untangle my limbs from the mess, but the damn hussy insisted that both needed to be a part of my life too.

Once done, I grabbed the offensive material and lifted it up. *Hm.* It was a similar garment to those the four aliens had worn. Had the Admiral left it here for me? It seemed a bit small for his frame, but it was a tad big for me. Yet its slick design and unusual texture made me curious to feel it on my body. *Should I put it on?* I didn't debate on the matter for long. The government would love to have a piece of alien technology, so I could wear it underneath my own suit.

I eyed it critically. It was a one-piece, and the opening was a vertical line down the front, similar to a jumpsuit. "Okay, let's see how this fits." Bunching the top part of the alien uniform, I put my right leg into the corresponding pant leg, then did the same for the left one. My skin tingled wherever the fabric touched it, so I waited a few seconds to see if I had any other reactions to it. When nothing else happened, I put my arms through the sleeves, and studied the two sides that made the front. The gap reached my belly button, revealing way too much skin for my liking.

Last thing I needed was Wravukians trying to cop a feel to see what it was like. Not that they'd given me such vibes, but this was one of those situations that one was better safe than sorry. Besides, the colorful aliens weren't trudging around with their chests exposed—although what a sight that'd be—so there had to be some kind of button….

"How the heck am I supposed to close it? There are no fastenings," I said to no one in particular as I brought the two edges together.

The suit's opening suddenly fused together as if the damn thing had heard my request. It started emanating a low crackle of static electricity before zapping me with light electric shocks all over while the alien fabric shrank and molded to my body. The process hadn't harmed me as I was still standing; it definitely was an unpleasant experience, though.

I moved my arms and legs, feeling completely naked—when in fact I was not—because the suit had become second skin. The tingling sensation started up again. It felt as if a thousand legs of tiny millipedes were crawling all over me. I tried pinching the fabric but couldn't get a good grasp and ended up pinching myself. "Ouch!"

How am I supposed to take it off?

The moment the thought crossed my mind, the suit reacted, freaking me out. I screamed as the deep-crimson material dissolved and burrowed under my skin in the blink of an eye, disappearing from sight.

I slapped my flesh while uncontrollable shudders swept through my entire body, bringing me to my knees.

An alien…thing was inside of me.

I had to get it out.

OhmyGod, ohmyGod, ohmyGod.

I had to get someone to help me—Callibohr would know what to do.

Chest heaving, I crawled toward my own uniform, needing to get dressed, when suddenly the freaking substance seeped out of my pores, then reformed and solidified into its initial deep-crimson form.

Now that it was out of me—where clothing should be—my terror subsided, and logic returned, along with my curiosity. Was this some kind of technology that reacted to the wearer's thought pattern? *One way to find out….*

I got off the floor and took a deep breath. Steady as can be, I pictured myself removing the suit. Before my eyes, it dissolved and receded somewhere beneath my skin where I couldn't see it.

"Whoa!"

Then I pictured myself dressed, and it emerge to the surface, once again covering my entire body.

"This is…crazy." The Admiral had a lot of explaining to do, but first things first, I had to find him. Then I'd kick his ass for undressing me; and after that, I'd ask him how to remove this uniform from myself.

Yes. That was a great plan.

I scanned the room, looking for the exit. There were two indentations on the wall across from each other. I picked the one that was closer, and it whooshed open when some kind of invisible sensor picked up my presence, but it wasn't the exit.

On the far right corner there was an enclosure I guessed was a shower, next to it stood some kind of weird looking bassinet, and across the length of the wall to my left there was a pool, albeit small, but still…a freaking pool. I stepped away from the bathroom, stirring up a new plan: find Callibohr. Kick his ass. Learn how to remove the suit. And then take a bath in that pool.

Yes, I liked this plan much better.

Still angry at the alien male, I resumed my stomping toward the other door, which also opened as soon as I approached it. Thank God, because if I had to search for a switch I might end up strangling someone.

They might have size and strength on their side, but I had agility and speed on mine. Not to mention my stubbornness as well as my secret ability, and my determination to teach a certain someone a lesson about respect and boundaries.

Hopefully, my attitude wouldn't jeopardize the negotiations General Foster had forgotten to mention were taking place. Although, given the fact they hadn't shared this itty-bitty detail with me, if something went sideways, I could plead the Fifth.

As I wandered around, some of the males I passed by paused and stared, while others ignored me completely. Weird, but since no one spoke or tried to stop me, I continued on the path I was on, eying my surroundings curiously and admiring the craftsmanship of their spaceship.

The floor was made of some type of rubbery substance, which was so dark in color that my black boots seemed to blend with its surface, giving the illusion that its top layer was a continuation of my own limbs. It also absorbed the sound of my steps, but despite its deceiving appearance, the alien material was hard enough that my feet didn't sink while I walked.

Concealed beams of light ran across the bottom of the white glossy walls that bracketed the wide corridor, casting their light upward, creating an ambient, almost dream-like atmosphere.

What is this made of? I trailed the tips of my fingers across its cool, velvety surface, seeking for an answer, but coming up empty when I failed to match the texture with what I knew metal or glass felt like.

I expected the ceiling to be made of the same soundproof material as the floor, since it was so quiet that not even the engines' humming could be heard. I craned my neck backward to check, only to gasp in awe. It looked like veins of lava intertwined at certain intervals with rivulets of liquid ice as they both flowed across its length, suspended high in the air by an invisible force.

Everywhere I looked, there were no visible seams I could detect. Each material flowed into the next, no matter their seeming incompatibility.

My feet carried me forward on their own accord until the corridor I was traipsing divided into three different hallways.

Which one to take?

Listening intently, I picked up the toned down ruckus coming from the one on the left. Before taking a step further, though, I paid attention to the signals my inner warning system was emitting. All I received was a gentle buzz, meaning nothing life threatening lay that way, so I followed the voices that'd caught my attention.

I'M MARRIED

LYRA

Soon, I was standing at the entrance of an indoor training area. The enormous room had several small arenas—almost all of them occupied, as well as many instruments scattered around the right side of the cavernous space. Weapons adorned the wall at the far end, and mats covered the floor of that area. This place had no windows, and the lighting was dimmed, but I could still see clearly various males in different states of undress engaging in hand-to-hand combat.

The skin at the back of my neck prickled, and my face heated.

I was used to being around handsome men. Hunter, with his model good looks had a ripped body, and most of the guys in my unit were very easy on the eyes, too, with physiques in tip-top shape.

There was nothing wrong with the type of woman that went after men just because they looked great, but I wasn't one of them. I needed the inner package to be equally, if not more, attractive, too.

But the males here? They were a sight to behold. Closest to me, a blue alien was lifting weights and had sweat dripping down his six, no eight, no wait…*what the heck, was that a ten pack?*

Wondering whether I was seeing things, I blinked several times, but the view didn't change. Lethal power barely restrained within slick physiques that didn't carry an ounce of fat. These aliens had muscles for days; and was it getting hot in here?

It required effort on my part, but I ignored the sudden increase in temperature and the veritable buffet in front of me to survey the rest of the soldiers until my eyes landed on Callibohr.

His pants rode low on his waist, the freaky material molding to each mound and valley of his bottom half, leaving little to the imagination. Although the bulge in his groin must have been some kind of protective padding, right? Because if it wasn't….

No, nope, I'm not going there. Lift your eyes, Lyra, I yelled at myself, and it did the trick.

His crimson torso glistened from exertion, highlighting the gold veins that ran along his skin, which seemed to disappear under his uniform.

Is that a tattoo?

But more importantly, my brain cut in, *Is he tattooed everywhere?*

Standing rooted to the spot, I studied him. He was facing a green-skinned soldier who was brandishing his sword at him. Callibohr parried the other's strikes with ease, his muscles bunching and releasing with every move he made. His legs with the girth of tree trunks kept him steady without hindering his agility. A scar across his back marred what otherwise looked like smooth flesh, but didn't detract from how mouth-watering he was.

This alien male had faced his enemies and come out on top.

He was strength personified.

He was a leader who didn't sit back while his troops fought his wars.

He was imposing.

Qualities I inherently found attractive. Butterflies took flight in the pit of my stomach, and my core repeated the stupid thing it did when I woke up—it clenched on air. Like kindling slowly catching fire, an ache bloomed in my chest. I tried to avert my gaze from the impressive male, but found I couldn't.

Guilt drenched me. I'd only ever felt such emotions for one man, until now.

Hunter was too good for me. If he could peek into my brain right now, he'd be devastated. I was quicksand—like my parents—slowly drawing him deeper, smothering his love and spirit in the process. I was unworthy.

The need to run away rose swiftly to the surface, but my feet didn't obey my command. My own body was rebelling against me.

Et tu, Brute?

My shame morphed into fury, and a wave of anger burst violently outward.

If my eyes hadn't been glued to the red-skinned alien's back, I'd have missed Callibohr's head snapping my way, giving the perfect opening to his opponent, who took advantage of the distraction and punched him in the face, causing him to stagger.

He totally deserved that punch, and I should have been elated, but I wasn't. I wanted to tackle the green-skinned guy and give him a taste of his own medicine.

The Admiral turned around, and a glint of metal drew my attention to his pectorals. *What's that?* I wondered as I squinted my eyes in an effort to see.

Fuck! His nipples are pierced.

Standing there ogling him, I almost missed his gesture beckoning me closer. The others in the room took notice, though, and stopped what they were doing to gawk at me.

Since my inner warning system remained quiet, I schooled my expression and paid no attention to them as I marched toward their leader with my chin high and my shoulders straight.

A relaxed smile crossed his face as his golden orbs scanned me from top to bottom, and I wondered whether he was pleased because I obeyed or because I was wearing their uniform.

No matter, the lesson I was about to teach him would wipe it out, anyway.

"Are you seriously thinking of sparring with her? She's a female...she's half your size, Callibohr. You'll squash her," the male next to him whisper-shouted in their native tongue.

Life had taught me it was important to establish dominance with this type of men. I doubted species mattered, so I spoke before he could. "It's your Admiral you should worry about, not me. Fuck you very much."

I could almost hear their jaws hit the floor, and judging by their reactions, my sarcasm was completely lost on them. Everyone but the red-skinned alien looked at me open-mouthed. Was it my words that had surprised them or the fact I understood their language? Maybe he hadn't shared the fact he'd ordered the doctor to hook me with a translator implant.

"Callibohr," the Admiral corrected. A smirk dancing on his lips.

First names implied intimacy, which was the last thing I needed between us—my libido was out of hand as it was. "Bring it on... Admiral." I put emphasis on his title, then fell into a defensive stance.

He was at least a foot taller than me. One of his kicks had the potential to break me, and if his broad shoulders and thick biceps wrapped around my torso, they could snap me like a twig. But even the strongest fighter had weak points, and I had an eye for spotting those weaknesses.

Earlier, I'd noticed his left side was the strongest one. He was quite flexible, but when he'd bent to avoid a kick to the head, the movement hadn't been as smooth. He'd favored his right leg just the slightest—maybe due to a past injury or due to the scar on his back.

Winning wasn't out of the realm of possibilities as long as I took him by surprise and subdued him fast. I doubted I'd overpower him in a fight otherwise.

Callibohr came at me first, but I could tell he was holding back.

I threw a few jabs and performed a couple of false attacks, making contact, but no damage while taking note of his reactions.

The noise around us picked up in volume. It was eerie how similar the soldiers surrounding us behaved to my brothers-in-arms. They were laughing and taking bets about who was going to win, but I ignored them. My focus remained solely on the red-skinned male because I'd get only one chance to throw him off balance and I had to time my moves just right.

I'd already formed a plan in my head and gone over the moves a few times when Callibohr charged me. He moved faster than I'd expected, but I'd make it work. At the last possible moment, I fell on my knees and slid on the floor right between his legs while his momentum carried him over me. As I'd anticipated, he bent to grab me, but I'd already propelled myself upward and had pivoted on the spot.

Using his calf as my stepping stone, I jumped on his back, then threw two punches at his lower back where I hoped his kidneys were, earning a pained grunt for my effort. It wasn't over yet, though, so I climbed higher and locked my legs around his neck before twisting clockwise while throwing my weight forward at the same time.

My action had the desired effect. Callibohr lost his balance and landed on his left forearm. I'd already jumped off him, but before he could pick himself off the floor, I landed on his back once again and delivered two more punches to his kidneys before grabbing his right wrist and pulling it upward at a sharp angle.

His body was too warm between my thighs, nearly distracting me from sensing his muscles clenching, readying for his next move.

It was over, though.

I leaned forward, trapping his forearm between our bodies, and he stilled. "Never undress others without permission, unless you want to lose certain body parts." As I delivered the threat, he lifted his head, tilting it slightly so that he could look at me, and my lips accidentally grazed the ridge of his ear, making him groan.

The vibration of the low sound went straight to my clit, igniting the forbidden desire all over again.

"I'll keep that in mind next time," he cheekily replied, and I flushed at my blatant mistake. "The Sirh bonded with you, and they'll protect you much better than your primitive uniform." It was not so much what he'd just said, even though I had questions, as it was the blatant hunger in his eyes.

My entire face caught fire, because the Wravukian body-hugging attire might have been technologically far advanced compared to ours, but it was also far more revealing than anything I'd ever worn, which reminded me again why I was angry in the first place.

"There won't be a next time, Admiral," I snarled, and if the buzzing in my head hadn't suddenly risen in volume, I wouldn't have noticed the two aliens who were stealthily inching closer.

Without missing a beat, I got up and put a few feet between Callibohr and me, lest his soldiers thought I intended to ill-treat their leader.

Still, the two kept advancing toward me, not getting the hint. Dammit, I couldn't fight two at a time without a weapon and come out of the quarrel unscathed. And the red-skinned alien was taking his sweet time lifting his big frame from the floor…actually, his shoulders were shaking and he wasn't even trying to get up. Had I inflicted more damage than I thought? My punches couldn't have been strong enough to injure him severely, could they?

"Admiral, are you all right?" His Second in Command broke through the circle that had formed around us and knelt next to his leader, then all but spat his next words, "Grab her."

I was fucked.

Suddenly, booming laughter echoed in the huge space, startling me. Then Callibohr raised his head and his wide grin took my breath away. He was freaking gorgeous, and he'd been the source of the loud sound.

"Let her be," he ordered before heaving himself off the floor, but he wasn't done. His eyes shone with mischief when he turned to Culhwch and added in a taunting tone, "She managed to do what none of you have in a while. Maybe I should make her my Second in Command."

Shoot. That last bit didn't bode well for me. Especially not when the blue-skinned alien spun and bared his teeth at me.

"No weapons," Callibohr clarified in a smooth, almost jovial voice.

The vein at the base of Culhwch's corded neck throbbed, and his nostrils flared.

Uh oh.

"Your luck has just run out, Earthling," he said through clenched teeth, and attacked like a bull in a china shop.

But as it turned out, my so-called luck hadn't run out, and upon realizing that, the blue-skinned alien quickly let his anger dictate his fighting style, rendering most of his moves ineffective as I easily avoided them while cooking up the best counterattack plan.

Culhwch was guarding his upper body tightly because he'd probably caught the tail of mine and Callibohr's fight. But he wasn't covering as carefully his lower half, and I was willing to bet these species had a sensitive area in common with human men. The moment the opening presented itself, I fell on my back and thrust both my feet toward his scrotum area, scoring a bull's-eye.

It was almost comical seeing the big alien go cross-eyed, clutch his family jewels, and drop to his knees before falling sideways on the floor.

Unfortunately, the second fight didn't deter the rest from wanting a chance against me too, and as soon as the blue-skinned male was out, another took his place.

But by the fifth soldier, my muscles were screaming at me. I stayed in top shape, exercising daily with my brothers-in-arms and then again a few times a week with Hunter, but it had been a while since I'd put my skills to the test.

My breathing had turned ragged and my heart rate was through the roof. I needed a break, but these aliens were impatient to get their turn. Each male angrier than the previous one, as if I'd somehow personally affronted them by winning these matches. Although, looking at the dark-blue guy currently facing me, who was taller and bigger than Callibohr, had me thinking that the outcome wouldn't be in my favor this time.

The loud buzzing in my head had brought on the mother of all headaches, by screaming *'danger, danger'* nonstop. And on this one occasion, I didn't need the warning to know this male was too much for my overexerted state. On top of that, I hadn't watched him fight, so I had no idea what his weak spot might be.

I wasn't a quitter, though, and I always loved a good challenge. "Let's dance, big guy."

The moment I shifted into a defensive stance, he charged.

The ground shook.

Fuck, this will hurt, I thought as I evaded by dropping to the left —hopefully low enough that his fist wouldn't fully connect to my head—and rolling away from him. Pain still bloomed from the spot his knuckles grazed, but I couldn't let it debilitate me.

Out of the blue, a gold blur swooped in front of me before colliding with the dark-blue soldier. Sounds of flesh hitting flesh echoed around me. The two figures moving too fast for my eyes to discern who was beating whom. The fight, though, was over a couple of minutes after it began with the blue-skinned giant unconscious on the floor.

The gold-skinned male pivoted on his heels and stalked toward the Admiral, stepping into his personal space and jabbing a finger in his chest. "Have you no regard for our mate's well-being? They could have caused irreparable damage!"

Holy smokes. The furious guy baring his teeth at Callibohr was the doctor. I might have swooned for a second there, but then his words *'our mate'* and the possessive vehemence in his tone registered. What the hell was he talking about? I wasn't theirs—the Admiral would tell him so.

But Brarn's words had stunned not only the red-skinned alien, but the rest of the soldiers too.

What's going on here?

Some kind of silent communication seemed to be happening between the two, before the doctor dismissed his superior officer and headed toward me.

He took my right hand in his and inspected the minor cuts on my knuckles. "I need to make sure you're not hurt. Will you allow me to do so, Lyra?"

"You don't have to. Nothing feels broken. I'm good."

"Please," he said, his voice sounding pained.

My gut warned me that he was asking for more than what he was expressing with his words, and I hesitated. On the other hand, though, I knew how difficult it was for Hunter to see someone hurt and do nothing about it, and Brarn was a doctor. It was probably all in my head, so I acquiesced in the end. "Um...okay."

He led me toward the door without dropping my hand. The moment we cleared out of the room I tried to disentangle myself, but long fingers wrapped around my arms, stopping me—and consequently Brarn—in our tracks.

I was trapped again. This time, it was hands with gold markings on crimson skin trapping me further.

"Callibohr," I sighed, my body relaxing under his hold of its own accord.

Heavy panting raffled the strands of my hair. "Are you certain?" he asked, but the question wasn't directed at me.

"Yes. I saw us," the doctor replied calmly, and let my hand go.

The Admiral spun me around, then pushed me against the gold-skinned male with his considerable bulk, before slamming his lips against mine in a hungry kiss.

With a mind of its own, my body reacted to his aggression. All rational thought deserted my brain, and my mouth opened of its own accord, eager to taste more of him.

Callibohr took advantage of the opportunity to explore. His tongue slipped through the opening to dance with mine. Its thickness and rough texture surprised me, and I was suddenly aching to discover how it'd feel sliding against other parts of my body.

But we weren't alone, and soon Brarn's lips trailed a fiery path with his small nibbles and tender kisses from the back of my neck to the sensitive spot between my neck and my shoulder, making me weak at the knees. His nimble hands traced slowly every one of my curves, exploring my body, setting it on fire and claiming ownership.

Their actions left no doubt as to what their intentions were, but what the fuck was I doing?

Even if they didn't have females waiting for them on their home planet, I wasn't available. Yet at the thought of other women owning their hearts, a low rumble from the back of my throat burst out of my mouth, confusing the heck out of me because I had no right to feel possessive over them.

Fighting the attraction between us was harder than it should be, but eventually, I managed to slap my palms on Callibohr's chest and push him away while wrenching my lips from his. Then I moved sideways, putting space between me and the gold-skinned alien as well. "Stop. We can't do this."

"Yes, we can. You're mine…ours," the Admiral growled, determination shining in his eyes.

"…No, I'm not." I hesitated. Why the fuck was I hesitating? He needed to know, and I needed the reminder as well. "I'm married."

He staggered backward, as if I had gotten in a physical blow rather than tell him the truth. "Is he your Fated Mate or your Chosen one?" he asked, confusing me.

What was the difference? Earlier, when he'd explained the concept, he hadn't made this distinction. "He's my husband."

"Did a line form when you completed your mating ritual? Or the first time he mated with you?" he insisted, his tone impatient.

"Um…no." Where was he going with this?

His shoulders sagged. "Then he's your Chosen Mate, and I can live with that."

"We both can," Brarn added.

"Live with that?" I mumbled under my breath, trying to grasp the meaning behind the words when a bulb lit above my head—the context of those words suddenly clear, and I shrieked, "What do you mean live with that?"

Callibohr closed the distance I'd put between us and bent to whisper in my ear, "It means that when the line forms after I and Brarn take you, which will prove what we already know is true, we will tolerate the presence of your Chosen Mate and not kill him."

"Unless he is our other Pair-bond," Brarn said and the Admiral's eyebrows almost reached his hairline.

All this was too much to unravel, and instinctively, I recoiled from his words—forgetting there was nowhere to go—and banged my head on the metal wall behind me. "What's true?"

He nuzzled the side of my neck, breathing me in, and when he spoke, reverence rang in his voice. "That you are our Sacred Mate."

"You're making way too many assumptions, Wravukian," I said and pushed him backward. I needed room to think without his spicy aroma meddling with my senses and arousing my libido.

Lust had blazed through my veins when my body was trapped between theirs, but I could not give them what they wanted—I couldn't become theirs. And when I returned to Earth, I wouldn't keep what had just happened a secret from the person I considered my soulmate because despite being loyal to Hunter, something deep in me yearned for these two males too, and that in itself was a serious betrayal.

It seemed wherever I went, someone always ended up hurting. I didn't deserve these aliens, and I definitely didn't deserve Hunter. Once this mission was over, I'd set the record straight and then find a way to continue alone.

Brarn lifted his hand and gently cupped the side of my face, pulling me out of my thoughts. "You are something else, little biska." The reverence in his deep voice made my heart clench. "We have a lot to talk about. I'm sure you have questions." He chuckled, then drew his hand back, making me miss his warmth. "Shall we continue the discussion in your personal quarters, Callibohr?"

The other male nodded, and I let them usher me back to where I had come from—the Admiral's room for I needed to get it into their heads that I wasn't the right gal for them...no matter that my heart insisted they both belonged to me and Hunter.

SACRED UNION

BRARN

On the way to Callibohr's personal quarters Lyra was wound up tighter than a spring, a fixed look of concentration masking her thoughts, whereas neither I nor my Pair-bond could contain our grins.

Upon looking at her, one would think we were leading her to the holding cells, not to explain what a Sacred Union was and how blessed we were.

All I wanted was to touch her. To affirm she was real and not a figment of my imagination. To shower her with affection, and get to know the female—her past, her likes and dislikes, her desires… anything and everything she was willing to share.

When Callibohr stepped into the chamber, she hesitated at the door—and that action was the only outward sign of the apprehension rolling off of her—before taking a deep breath and following him to the sitting area with me bringing up the rear.

Unlike her bulky suit, the new Sirh uniform molded to the contours of her body. Lyra was gorgeous, and I couldn't wait to familiarize myself with every fingerbreadth of her skin, but she chose to sit on the edge of the couch. Her back was ramrod straight, shoulders pushed back and her chest jutted out. This wasn't the right time for all the tantalizing thoughts crossing my mind because her defensive posture screamed 'stay away', even though she hadn't uttered the words.

Holding back would be torture. Yet there was no other option but to respect her wish. I was certain the last thing my Pair-bond wanted was to stress her out, so we both kept our distance and sat across from her.

"Whatever you think is going on between us, you're mistaken," she said, getting straight to the point.

Callibohr raked his fingers through his hair, frowning. "You feel the bond; you surrendered in our arms earlier. Your heart knows the truth, even if you don't want to admit it."

Lyra jerked as if he'd slapped her. "That was a lapse in judgment on my part." She crossed her arms and added, "Just because I might find someone attractive to look at doesn't mean I want to have a relationship with him." Her tone was higher than before, signaling a rising temper.

My hearts skipped a bit. She admitted she found us attractive. The mate bond didn't seem to affect her the same way as us, but at least she wasn't unaffected. We could work with that.

"Brarn's visions always show the truth," my Pair-bond said.

For those who knew me or of me that might have been enough of an explanation…but not for our mate, who rolled her eyes at us.

It was time I intervened lest the situation escalate into a fight. "You don't know us, and you have every right to doubt our words. Please allow us to explain." My cajoling tone had an immediate effect—her body relaxed, and she leaned backward against the couch in a more casual position.

"All right. I'm listening," she said.

"Unlike humans, every Wravukian is born with a gift, a natural ability if you like, that allows them superiority over others. For example, my main gift is healing. Just by being in another's proximity, I can detect the location and severity of any potential health issues that individual might have, and instinctively know what to do to heal them." I stopped to let her absorb what I'd shared and give her the opportunity to ask questions. I imagined she'd have a few, but she remained silent, so I continued. "Sometimes, one has more than one gift. Mine isn't strong, and I can't control it, but sometimes when I touch another being I see parts of their past or their future. Earlier, when I shook your hand, I had a vision." Her lack of reaction made me pause. She sat motionless, not even blinking. Was all this too much for her?

Before I had a chance to ask, Lyra cleared her throat, but her voice still came out raspy when she asked, "What did you see?"

My Pair-bond rose and walked toward the window covering this side of the chamber. His lips pressed into a thin line, and a haziness covered his eyes—he was lost in thought. What I was about to reveal would cause issues the moment it reached our people's ears, but we'd cross that bridge when we came to it. I redirected my attention to our mate and answered her. "Proof that we formed a Sacred Union. But before I go into detail about what that means, do you have any questions?" When my inquiry was met with silence, I tensed. Was she not comprehending what I was saying or purposefully rejecting every word coming out of my mouth? "I expected you'd have a few questions—"

"She doesn't because she has a gift of her own," Callibohr cut in, his back turned to us. "She's a Shield."

Her widened eyes snapped to him.

"Humans don't have abilities," she disagreed without really denying my Pair-bond's claim.

"Do all Humans lie with their words?" he asked, still facing the window. His gravelly tone ominous.

It seemed our mate had the uncanny ability to ruffle his feathers. "Callibohr," I warned, but didn't miss the fact that she hadn't answered.

He pivoted and stomped straight toward Lyra. He bent over her, making her lean deeper into the couch, as he gripped its back, caging her in. "Ask me what my gift is."

"I don't need to kn—"

"Ask me," he growled. "For I won't tolerate my Mate lying to me."

She lifted her chin in defiance. "There's no point. I'm. Not. Your. Mate."

Wrong answer, little biska.

"I can tell what you'll do..." he said and dragged the tip of his finger from her temple downward, "...the moment the idea solidifies in your consciousness." He slid his digit over her bottom lip before continuing the descending path down her neck. "I can tell when you're lying," he warned, looking straight into her eyes.

His finger trailed further south, over the middle of her clothed breasts and down her taut stomach.

Suddenly, she snatched his wrist, stopping his momentum, but failing to dissuade him from making a point.

Callibohr's nostrils flared, right before the sweet scent of her arousal filled my lungs.

"I can tell when your body gets all slick for me, like right now," he said, pulling his hand away. "Your own energy betrays you." She broke eye contact, deflating on the spot.

That action seemed to mollify him because when he spoke next, his tone was much gentler, almost reverent. "Being a Shield is an extremely rare gift. Do you know how I can tell you are one? Everyone and everything emits vibrations. Non-stop. It's a superb weapon to have in one's arsenal, but the price one pays..." He seemed lost for words as he gritted his teeth in an effort to rein in the anguish I could sense coursing through him. "It's a torture living with my ability. But you...you're giving me a priceless gift. You quiet all the noise."

She slowly raised a trembling hand as if to cup his face, but then dropped it to her lap, her cheeks flushing a rosy color. "I'm sorry," she said, but I wasn't sure whether she was apologizing for denying him her touch or for something she had no say in—his power.

"You are gifted," he reiterated. "And something tells me you have more than one ability. But you can keep your secrets for now because once we complete the Mating Ritual, there'll be none left between us." He straightened and returned to the couch next to me.

Lyra drew a deep breath and let it out slowly, as if steeling herself. "You're right. I've always known I was different to most humans. My inner warning system set me apart. It shows me how and where to attack or when to retreat. My gift was the reason I was able to take you and your warriors down. You claim I'm a Shield, but I didn't know I could do that."

"Is your Chosen Mate gifted too?" I asked.

She didn't hesitate this time. "Yes. He's a doctor...a Healer like you."

"Do you think he's our Pair-bond?"

Callibohr's question was valid. I took a few ticks to think it through. "He could be. A Sacred Mate carries one part of a soul, and they gravitate toward the rest of the parts, needing the fulfillment the completion will give them," I replied carefully. "He could be the male in my vision, but I can't be certain, not until I meet him."

Lyra's eyebrows squished together, and she pursed her lips. She looked even more adorable in her confused state. "What is a Pair-bond? And what are Sacred Mates?"

"In a Sacred Union, the males are bound to their female. The needs to provide, protect, and please her are as intrinsic as breathing. The same bond exists between the males as well, although it doesn't always lead to a sexual connection. And that's why we are called Pair-bonds," Callibohr said, and she stiffened.

With how skittish our female was, the subject needed to be handled with subtlety, so I took over. "There are three types of unions. The most common one is formed when two individuals want to spend their life together and decide to complete the Mating Ritual, thus becoming Chosen Mates. Marriage is the human equivalent to that, but Wravukians mate for life." She nodded her understanding, so I continued, "Fated Mates, the second type is less ordinary but not too infrequent. The couple has one pneuma, and when they mate for the first time, the Fated Line manifests, forming a circle that unites the two halves into a stronger whole." I paused to get a feel for where her head was at, though I couldn't decipher her expression.

"And the third one?" she asked somewhat impatiently, making me wonder if it was annoyance lacing her voice.

I couldn't wait to get to know her better and familiarize myself with all the nuances that were uniquely hers. *All in good time,* I thought and continued, "The third type—ours—is quite powerful, but extremely rare. A Sacred Union forms when there are more than two Fated Mates in a pairing. It's one of the greatest blessings, but the cost to having just a piece of pneuma is always feeling something isn't right without knowing what exactly. During their first mating, once again, the Line will form a circle that will connect the Mates, and interlace the incomplete pieces of their pneuma with one another until it's whole again."

"And prior to my brother meeting his Sacred Mates, there had never been an interspecies Union," Callibohr added.

What we'd shared with her was a lot, and Lyra remained silent while mulling over what she'd learned. Though, not too long after, she asked, "What happens if the female chooses someone before she finds her Fated Mates?"

"The Fated Males would tolerate the Chosen one, and maybe in time come to care for him the way they would for their Pair-bonds," Callibohr said. "No one would risk the female refusing them. A rejection would lead to the males' demise, and ultimately hers too."

But there was more to it and she needed to know, so I explained, "The fundamental difference between Chosen Mates and the other two unions is that when the latter manifests, the Mates don't have a choice. It's not simply a want to complete the Mating Ritual, but a compulsion that cannot be denied. The physical attraction between them is fierce and the level of its intensity escalates the longer they take to complete it. They're incapable of staying apart for long—the need to see to each other's well-being is far too great. Separation before the Union is established leads to inability to focus on anything else that gradually morphs into agony, which eventually becomes unbearable."

I watched, enthralled as a plethora of emotions crossed her face

—too fast for me to comprehend—while Lyra chewed on her bottom lip. Then, seemingly coming to a decision, she nodded to herself. "And what did your vision show you?"

"The moment when a gold line formed a circle, uniting Callibohr, you, me, and another human male. We are Sacred Mates, little biska."

"And your visions have never been wrong?"

I furrowed my brows, searching my memories. There'd never been an incident where they were proven incorrect. "Never."

"Right. Well, I'm Human not Wravukian and…um…I need time to think about everything you told me."

"You've got until we pick up your Chosen Mate. If he's our Pair-bond, we'll retrieve him and set course for Wravuk. If he isn't, we'll search for the male that will complete our Union before we return home." Callibohr's plan was sound, and I fully agreed.

If needed, I'd sketch our missing Pair-bond's portrait and give it to Axr, who could access Earth's online databases to find him.

"In the meantime, you'll stay here with us, where we can get to know each other better."

I saw her bristle at his order, right before she shot off the couch. "I can't do that. Besides, it's past time I reported to my superiors, so if you'll excuse me, I need to go to my spaceship," she said and stepped away, increasing the distance between us, readying to flee.

We both rose, but she lifted her hands, palms towards us, in the universal sign for stop. Her rigid body posture screamed stay away, and as I let my senses expand to examine her, I found her temperature had increased and her heart was beating wildly—both signs of a being riddled with anxiety.

The need to comfort her rode me, but she wouldn't allow me to so much as approach her, let alone envelop her in my arms. If we insisted on escorting her to her ship, we'd only stress her further.

"Axr, inform Denkal to come to the Admiral's quarters immediately," I ordered the ship's AI, before turning to Lyra. "The soldier will accompany you to your ship."

Callibohr opened his mouth to disagree, but a warning look from me stopped him from speaking.

"Thank you," she said, and not long after, she was gone.

When the door closed behind her, my Pair-bond muttered, "What the fuck just happened?" Echoing my thoughts exactly.

How could she not be feeling the developing connection between us? I wasn't mistaken when I said we were Mates, but maybe we needed our other Pair-bond present for her to start feeling the Sacred Bond.

"It seems…" I hesitated, searching for the right words, the right explanation. This was uncharted territory. "…Human Fated Mates don't feel what Wravukians do."

He began pacing perpendicular to the length of the floor to ceiling window, taking measured breaths and rolling his shoulders in an attempt to release the restless energy riding him. "Fuck! We'll get enough pushback from the Council and the elitist nobles as it is. They will challenge me…us for the throne. We can't have our Earthlings pushing us away, too."

"She's attracted to us—her body told us as much. So we find a way to convince her mind that she's the one for us." As the words flew out of my mouth, a plan formed in my head. Callibohr sensed the change in me and stopped pacing, giving me his full attention. "We should spend time with her. Get to know her. Give our Bond a chance to strengthen. Make it impossible for her to reject us. And afterwards? We retrieve our Pair-bond and complete the Mating Ritual to establish our Union."

"You know? I think your plan might just work," he said, and we both sat down to iron the details.

By the time we'd be done with her, she wouldn't want to leave us. Ever.

CREATOR WAS MY WITNESS

CALLIBOHR

Step one of the *'Make Lyra fall in love with us'* plan was complete.

Although if I was being honest with myself, it had backfired. The goal was to make her fall in love with us, but I was already halfway there. I couldn't stop thinking about her every tick we were apart. Her scent lingered in my chambers—even though she'd only spent a few spires in it on her first circle on the Imperial—driving me crazy with lust. And when I closed my eyes to sleep, rest was the last thing I was getting…more like a rock hard cock that I had to take care of as soon as I woke up lest it broke from the tension.

I bet Brarn felt the same, but we'd agreed to take it slow, and to woo her separately in the beginning, to avoid overwhelming her.

The first seven circles were mine, while the next seven his. I'd spent the past three in the Simulations chamber, training our mate on how to fly our small Destroyers.

There were always other warriors practicing as well, and as I'd hoped, their attendance helped put her at ease. Initially, she'd been detached and formal with me but, little by little, she began relaxing and getting more comfortable in my presence.

Of course, it might have helped that she found the activity I'd chosen for our time together fascinating.

During the spires I spent teaching her, I discovered she had an aptitude for flying. She was a quick study, retaining all the information after listening to me point them out once. Curious to see how well she'd do if I put her abilities to the test, I'd arranged for us to fly a Destroyer together.

But first, I had to finish one last task. I was on the Bridge, going over the reports Ilark had sent. He was the Admiral of the Fourth Fleet of Wravuk, and they had recently intercepted one of the Order of the Prime's units that had been heading toward Wravuk.

Ilark noted that the weapons Brarn had helped create by mapping the Pawn and Trojan's genomes had been a hundred percent effective, giving our troops the upper hand, and allowing them to win without casualties on our side.

That was excellent news my Pair-bond would love to hear.

"Admiral," Forsa said, lowering the headpiece that allowed him to monitor communications. "Captain Lyra Hogan has received an incoming call. I believe you should listen in on their conversation."

Violent vibrations that lashed at everything in their path were rolling off of him. The turbulent waves headed straight toward me, but my mental shields held strong, keeping them from overwhelming my senses.

Something had angered him, and it had to do with my mate.

"Send the link to the transmitter at my office," I said and headed there myself. Once inside, I sat at my desk and activated the link that would allow me to tap into their communications channel without worrying about being detected.

Forsa's dominant gift allowed him to understand and interact with everything that had a circuit. He could manipulate technology in a way I didn't understand. My Third in Command was the best at what he did, though, and had my full trust.

"No, Sir." Lyra's terse voice filled my space.

I'd missed part of their discussion, but it didn't matter. I'd listen to the recording later.

"This is your last warning." A male's booming voice blasted through the speakers. "The information you've sent is more than enough. Your new mission is effective immediately. As I've already said, you are to retrieve a sample of their alien tech by any means necessary, and return to base right away."

"But...that's stealing."

"Captain," came his swift rebuke. "Unless you want to be court-martialed, you'll follow your orders to the T. Am I clear?" he growled, and I wanted to smash my fist in his face for the way he was speaking to my mate.

"Sir. Yes, sir!" she said before terminating the call.

Time stood still.

Her assent acted like the toxic bite of a sharacval, its venom invading my being and paralyzing my limbs, rendering my mind unable to compute what I'd had heard.

She'd been sending information? And she'd just agreed to steal from us? Raking my hands through my hair, I pulled at the strands. "Fuck!" I yelled and threw the first thing I grabbed at the wall.

Upon impact, a loud ringing grated my ears before the transmitter broke at the seams, and exploded into fragments. As the shattered bits fell on the floor, a shower of soft pitter-patter disrupted the sudden silence in the room.

Lyra's betrayal felt like my hearts were slowly being sawed into pieces by a dull dagger.

A small voice inside my head reminded me she hadn't betrayed me yet and insisted that I give my mate the benefit of the doubt… trust in her more.

She hadn't shared the fact that she was already in possession of alien technology—the Sirh suit. But whether it was because our developing bond kept her from betraying us, or because she guessed they wouldn't be able to remove it without killing her first, I did not know.

Well then, it was time to find out what she would choose.

If she went against her superior's orders, I'd protect her.

If she proved to be a thief, I'd chase her to the edge of the universe until I captured her. And once she was in my custody, I'd make sure she never chose another over her mates again.

Having settled on which path to take, my mind conjured images of all the deliciously erotic ways I could punish her for her transgression—for not coming to me first. But I was getting ahead of myself. It was still to be seen if we'd go down that path, so I stormed out of the Bridge, ignoring the sideway glances I got from my crew, and headed toward the arenas.

I needed to expel the anger that was riding me hard, because I would end up doing something stupid like tying her to my bed and spanking her firm ass until her smooth skin turned red and she confessed her plans to me.

A few spires later, sweat was dripping from my body, and my muscles had turned to jelly from the exertion.

It was also near the time I'd told Lyra we'd fly the Destroyer, so I returned to my quarters, bathed, got ready, and headed to our meeting point—her ship.

She was standing next to its lowered ramp, talking to Brarn, and when I approached them, she greeted me with a wide smile that lit up her eyes.

It was the first one she gave me, but I couldn't bask in the warmth she was exuding. I had to know, and going in circles wasn't my style, so I got straight to the point. "Everything all right with your superior officers?"

Her smile dimmed, then disappeared. "Yes. It was just routine stuff. Everything is fine."

Suddenly, my chest tightened.

Brarn's eyes snapped to mine before he cocked his head and zeroed in on the vein twitching at the base of my neck.

Lyra would have fooled me with how easily the lies rolled off her tongue if I hadn't known the truth. Her betrayal hurt, but I'd give her one more opportunity to open up to me and come clean.

"If staying on the Imperial is an issue, I'd be happy to speak to them."

"No, it's not," she replied fast. Too fast, but she continued smoothly, "They anticipated I'd make contact. As long as I don't delay the reports they expect from me, I have the freedom to explore."

The pounding in my ears increased with every new word spewing out of her mouth. I pressed the heel of my palm over one of my hearts, hoping to alleviate some of the pain racking the damn organs.

"But I will need to return to base soon," she added as an afterthought, and my blood turned cold.

She'd made her choice, and it wasn't in our favor.

I locked down on my emotions and pushed them far away to the recesses of my mind, but staying with her in my current state wasn't an option. "Sorry to cancel on you, but I came here to inform Brarn we've got urgent business to attend to." Improvising on the spot, I lied just as easily as she had. Now, though, it was time to help her fulfill her mission. "I've already instructed my soldiers to prepare a Destroyer, and one of them will come get you soon." I smiled, but suspected it was more a show of teeth than an actual smile. "Take it for a ride. I trust in your ability to fly, and your training shouldn't go to waste."

"It's not neces—"

"I insist," I cut in, my tone more abrupt than I would have liked, but damn it, if I didn't get away, I'd end up doing something I regretted, like fucking the lies out of her when she wasn't ready to go there with us. "No reason you can't have fun," I said, and without waiting for a reply, gestured at Brarn to follow me, leaving a wide-eyed Lyra behind.

Every step that took me farther away from her had my soul crying out for the connection and true trust we would never have. But she'd made her choice, and we'd all have to live with the consequences. So now, I was making mine, too. I'd never allow the Mating Fever to lay a claim on mine and Brarn's lives, and that meant we were keeping her and our Human Pair-bond…even if she didn't want us to.

Brarn had remained silent, observing mine and Lyra's interaction without interfering. Now that we had cleared the Docking Bay, though, he spoke up. "What was that?"

"I just gave our Mate the opening to follow her orders," I growled, done with hiding the fury churning in me, turning the pit of my stomach hard as a rock.

"Her orders?" he asked, not comprehending.

So, on the way to the Bridge where we could monitor her flight, I explained what had happened from the moment Forsa intercepted her communication until now.

A pensive frown marred Brarn's face while he listened with rapt attention to the recount of events. "I don't think she'll go through with it," he said as we stepped into my domain.

I wished I had his optimism.

"Forsa, activate the video feed from the cameras inside the Destroyer and put it, along with Lyra's coordinates, up on the main viewscreen. Keep monitoring the space traffic in relation to her position," I ordered my Third, before turning to my Pair-bond. "I guess we're about to find out."

"Sacred Mates can't betray one another. You know that as well as I do." Forsa and Eoin, who'd been standing next to our sides, jerked toward us—mouths agape. Sudden sharp indrawn breaths sounded from behind us, and I was certain if I turned to look at their faces, they'd be donning the same shocked expression. "She will not betray us," he reiterated, ignoring everyone else. "But know this. Even if she ends up making a mistake, there is no alternative where she and our Human Pair-bond don't end up with us."

I didn't need the ultimatum. However, I was glad we were on the same wavelength. "We'll settle for nothing less," I vowed as Lyra's face lit up on the wide screen in front of us.

Silence fell across the chamber as we waited for her to complete the initiation sequence, but the sparky vibrations incessantly battering at my mental walls exhibited the fascination and curiosity of the individuals surrounding me in a way their stillness didn't.

"Preflight check concluded. Take off is a go, Lyra," Culhwch said, giving her the green light to fire up her Destroyer.

Everyone watched, enthralled, as the small fighter jet shot out of the Docking Bay and out into space.

Suddenly, the muscles across the scar on my back spasmed, and a grunt of pain escaped through my clenched teeth. A sharp sting zapped my spinal cord and was followed by agony. It felt like something was trying to drill a hole out of my spine.

Brarn's whole body jerked, and he inhaled sharply. "Callibohr, I'm sensing…" His voice trailed off as he palpated the exact spot the pain originated, but the moment his fingers applied pressure on top of my uniform, the torturous sensation ceased.

"I'm fine."

His brows pulled downward, and his lips formed a thin line. His worry beat at me, and it was the last thing I wanted.

"I'm fine," I repeated and redirected my attention to the viewscreen.

At that moment, our mate's giggle sounded through the Bridge's speakers as she performed a few perfectly timed orbital maneuvers to spin the Destroyer tail over nose without losing control.

"Damn," she whispered. "This ship is something else," she said, awed, and I expected her to make a run for it any tick now.

My Second in Command, who didn't yet know what Lyra's new mission was, replied dryly, "Of course it is. Wravukians made it."

"Shit! You can hear me?" she asked, sounding breathless.

Culhwch chuckled, but the loud rhythmic noise of the alarm blaring cut the sound of mirth short.

Everyone scrambled to their positions, and a cacophony of voices rose in the air as each reported from their stations.

"U.E.F. detected," Forsa added before cursing under his breath. "The Captain is heading straight toward it."

Fuck. Unstable Electromagnetic Fields were the precursor to temporary and quite volatile wormholes. "Lyra, return to the Imperial immediately." Static followed my order. I turned to my Third in Command. "Something's wrong. Is it on our end or hers, Forsa?"

His fingers flew over the comms' control panel. "Ours is fully functional. The Destroyer's...hm...oh, shit! The signal is being jammed."

He hadn't even finished the sentence when a spacecraft, double the size of Lyra's, zoomed out of the wormhole and straight toward the Destroyer.

"Space pirates," my Second in Command spat and set course to intercept.

"Activate shields, but do not fire. Lyra will be caught in the crossfire," I ordered. "Culhwch, what's our ETA? Rohan, have you identified their ship yet?"

A metallic groan reached my ears. I was clutching the main control panel so hard that its materials protested, and my fingers had gone numb.

"We aren't goi—"

His answer was cut short when the space scums opened fire, hitting the Destroyer carrying my mate, wrecking the ship's engine. Then they opened fire at us, slowing us down significantly because we couldn't retaliate, not without risking the female that held my life in her hands.

"Stand down," I reinforced my earlier command in case someone got trigger-happy.

No one did. We all watched helplessly the as events unfolded.

As panic set in because we wouldn't reach her in time, my hearts threatened to burst from my chest, and black spots filled the edges of my vision, obscuring Brarn, who was pressing his palm against his chest as if trying to keep his own hearts inside his body.

"Admiral, identification process is at ninety percent," Rohan said at the same time cables that had hooked edges shot out of the hostile craft and latched on to Lyra's before reeling it in.

"Increase our speed by eighty percent," I ordered. Raising it higher would get us there faster, but we'd compromise the Imperial's shields' integrity and the safety of my warriors. I couldn't do that no matter how much my soul screamed that we needed to reach our mate before they took her away.

"Identification complete." And no sooner were Rohan's words out, than we watched the hostiles re-enter the wormhole, taking Lyra with them, right before it collapsed, blocking the path that would lead us straight to them. "That was a Crootan ship, Admiral."

I dropped to the chair behind me, and hung my head, covering my face with my hands, as my thoughts became too loud, drowning me in despair.

Everyone I loved was taken from me. What was purer in this world than an offspring's love? Yet it wasn't enough to keep my mother in my life…the Creator had taken her. On that fateful circle, my sire's love for her—the love of a Fated Mate—had nearly driven him mad when she'd drawn her last breath. He might still be alive, but since then, he'd never been the same, and loving him only ended in disappointment and pain.

Loving someone always ended in pain. And if the agony coursing through my system was any indication, I loved the human female too.

Fuck! I love her.

The realization stunned me, for Lyra had slipped through my defenses and had burrowed into my heart without even trying.

And now a species that had no regard for their own mothers and offspring had abducted my mate.

If they dared harm a single strand of her hair, their lives would be forfeit, and I wouldn't stop until I killed every last one of them.

"She's got the tracker," Brarn said, and I couldn't remember the last time his voice had sounded shaken. "Can you trace it, Forsa?"

I got up and walked toward him. He looked at me, and the pain in his eyes mirrored mine. Wrapping my arm around him, I pulled him in a tight embrace. "I promise you, I'll bring our mate back."

His Adam's apple bobbed a few times, before he shut his eyes and breathed deeply, in an effort to steel himself. When he opened them again, he gave me a stiff nod and let go so that I could take my position at the helm.

"The moment they stop using a signal blocker, we'll be able to pinpoint her exact location, but until then, I'll keep trying to force a connection," Forsa replied to my Pair-bond while his hands kept flying over the comms' control panel.

Culhwch—I noticed—was going over the neighboring systems' maps searching for potential exit points.

One thing we had going for us was that ships couldn't travel far through these volatile wormholes. And there weren't many places space pirates like the Crootan took their fare to, so we would find her sooner rather than later—Creator was my witness.

Thank you for reading Broken Warriors!

Callibohr, Brarn, Hunter, & Lyra will get their happily ever after in Healed Warriors, book 5 in the Intergalactic Enosis: The Pyxis System series.

GLOSSARY

Astronomical Unit (AU): AU is the distance between Earth and the sun.

Biska: Explorer.

Circle: A full circle is the Saberian day and is equivalent to twenty-eight hours.

Cycle: A full cycle is the Saberian month and is equivalent to thirty-eight circles.

Monakrivimou: My precious, my one and only.

Pallium: A rectangular length of cloth, worn around the waist and over one shoulder. The Saberians used it as a cloak.

Psehimou: My soul.

Pneuma: Soul.

Rotation: A full rotation is the Saberian year and is equivalent to eighteen cycles.

Scaths: Weight measurement equivalent to kilos/pounds.

Sharacval: A venomous snake-like species.

Spires: Equivalent to one hour.

Stridulate: To produce a shrill, grating sound, as a cricket does, by rubbing together certain parts of the body; shrill.

Tick: Second, moment.

Torsek: A domesticated species that looks like a four-legged phoenix and are excellent companions.

Vackal: Asshole.

ABOUT THE AUTHOR

Aurora Welkin is a sci-fi and paranormal romance author. She lives in Sydney, Australia. She enjoys reading a little too much, and her loved ones usually find her with her nose in a book. In her free time, you'll find her strolling along the beach with her husband, savoring a cup of cocoa and watching their little prince explore the world.

www.aurorawelkin.com

Aurora loves to hear from readers! The best way to connect with her online is via her newsletter. You can sign up here: www.aurorawelkin.com/mailing-list

www.ingramcontent.com/pod-product-compliance
Lightning Source LLC
Chambersburg PA
CBHW020500310726
48979CB00016B/2740/J

* 9 7 8 0 6 4 5 4 8 2 5 4 6 *